The Pastor's Perfect Wife

Jane Daly

ISBN-13: 978-1-962168-97-7

Chapter 1

Mariah slid one long red fingernail under the flap of the envelope and pulled out a sheet of paper.

"Finally," she said, scanning the approval letter and the request for references.

There was only one problem. Finding three people to give her a good reference. Pastor Roy would be the first one she asked.

In her bedroom, she pulled on a pair of black running tights and a snug top and headed to the bathroom to gather her black mane into a neat ponytail. A quick swipe of red lipstick, and she was ready.

With earbuds shoved into her ears, Mariah warmed up with a slow jog. At this pace, she'd reach Main Community Church in about fifteen minutes. Plenty of time to burn off the microwaved burrito she'd eaten for dinner the night before. With the kitchen torn apart, she had three choices. Frozen dinners, take out, or starve.

Mariah's pace increased the closer she got to the

church. Soon she'd be a part of the Safe Families for Children program, hosting children whose parents needed temporary respite. Whether it was a homeless family living in their car and trying to get back on their feet, or a mom with court-ordered rehab, Mariah could finally feel like a mom, even a temporary one. If - and it was a big if, she could find two others besides Pastor Roy to write a glowing reference.

Since her breakup with her fiancé, Mariah had to pull her self-esteem out of the depths. Mariah wanted kids, Scott didn't. End of story. Well, that and the fact she'd recently made a commitment to Jesus. Scott wasn't interested in competing with God.

From now on, her life would be great. She had a house and a new opportunity to serve. *Who needs a man?*

Mariah slowed her pace as the church spire came into view. She stopped, leaning over with her hands on her thighs to slow her breathing, admiring the green ivy crawling up the sides of the white clapboard building. The church was one of the first buildings raised after the founding of Main, Oregon in the mid-1800s.

When her breathing returned to normal, Mariah pulled open the side door. She stepped into the church office and looked around. The reception desk sat empty. Maybe Pastor Roy's wife, Susan was on a break. Mariah tiptoed down the hall toward Pastor Roy's office. The door was open, but the office was empty as well.

Her Asics running shoes squeaked on the tile floor as she made an about-face and headed back toward the sanctuary. She peeked into the room and spotted a man swishing a rope-type mop under the rows of pews. He whistled along to some tune only he could hear. Black ear buds stuck out from his ears like dual antennas.

Mariah's heart sped up and her mouth went dry. She cleared her throat, hoping to get the man's attention. He continued to push the mop back and forth, leaving wet streaks on the tile floor.

"God has not given me a spirit of fear," Mariah whispered, desperately trying to remember Pastor Roy's counsel.

"Not every man in a church is a predator," he'd said during one of their counseling sessions with his wife, Susan. Mariah's brain knew this as truth, but her legs refused to move.

"Hey." Mariah's voice echoed in the sanctuary.

The man whirled around with a look of surprise.

Pulling the earbuds out one at a time, the man looked her up and down. Mariah squirmed under his appraisal. If he made a move toward her, she'd bolt for the door.

"May I help you?"

He leaned the mop against the wall and wiped one hand down the leg of his jeans. Mariah turned up her nose at his faded yellow shirt dotted with enough holes to pass for a slice of Swiss cheese. The paint-stained pants weren't much better. When did Pastor Roy hire a homeless guy to help clean the church?

"I'm looking for Pastor Roy."

"He isn't here right now."

Mariah felt her shoulders drop with disappointment, then tense with irritation. Who was this rude guy?

Mariah eyed him with a bit of suspicion. "I didn't realize we hired a new custodian," she said, crossing her arms.

"We?" he asked.

Her face grew hot. "The church. I didn't realize the church hired a new custodian."

He seemed to consider her answer. "Are you on the church board?"

"What difference does that make?" Mariah bit her lip before her quick temper could spark into flame. This guy was getting on her last nerve.

The man shrugged. "No difference."

"Do you know when Pastor Roy will return?" Mariah gave him her best frosty look.

He cracked a smile. "No, I don't. Sorry. But I'm glad to pass a message along to him."

Mariah dug in her bag and pulled out the reference form, slapping it against her leg. "I'll drop this on his desk and leave him a note."

She'd wanted to give Pastor Roy the form and talk about who else she could ask. There weren't many people in town who would give her a glowing review. Her reputation as a 'mean girl' didn't disappear the minute she decided to follow Christ.

Mariah strode back the way she came and grabbed a piece of scratch paper and a pen from the reception area. After scrawling a note, she placed the form and the note on Pastor Roy's desk.

On the way back to her house, her feet pounded the pavement with annoyance directed toward the rude man at the church. If he was their new janitor, he needed some lessons on courtesy. She directed her angst toward him rather than focusing on how she'd be able to get two more references.

~

Ethan watched the woman stride out of the sanctuary, black ponytail swishing. Beautiful woman but tightly wound. Not that he'd noticed her beauty. Much. Since his wife's death, he'd made a conscious effort *not* to notice women.

When he finished mopping the floor, he headed to Pastor Roy's office and sat behind the scarred desk. He picked up his cell phone and tapped out a number.

"Ethan, my boy. How is everything going?" Pastor Roy's voice boomed over the phone.

"Good. Jayden and I are settling in. Thanks for letting me stay at your house. How's your sister-in-law?"

Roy's sighed. "Not well. Instead of releasing her from the hospital, they had to drain two liters of fluid from her lungs. They're keeping her for another couple of days."

"I'll bet Susan is stressed."

"We're holding each other up in prayer. I can't thank you enough for filling my pulpit."

Ethan experienced a stab of guilt. His faith had been shaken when his wife, Angela, was killed by a drunk driver. Two years later, he still felt like he was going through the motions. He'd asked for a leave from his pastorate in Seattle and had been living off the proceeds from Angela's life insurance. 'Leave of absence' wasn't the right phrase, but it soothed his ego.

Roy's call offered him a lifeline, and Ethan jumped at the chance. Perhaps this temporary pastorate in a tiny community would help him rekindle his faith.

"I'll be praying for you." Ethan said the expected words, knowing his prayers would be weak. "By the way, a woman came in today asking for you." He picked up the folded paper and tapped it idly on the desk.

"Who?"

Ethan squinted at the signature on the note. "Mariah."

"Ah yes. Pretty girl. I've been working with her for a couple of months. Great story of God moving in her life. You'll have to ask her about it."

Ethan doubted she'd deign to speak to him again. His holey work clothes contrasted sharply with her perfectly put together look. *Jogger Barbie.*

"She dropped something on your desk. Want me to scan it to you?"

"What is it?"

Ethan unfolded the document, looking toward the door in case the woman came charging through, accusing him of violating her boundaries or something.

"It's a request for personal reference from Safe Families For Children."

"Oh, right. I forgot I told Mariah I would give her a reference. Please send it and I'll fill it out after we leave the hospital."

"Will do." Ethan moved to the scanner, remembering how the woman eyed him up and down as if he was gum stuck to the bottom of her expensive running shoes. If God had done some miraculous moving in her life, why was she super judge-y?

Ethan's thoughts were interrupted by the pattering of feet dashing down the hall toward his office. A small bundle of energy launched onto his lap.

"Dad! Me and Miss Sarah baked cookies today."

Ethan returned Jayden's enthusiastic hug as Sarah stepped into the room with a bright smile.

"Jayden is a master cookie maker," Sarah told him.

Ethan set Jayden on his feet. "Are you now?"

Jayden nodded hard enough for Ethan to hear his neck crack. "That's right. Tomorrow we're gonna work in the garden."

"Did you tell Miss Sarah thank you?"

Jayden ran to Sarah, hugging her around the knees. "Thank you, Miss Sarah."

Sarah patted him on the head. "You are quite

welcome. I enjoyed it."

Ethan stood. "Thank you for watching him. He'd be bored hanging out here all day."

"Tsk. It's no problem. You need quiet time to prepare your message."

Ethan cringed. He'd swept and mopped the sanctuary floor, tightened the hinges on the bathroom stalls, and blown the leaves off the church steps. Anything other than preparing his message.

"Well, thanks again. I'll drop him by tomorrow at the same time."

Miss Sarah moved in for a hug. Ethan gulped, trying for the 'tent hug' to no avail. The older woman was as enthusiastic with her affection as Jayden. She pulled him close enough for him to smell the scent of gardenia perfume on her neck.

"Bye-bye, Jayden." Sarah waved her fingers and turned to go. "Oh, I almost forgot. I brought a Tupperware container of cookies. They're sitting on the front desk. Enjoy!" With a waft of fragrance, she was gone.

"Well, J-man, ready to help me tighten up some squeaky pews?"

Jayden jumped up and down with a fist pump. "Yeah!"

Ethan grabbed his tools and they headed into the sanctuary. Perhaps the act of working with his hands would spark inspiration for Sunday's message. Either that, or he'd pull an old one out of his archives, dust it off, and pass it as new.

"Test each pew for squeaks, okay?" Ethan knew which of the fifty-plus pews needed screws tightened, but it would give Jayden something to do with his endless energy. And something to keep himself from working on the sermon.

While Jayden slid along each pew, Ethan thought about the life he'd been handed by the Lord. When he and Angela met in Seminary, they'd had big plans. Marriage, children, serve the less fortunate in their community, preach the Gospel with words and actions. Maybe some short-term missionary work.

That had come to a jarring halt when Angela was killed. Even now, his grip tightened on the screwdriver until his knuckles turned white at the thought of the accident. A drunk driver crossed the median and hit her head-on. Why hadn't he insisted she take the minivan instead of her little puddle-jumper? Maybe she would have survived the impact.

Jayden's voice pulled him from his dark thoughts. "Dad? Someone's here to see you."

Ethan stood and tossed the screwdriver into the toolbox, hoping it wasn't a rerun of Jogger Barbie.

He relaxed when he saw it was a man about his own age. "May I help you?" Ethan asked as the man approached.

"Hi. I'm looking for Pastor Roy."

You and everyone else. Ethan's thoughts went to Mariah. If only Roy and Susan had had time to explain their absence to the congregation.

"Pastor Roy is on an extended leave of absence. Can I help you with something?"

The man's face fell. "I'm sorry to hear that. Is everything okay? Well, obviously everything is not okay, or he wouldn't be on a leave of absence." The man stuck out his hand. "I'm Roman. I came to ask Roy and Susan to lunch after church Sunday."

Ethan shook Roman's hand. "I'm Ethan. I'll be filling in while they're gone."

"Great. I mean great that you're filling in, not that it's great Roy's gone. I mean, not that we're not glad to welcome you, but…" Roman's voice trailed off.

Ethan smothered a grin. The guy seemed flustered.

"Well, anyway," Roman continued. "Since Pastor Roy isn't here, maybe you and your wife would like to come? My wife, Lizzy, is cooking something special. She won't tell me what, but her food is always good."

Ethan froze. After Angie's death, friends invited him for meals and game nights. At first, he turned down every invitation. Finally, they stopped asking.

"Uh—" Before Ethan could complete a response, Jayden ran to him.

"Can we go, Dad? Please? I'm tired of your cooking." Jayden pulled on Ethan's hand.

"Hey, little man. What's your name?" Roman asked.

"I'm Jayden. I'm five. We live here now. Do you have kids?"

"Jayden, that's enough." Ethan was ready to decline the invitation.

"We have a daughter. She's eleven. I'm sure she'd love to meet you." Roman looked to Ethan. "We'll give you the address after church. Our neighbor is coming too. It'll be a party."

Roman stalked down the center aisle toward the door, hitting his forehead with the heel of one hand.

"Yay!" Jayden shouted. "We're going to a party, we're going to a party." He danced in a circle with his arms extended like an airplane.

Was his son so desperate for fellowship that one lunch invitation had him over-the-top excited? Ethan struggled with his single dad-ness every day, always questioning if he was doing a good enough job. Was Jayden happy, did he miss his mom, was he depressed? He had thirteen more years of this.

Angela and he had never talked about what they would do if one of them died. Their whole lives spread out before them like an unending feast. Until it didn't. Would Angela have wanted him to marry again?

Chapter 2

Mariah arrived home to find a large box on the porch. She examined it for the shipping label to see it was the crib she'd ordered online. The extra downstairs bedroom was equipped with a twin bed, and Mariah wanted to be prepared in case she was assigned a little one by Safe Homes for Children.

Stepping through the front door, she called, "Grady, you still here?" At his affirmative grunt, she said, "Can you help me bring in this box?"

Between the two of them, they hefted the box into the spare bedroom.

"You need help putting it together?" Grady asked, pulling off his ball cap and scratching his head.

"No, I've got this. I'm sure there are directions. Go on back to what you were doing."

Grady shambled back toward the kitchen. "Your cabinets were delivered today. To my shop. I'll bring them around tomorrow."

Mariah beamed. "That's great. I can't wait to get

them installed. How's the floor coming?"

Grady adjusted his cap. "Okay, I reckon. Got a bit of clean up and I'll be done for the day."

Mariah nodded. Had she made a mistake in hiring the old geezer? He came well recommended, but maybe somebody younger would work faster. His references said he was slow but thorough.

She sighed, wishing she'd listened more carefully to her dad's recommendations. She'd been determined to do this on her own and this decision may have cost her precious time.

"Shall I write you a check for everything you've done so far?"

"That would be mighty nice of ya."

Mariah retrieved her rarely used checkbook from the bedroom and carried it into the living room. Grady shifted his weight from one leg to another while Mariah filled in the date.

"Do ya want an invoice first?" he asked.

Mariah squinted up at him. "You can bring it next time you come. How much do I owe you?"

Grady quoted a figure. "Ya know, folks around here said I shouldn't work for ya. But ya ain't been so bad." He rubbed a hand across his face.

Mariah stopped writing as anger flared. "Excuse me?"

A flush worked its way up from the old man's neck to his cheeks. "They said you was difficult."

Mariah pressed her lips together and gripped the

pen with white knuckles. Living in a small town was both a blessing and a curse. Shedding her mean girl reputation hadn't disappeared simply because she'd made a profession of faith.

"Anyhow," Grady said. "Thanks for the job." He shrugged then let his arms drop to his sides.

Mariah clamped her lips together and handed him the check. Grady shuffled into the kitchen. Soon the sounds of tools clanging into his toolbox drowned out the country music coming from Grady's radio.

When Grady collected his tools and said goodbye, Mariah collapsed onto the sofa with a bottle of water from the only source of refrigeration she had - an ice chest. Maybe the ice-cold water would cool her anger over Grady's words. Small towns thrived on gossip. She should know. She'd used ugly half-truths herself to destroy someone's reputation.

As she was chugging the water, the doorbell sounded, and a familiar face popped through the door.

"Hi – it was unlocked so I let myself in."

Speaking of destroying someone's reputation. Lizzy was proof of Mariah's past reputation. "Hey, Lizzy. Come on in and sit."

They were friends now, thanks to Mariah's heart change. Lizzy plopped down on the sofa.

Mariah eyed her up and down. Lizzy's hair, normally up in a neat pony fell around her shoulders in a tangled mess. Her face was splotchy, as if she'd been crying.

"You look awful."

"Gee, thanks, Mariah. I can always count on you to be brutally honest."

Mariah immediately regretted her forthrightness. She and Lizzy had only recently become friends after years of animosity. Mostly because Mariah had bullied Lizzy and her friend Simone since middle school. It wasn't until she started meeting with Pastor Roy that she realized how wrong it was. The thought of Pastor Roy brought the unwelcome thought of that rude janitor at the church.

Shaking it off, Mariah grabbed Lizzy's hands in hers. "I'm sorry. What's wrong?"

Lizzy snuffled as tears formed in the corners of her eyes. "Everything's wrong. Roman and I are getting on each other's nerves. Abby wants to spend a whole month with her dad and stepmom in Portland. And I'm pregnant!"

"You're pregnant?" Roman and Lizzy had talked about having a baby, now that they'd been married almost a year.

Lizzy nodded.

"I thought you wanted to have a baby." Mariah spoke slowly, trying to understand her friend's angst.

"I do. It's these hormones are making me crazy. And I'm making Roman crazy. No wonder Abby wants to spend more time with her dad."

Mariah got up and snagged some tissues from the bathroom, handing them to Lizzy.

"Anything else?"

Lizzy nodded again. "I kind of went crazy on him when he got home today. He biked down to the church to ask Pastor Roy and Susan to lunch after church Sunday." She dabbed her eyes. "You are coming, aren't you?"

It was Mariah's turn to nod. Any meal that didn't come out of a box was a welcome change.

Lizzy blew her nose with a loud honk. "Anyway, I wanted to come over and tell you the news. I have a doctor's appointment in two weeks."

Mariah thought back to when Lizzy worked at the Pill Shoppe drug store and had rung up several purchases of home pregnancy tests for her. Mariah and Scott were living together at the time. When Scott found out she was deliberately trying to get pregnant, he dropped her like a hot massage stone.

"That's exciting! Does Simone know?" Mariah had no doubt Simone was told the news first. Mariah was third in their little triangle. A tiny bit of jealousy slithered up her back.

"I sent her a text, but she hasn't responded. She's probably with a client." Lizzy stood. "I should get back. Abby and Roman are probably plotting to lock me away until my hormones settle down."

Mariah stood and the two women hugged. "Let me know if you need anything."

Lizzy smiled. "Thanks. I will. Anyway, see you Sunday at church. And after for lunch."

Mariah plopped back down on the sofa. Roman must have caught up with Pastor Roy after she left the church. Maybe he'd have her reference filled out and would bring it. She sat back with a sigh. Things were starting to look up. Soon she'd be caring for a child, or maybe two. Tomorrow she'd unpack the crib and assemble it. Grady would deliver the kitchen cabinets and begin to install them. She'd schedule delivery of the new appliances and get ready to greet her new temporary family.

~

Ethan stared at the blank screen of his laptop while Jayden played on the floor by the kitchen table. The blinking curser mocked him from the flush left margin. In another lifetime, he'd be putting the finishing touches on his sermon instead of starting.

What could he possibly say to encourage and exhort these strangers? How could he preach about hope when he had none? He reached for his iPad and did a Bible search for the word 'hope.' Perhaps he could cobble something together from the fifty-three references in the New Testament.

After two sentences, Ethan's laptop dinged with an incoming email. Pastor Roy had scanned him Mariah's reference. Ethan printed it out and glanced at it before setting it aside to continue typing.

What is our hope? Is it only for eternal life? The Apostle Paul says if we only hope in that one thing, we are miserable. Why did he say that?

Ethan tried to continue typing, but the reference form pulled him. Would it be intrusive if he read what his old friend said about Mariah? What good things could he say about the woman who looked down on someone she perceived as lesser than? Ethan snorted. She wanted to take care of kids. Not a chance, lady. He was pretty sure eating kids for breakfast was not part of the program.

Although no one was in the house except for himself and Jayden, Ethan sent a furtive glance around the room before reaching for the paper.

He read it through several times, trying not to laugh. Roy had given Mariah glowing praise about her integrity, character, and compassion. Either Roy had her pegged incorrectly, or she was very good at hiding her true personality.

Ethan folded the sheet into thirds, thrust it into an envelope and sealed it. If she was at church tomorrow, he'd hand it to her then. He shook his head, then went back to preparing a sermon he hoped would impress his new, temporary congregation.

~

Mariah slipped on a yellow and turquoise sundress, admiring the way it contrasted with her sheath of black hair. Her carefully painted toenails peeked out from yellow strappy sandals. She'd paid way too much for the Steve Madden's, but seeing how they made her outfit, she was glad.

Another quick turn in the full-length mirror and

she was ready to don a short turquoise sweater and hop in her BMW to head to the church. Attending Sunday service without Scott beside her was difficult, but Lizzy and Roman usually saved her a place. Mariah silently thanked God Scott had moved out of the area, so she didn't have to face the humiliation of seeing his face after he dumped her.

Mariah shook her head, remembering how they attended church together, even after moving in together. How dumb she'd been, thinking it was okay to live with someone without being married. That was BC, she reminded herself.

At the church, Mariah parked and strode up the concrete steps to the main door, skirt swishing around her knees. A couple of people greeted her. Roman, Lizzy, and Abby hadn't arrived yet, so Mariah took a seat in their normal spot to wait.

As the church filled, Mariah thought about how much her life had changed in only a few months. When she and Scott broke up, she'd been devastated, seeking counsel from her pastor. He'd gently showed her the path to salvation. Pastor Roy helped her see she didn't need a man to complete her, she needed Jesus. With painful clarity, Mariah saw how many people she'd hurt by her own insecurity over her past trauma.

She'd made amends with Lizzy and Simone and was about to embark on a new adventure; caring for children whose parents needed a little respite. For the first time since high school, Mariah didn't have a man by her side. Who needs a man when she had two new best friends?

A few minutes later, Roman and Lizzy squeezed into the pew, Abby a few steps behind. After whispered 'good mornings,' they settled in to listen to the worship team begin. From her vantage point, Mariah didn't see Pastor Roy and Susan sitting in their usual spots in the front row, left side. When they stood to sing, Mariah saw an unfamiliar man sitting in the Pastor's spot. Only the back of his head was visible. His brown hair curled over the collar of his dress shirt. A small boy stood on the pew by his side.

When worship ended, everyone sat. Except for one man, the one who'd sat in the pastor's normal place. He strode up the two steps to the platform, set an iPad on the pulpit, and smiled.

Mariah stifled a gasp. She wouldn't have recognized him as the same guy who'd been mopping the floor two days ago, except for those green eyes that seemed to pierce her very soul. She slid down in the pew. Maybe he wouldn't notice her.

"I am not Pastor Roy," he began. This brought on a few titters from the congregation. "Pastor Roy and Susan asked me to pass along their apologies for leaving without being able to notify you all. Susan's sister had a heart attack and was rushed into emergency open-heart surgery." This brought a few gasps and murmurs. "Your pastor asked me to step in and temporarily take his place. Now, I know I have huge shoes to fill, and I ask for your forgiveness in advance. My name is Ethan Walsh and my son is Jayden."

He went on to give a bit of his background while Mariah sat in shamed mortification. She'd mistaken him for the janitor! Once again, her old nature had asserted itself and had judged him harshly for the way he dressed. Lizzy glanced at her sideways as Mariah slid further down in the pew, praying for the service to end.

When the worship team started the final song, Mariah jumped to her feet. "I'll see you two in a bit," she said to Lizzy. Mariah rushed out the back door and dashed to her car before anyone could stop her.

~

Ethan's eyes locked on Mariah the minute he stepped to the pulpit. No one should be allowed to look that good. The blue of her sweater brought out the color of her eyes. She was beautiful. Too bad her personality didn't match. Maybe Pastor Roy didn't know Mariah as well as he thought.

At the end of the service, Ethan strode to the door to greet his new flock. He spotted Jayden running around the grass with some boys while women clustered around him like hens.

"Welcome to Main, Pastor Ethan," a youngish woman said with a smile.

The questions came fast and furious.

"How long will you be here?"

"How old is your son?"

"Are you married?" This from a short red-haired woman who looked to be around his own age.

"Do you need some meals delivered? We can set you up on our rotation."

"Are you free for lunch?" one bold woman with glasses and a baseball cap asked.

Ethan spied Roman and a woman he assumed to be Roman's wife push through the throng. "He's coming to our house. Roman and I asked him two days ago." She turned to Ethan with her hand extended. "I'm Lizzy. Nice to meet you."

"You too," Ethan said, shaking her hand.

Ethan sighed with relief as the group of chattering ladies melted away. Some gave him lingering gazes as they moved toward the parking lot.

He hated this. Single women and their assertiveness was another reason he'd left his church in Seattle. Since Angela's death, women seemed to think he was husband material. He was not interested. Period. End of story.

The only one who piqued his interest was the one with the blue eyes and black hair. The contradiction of Roy's assessment and her seeming snobbishness made him want to know more. That was not a good idea. Best to keep the door to his heart closed and locked.

When the last hand had been shaken and the doors to the church were firmly closed, Ethan gathered up his son and climbed into his truck for the short drive to Roman's house.

Jayden kept up constant chatter about his new friends. "There's lots of boys at this church. We played soccer and they said we could come over to play video games at their house. Can we, Dad?"

Ethan mumbled his response, exhausted over the effort to remember names and faces from the introductions after church. He'd rather go home and take a nap than have to make nice with new people over lunch. Although a home-cooked meal did sound good about now.

He pulled up to a cozy stucco home painted light gray with dark blue accents. "Jayden, remember your manners, okay?"

"Okay, Dad."

They climbed out of the vehicle and approached the front door. Before they made it halfway up the driveway, the front door flew open, and a girl raced toward them.

"Hi. I'm Abigail. I'm eleven. We're having pasta fagioli for lunch. Do you know what fagioli is? It's Italian. My stepdad is Italian. His name is Roman."

Ethan grinned. His son had met his match. Abigail grabbed Jayden's hand and pulled him into the garage. "Let's ride bikes," she said. "You can ride my scooter."

Ethan heard their excited babble as he approached the open front door.

"Hello," he called.

Roman came to the door wiping his hands on a towel. "Welcome. I see you've met Hurricane Abby."

Ethan stepped into the house with a grin. "Yup. She and my son, Jayden, are cut from the same cloth."

Roman's wife stepped into view. "Come on in, Pastor Ethan. Lunch will be ready in a few."

"It's just Ethan," he said, following Roman into the living room. A gray sofa along one wall held colorful pillows. Silk plants with fairy lights sat in two of the corners.

Roman sat in a red and gray plaid lounger. They stared at each other until Ethan broke the silence.

"Nice place you have here."

"Thanks."

Uncomfortable silence followed until Lizzy stepped into the room while removing her apron.

"We're waiting for my friend, Mariah," Lizzy said, patting Roman on the shoulder before she sat on the sofa.

It took a minute for her words to sink in.

"Mariah?" Ethan asked with a bolt of panic.

Lizzy nodded. "She should be here any minute. Have you met her yet? She and I have known each other forever. We went to school together."

Ethan had a hard time connecting Lizzy's warmth with Mariah's coldness.

The doorbell rang, keeping Ethan from having to respond. He sent Roman a weak smile.

Ethan kept his gaze on Roman, hearing Lizzy in the background. "Come on in, Mariah. Pastor Ethan is already here. And his son, too. I guess you heard today about Pastor Roy and Susan."

Lizzy's chatter continued as Mariah stepped into view. Like trying to look away from a car accident, Ethan's gaze swept to the woman stepping into the room behind Lizzy followed by Jayden and Abigail.

Mariah's blue eyes searched his for a moment, then she looked down. For a moment, he caught a glimpse of red starting on her neck and working its way up to her cheeks. He hid a smile. So, she was embarrassed over their initial meeting. Interesting.

Chapter 3

It wasn't until Mariah pulled to a stop in front of Lizzy's house that she realized she should have cancelled lunch. She could have made up some story about food poisoning. Or a sudden onset of hives. Or pneumonia.

She remembered Lizzy mentioning the other day about Roman asking Pastor Roy and Susan to lunch. Lizzy or Roman must have asked the new interim preacher to lunch instead. Now Mariah would be stuck making nice with the man she'd been rude to. A pastor, to boot. Surely there was some special punishment from God for being mean to a man of the cloth.

Yeah, there was. Having lunch with him at a friend's house and having to decide whether or not to apologize. She shuddered.

"Thanks, God."

Mariah climbed out of her BMW and made her way up the driveway.

"Hi, kids." Mariah waved at Abby and the boy she assumed was Pastor Ethan's son.

"Hi, Mariah," Abby said. "This is Jayden. He's

five. Miss Sarah is babysitting him while his dad works. If he's still here when school starts, he'll be in first grade. We'll be in different schools, though, cuz I'll be in fifth grade."

Mariah crouched down to give Abby a hug. "Sounds like you've got it all figured out."

Not to be outdone, Jayden opened his mouth and let loose a torrent of words. "I'm Jayden. My dad is a pastor. We're living in Mr. Roy's house until, well, I don't know. My mom's dead."

Mariah inhaled sharply. Poor kid. It must be hard to grow up without a mom. "It's nice to meet you, Jayden. I hope you're happy here. I've lived here all my life and I like it."

"We lived in Seattle before. I liked it there. We did a lot of stuff. Like hiking and riding bikes and stuff."

Mariah's stomach growled, reminding her of the reason she was here at Lizzy and Roman's.

"Let's go check on lunch, shall we?" Mariah asked, holding out her hands for the kids to take.

The front door stood open. Mariah stepped across the threshold. Lizzy grabbed her in a warm hug, then led her and the kids into the house. Mariah glanced at Roman, then Ethan, and looked down. Her face grew warm as Lizzy made introductions.

"Come on to the table. I'm sure everyone's hungry." Lizzy indicated where everyone should sit. "I'll get the soup off the stove and dish up." She returned to the dining area a moment later carrying a huge tureen.

Roman popped up from his seat. "Let me get that." Mariah heard him whisper, "You shouldn't be carrying anything heavy."

The look Lizzy sent him was pure adoration. A wave of jealousy washed over Mariah. Would anyone look at her that way again?

After Roman said grace and everyone's bowls were filled, Lizzy passed a green salad and a basket of rolls around the table.

"This soup is amazing. What is it?" Ethan asked.

"It's called Pasta y Fagioli. Roman's mom has been teaching me some of the family's favorite recipes."

Roman rested his hand on Lizzy's. "She's a quick learner." They smiled at each other like newlyweds.

Mariah stayed quiet as the conversation rolled around her. Pastor Ethan talked about moving from Seattle with Jayden. Roman and Lizzy extolled the virtues of living in a small town.

"You've been quiet, Mariah," Lizzy said.

Mariah startled. "Um, yes. I'm enjoying this good food. Until my kitchen is finished, I'll continue eating frozen dinners and takeout."

Pastor Ethan met her gaze across the table. "You're redoing your kitchen?"

Mariah took a bite of salad and nodded. Lizzy took the opportunity to launch into the story of the house lottery and how Mariah had won. The contract with the

City of Main stated she had to live in the house for at least a year and pay all taxes owed.

"She's doing some upgrades, too. The house is over ninety years old. The last time anyone did improvements was probably forty years ago." Lizzy got up and went into the kitchen, returning with a pitcher of ice water.

"The house was *uuuugly,*" Abby piped up.

Mariah agreed. She and Lizzy had gone round and round with what should be done first. Lizzy itched to put her design ideas into practical use on Mariah's snug little bungalow.

"When will the kitchen be finished?" Roman asked.

Mariah shrugged. "Soon, I hope. Grady delivered the cabinets yesterday. He's done scraping the old linoleum off and as soon as he gets the floor down, he'll install the cabinets and counter tops."

"Did you get your crib set up?" Lizzy asked.

"Crib?" Ethan asked, looking confused. "Do you have kids?"

Lizzy leaned across the table with a huge smile. "Wait until you hear this. Mariah is preparing her home so she can take in kids whose parents need some respite. It's like foster care, but you don't get paid, and the kids aren't in the system. It's really cool. Tell him about it, Mariah."

Mariah gulped, anxious to turn the attention away from herself, a totally new sensation. Was it because

Ethan's hazel eyes bored into hers, challenging her?

Ethan snapped his fingers. "I just remembered something. I left it in the car. It's from Pastor Roy. I think it has to do with your program."

Mariah cringed. What had Pastor Roy written on the reference sheet? Did Ethan read it? Ugh. Why couldn't she be more like Lizzy? Her inner demons continued to hammer away at her self-esteem.

Ethan pushed back from the table, returning a few minutes later. He handed the envelope to Mariah.

"Thanks," she murmured.

Jayden and Abby started to get restless. Mariah turned her attention to them. "Wait until you see the playroom I made. It has everything a kid could want."

Abby bounced in her seat. "When can we see it? Can we go today?"

Mariah smiled. "Sure, if your mom and Roman don't mind."

Abby turned to Lizzy. "Can we go now? I'm all done eating."

Jayden turned to his dad. "Yeah, Dad. Can we go see it now?"

Before they could answer, Mariah said, "Let's help your mom clean up. Then we'll go."

"Let's all go," Lizzy said. "We'll clean up later."

Roman stood and tossed his napkin on the table. "It's such a beautiful afternoon, let's walk."

The six of them trooped down the driveway and onto the sidewalk. Roman and Lizzy held hands, Jayden and Abby talked over each other, and Mariah and Ethan ended up walking side by side.

"Tell me more about this program. How did you get interested in it?" Ethan asked.

Mariah hesitated, her heart torn in two. She wanted to tell him the story of how her life had changed since Scott had refused to have children and how he'd left her. But it was a new and fragile tale, one she wasn't sure he was ready to hear. "It's a long story," she said, struggling with her inner turmoil. "Maybe I should tell you another time."

Ethan nodded. "Okay."

They walked in silence around the corner and up the hill to Mariah's home. She unlocked the door and let everyone pass by before closing the door behind them. She led the way to the narrow staircase at the end of a short hall.

Lizzy peeked into the guest room as she passed from the living room. "Is that the crib?" She pointed to the large box leaning against one wall.

Mariah nodded. "Yes. I was going to unpack it yesterday, but it's too unwieldy."

"Maybe Roman can help," Lizzy said, glancing behind her at her husband. Roman shrugged noncommittally.

The kids raced up the stairs while the adults followed.

"Wow!" Abby exclaimed.

Mariah had painted the room a bright yellow.

Windows on either side of the room let in an abundance of light. The slanted ceiling met in the middle of the room, tapering down each side, giving the space a cozy feeling.

"I bought at child-sized easel and paint set." Mariah pointed to one corner. "There's tubs of Legos and another of Blume dolls."

A couple of bean bag chairs invited one to sit.

"You have a TV up here too?" Lizzy asked.

"Yes, and a PlayStation." Mariah wiggled her eyebrows at the kids.

"Can we play?" Abby asked, jumping up and down.

"No, Ladybug, I'm sure Mariah has tons of stuff to do. Maybe another day."

Mariah crouched down to Abby's level. "It's okay with me if it's okay with your mom."

Abby clasped her hands and gave her mother a prayerful look. "Pleeeeeze, Mom?"

Lizzy sighed. "Okay, fine. But only until Mariah gets tired of you."

Jayden grabbed Ethan's hand. "Can I stay too, Dad? Please?"

Mariah stood and faced Ethan. "I really don't mind. It's more fun with two players."

Ethan looked undecided, then said, "It's all right, I guess. For a little while."

Lizzy covered her mouth as she yawned. "I'm heading back home for a nap."

"I'll do the dishes," Roman said.

The adults trooped back down the stairs. Roman and Lizzy said their goodbyes.

Ethan turned to Mariah. "Are you sure they won't be too much trouble?"

She shook her head. "I'm going to wrestle with the crib box, then see if I can get the crib set up. They can hang out while I'm doing that." She motioned into the spare room.

"I could help you," Ethan said.

~

As soon as the words disappeared into the air, Ethan wanted to grab them and pull them back. Why did he offer to help this dichotomy of a woman? Brittle with adults, soft with kids. Right now, he'd rather be slumped on Roy's comfy sofa, snoozing while today's baseball game filled the room with noise.

Instead, he was sharing a task with a woman he couldn't figure out.

Mariah released the blade on a box cutter and sliced along the edge of the box. She handed the cutter to Ethan, and he did the same on the opposite side.

Mariah grabbed the cardboard and pulled. "Ow. Ow. Ow." She sat back on her heels, cradling one hand in the other. "I broke a nail!" she moaned.

Figured. Miss Perfect would be out of commission the rest of the day.

"It's just a nail," Ethan murmured.

"But I'm bleeding." Mariah jumped to her feet.

"Let me get a band-aid and we can finish."

By the time she returned to the bedroom, Ethan had removed the crib from the fingernail-attacking box. "Let's lay out all the bags of parts before we do anything else."

Mariah knelt on the floor in the doorway, a good six feet away and grabbed a handful of tiny bags containing screws and other objects she couldn't identify. "Here's the instructions." She extended her arm toward him, holding the folded sheaf of paper. Ethan reached across the expanse and took the single sheet of paper.

Her scent wafted toward him; a cool, minty fragrance, indicative of her personality. Both cool and warm. Ethan got to his feet. "I should go check on the kids."

Mariah scooted back into the living room to allow him to pass. "I'm sure they're fine."

Ethan brushed past her, anxious to escape the intimacy of building a crib in a cozy room with a beautiful woman. He bounded up the stairs and practically fell into the open space.

"Check this out, Dad, they have the Spiderman game." Jayden barely acknowledged him as he turned his attention back to the game.

"Great. Well, have fun. We'll be leaving soon." Ethan raked a hand through his hair. What was wrong with him? Angie had been gone two years. He still grieved for her. Why was he attracted to someone else?

Ethan lingered for a few moments, watching Spidey climb tall buildings with his super-power and Jayden's delight at playing the latest and greatest video game.

"Bam!" Abby exclaimed, waving the controller as she completed some stunt.

Ethan turned and trudged down the stairs. If only he could have a super-power. What would he choose? To be able to preach like Franklin Graham? Maybe something as simple as hearing from God again. He'd been silent since his wife's death.

With a sigh, Ethan returned to the task at hand. Mariah had kicked off her sandals and sat with her back against the doorframe. Her long, tanned legs stretched out in front of her as she held the directions. The bags of parts lay in neat rows, one numerically and one alphabetically.

"Here," she said, handing him the instructions. "I can't make heads nor tails of this."

Ethan stepped over Mariah's legs and sank to a crisscross position. "Let me see if I can decipher it." The instructions seemed to be written in another language before being translated into English. With a groan of frustration, he set the pages on the floor.

"Do you have a screwdriver?" Ethan doubted she knew what a screwdriver was.

Mariah gathered her legs under her and rose gracefully to her feet. "Be right back." She disappeared, reappearing a few moments later carrying a small pink toolbox.

Ethan quirked an eyebrow. "Seriously? Pink?"

Mariah shrugged. "Tools don't have to only be utilitarian you know." She knelt down and popped open the ridiculously pink toolbox.

All the tools inside had pink handles. "I think I just lost my man card." Using his thumb and forefinger, he gingerly removed the screwdriver from its slot.

"Oh, good grief. Get over yourself," Mariah snapped.

Ethan grinned despite himself. She was back to being snotty. He was more comfortable with that side of her.

Between the two of them, they wrestled the crib parts into submission. By the time they finished an hour later, Ethan had sweated through his shirt. He sank back against the wall and swiped a hand across his forehead.

"Whew. Glad that's done."

Mariah seemed not to have oozed a drop of perspiration. Her hair stayed neatly clipped at the nape of her neck, and her dress remained crisply ironed. Even her lipstick stayed intact. Ethan pulled his gaze away from her lips with a huge effort.

"Let me get us some water." Mariah returned to the room with two wet bottles of water and a neatly folded towel. "Sorry they're so wet. I grabbed them from the cooler." She wiped one of the bottles and handed it to him. "I don't have a refrigerator yet."

"No problem." He opened the water and guzzled

down half of it before rolling the bottle across his forehead. "I'm exhausted," Ethan said, struggling to his feet.

"I'll bet you are." Mariah appraised him from her stance at the door. "Pastor Roy said he looked forward to his Sunday afternoon nap."

"Let me gather Jayden up, and I'll get out of your hair."

Mariah moved to let him pass. "Thanks for your help. I could never have done that by myself."

"No problem," Ethan repeated. He was starting to sound like a robot.

By the time he'd convinced Jayden and Abby to exit their game and grudgingly head down the steep staircase, Ethan's limbs felt heavy with fatigue.

"I'll walk you back home," Ethan said to Abby.

"That was super fun," Jayden exclaimed. "Can we come over again?"

Ethan glanced at Mariah, who knelt down to Jayden's level. "I'm glad you had fun. You can come back any time, as long as your dad says it's okay."

"Can we dad?" Jayden looked up imploringly.

Too tired to do much more than nod, he took his son's hand and led Abby out the door.

"Thanks again for your help with the crib," Mariah said.

Ethan was caught off guard when her lips stretched into a smile. With a curt nod, he ushered the kids out the door. He would not be attracted to this woman.

Chapter 4

Mariah closed the front door behind the trio and stood with her head resting on the cool wood. Ethan's presence had rattled her more than she wanted to admit. Pastor Roy's words echoed in her ear.

"Not every clergyman is a predator, Mariah. Most of us are decent, God-fearing men and women."

Working on the crib with Ethan had notched up her pulse and caused her stomach to churn.

"You're an adult," Mariah said out loud. "Not a stupid twelve-year-old. You can defend yourself."

She sucked in a lungful of air and blew it out to the count of five. Again. A nice, long run would calm her jangled nerves. And allow her to retrieve her car from Lizzy's house.

Forty minutes later, Mariah arrived home sweaty and exhausted. Her phone pinged with a text from Lizzy.

Our new pastor is cute, right?

This was followed by a smiley face. Mariah's grip

on her phone tightened. The last thing she needed was for her new best friend to set her up with someone, much less a pastor. She had a mission – provide a safe and temporary shelter for kids whose parents needed a little help. It was time to shrug off her mean girl reputation and do something to make her life count.

Mariah ignored the text. After a shower and a quick snack, she responded.

Not interested!

No more than three minutes later, her phone rang and her brother's photo filled the screen.

"Hey, sis. I need a favor."

Mariah rolled her eyes. Daniel's favors usually involved something Mariah didn't want to do.

"Mom and Dad are hosting a fundraiser in two months, and they need your expert planning skills."

Mariah scowled. "I told you I don't do that anymore. I'm super busy, Daniel. The house remodel, the Safe Families thing, you know."

"Ah, come on, sis. We need you. Please."

"Don't beg. It's unbecoming."

"But effective." Mariah detected the humor in his voice.

"Not this time, Danny." He hated his nickname.

"If you don't say yes, Mom will be calling you."

"What is this, 'I'll tell mom?' I thought we outgrew that."

"Do you really want Mom to call you?

Mariah sighed. Mom was a force of nature. Gee,

wonder where Mariah got it from? Look no further than one branch up the family tree.

"Fine," she snapped.

Daniel had the nerve to laugh. "I'll text you the deets. Meeting tomorrow here at the ranch."

To call their home a ranch was a misnomer. Dad had made a fortune in real estate and built their homestead on a hill outside of Main, Oregon. He spent his days pretending to be a rancher, farmer, and vineyard worker. He provided his two offspring with a hefty monthly allowance, enabling them to pursue their own interests.

Daniel's voice turned serious. "How are you doing, really, Mariah?"

"Fine. Why?"

"Since Scott, you know—"

"Dumped me? I'm fine." Which was half true. While his mad dash to leave her and Main for Portland had stung, Mariah took partial blame for his hasty departure. She'd tried to trap him into marriage by trying to get pregnant. When he discovered her scheme, he'd moved out.

Looking back, it was all part of God's plan. Mariah had run to Pastor Roy and discovered the love and forgiveness she'd been searching for. If only it was that easy to shed the mean girl persona she'd carried since she was twelve.

"Ancient history," Mariah said.

"Okay, then, if you say so. Later." Daniel

disconnected.

Mariah turned the phone over and over in her lap. Her family didn't understand her new-found faith. Mariah still hadn't found the right words to convey that even though she'd attended church with Scott, their living situation wasn't honoring to God.

With a growl of frustration, Mariah opened the notes app on her phone and started a list.

Possible people to ask for a personal reference

The Safe Families organization asked for three. Pastor Roy was the first ask. She'd tossed the envelope Pastor Ethan had given her on the small table inside the front door.

"Think, Mariah." Surely there was someone else who might provide a reference. She could ask Lizzy or Roman. They'd become good friends since Mariah had made the decision to follow Jesus. Mariah squirmed with embarrassment, remembering how she'd flirted with Roman before he and Lizzy had gotten married. He'd run out of the gym like his hair was on fire.

Since middle school, Lizzy had been on the receiving end of Mariah's torture. She'd taken every opportunity to belittle and bully Lizzy over her clothes, her hair, and her unexpected pregnancy at sixteen.

Okay, don't ask either of them.

Mariah's eyes filled with tears. For too long, she'd been brittle and abrasive to almost everyone. Now her life had changed, but everyone remembered her as Mean Mariah. Everyone except the few who knew her now.

Lizzy, Roman, Simone, and a few ladies at church. Mariah folded her hands and sent up a prayer for divine inspiration.

~

Ethan woke Monday morning with a start. Jayden stood by the side of the bed, staring. "What are you doing up, J-Man?"

"I couldn't sleep."

Ethan sat up and pulled his son into bed. "Let's snuggle, okay?"

Jayden curled up like a puppy next to him as they spooned.

"I miss Mommy. She was the best snuggler."

Ethan's heart hurt. "I know, buddy. I miss her too."

Two years. Two long, lonely years. All Ethan had ever wanted was to get married, go into ministry, and have a family. The pitiful shell of his current life was like an egg dropped from a cozy nest onto the hard ground. Shattered outside and all the insides leaking out.

Angela had been everything a pastor's wife should be. She played the piano, sang in the choir, and happily led children's church. Equally adept at teaching toddlers and women's Bible studies.

They'd met in Bible School. Angela wanted to become a missionary, hoping to serve overseas in Africa or Thailand. She'd laid it aside to become Mrs. Pastor Ethan Walsh and serve in Seattle, Washington.

Ethan sometimes found her searching the internet for mission opportunities in those countries. It was a source of irritation in their marriage, but never to the point of conflict. When Jayden was born, Angie had seemed content to lay aside her desires and be a mom.

Until a drunk driver took her. Ethan's arm around Jayden tightened. He'd stopped asking God 'why' because he'd never gotten an answer. God had been silent for too long. Now he was here in Main, Oregon, stuck in this tiny town. Like spiritual purgatory. Maybe here he'd find the peace that had eluded him since Angie's death.

Pastor Roy's call had come at the time Ethan was ready to call it quits. His recycled sermons had raised the ire of the church board. Ethan felt their displeasure. When Roy asked him to fill in, Ethan jumped at the opportunity. His home church graciously gave him a three-month leave of absence, telling him in so many words to get his life back in order.

As if it were that easy. At least here in the little town of Main, population 10,201, he wouldn't have to avoid the intersection where his wife had been killed. He wouldn't have to face the pitying looks on his congregants' faces. Hopeful young women, looking for a husband, wouldn't bring him food, invite him for coffee, or try to get him alone.

Jayden stirred and pulled out of Ethan's embrace.

"What are we doing today, Daddy? Can we play more video games at that lady's house?"

"That lady's name is Miss Mariah and no, we can't go there today. She's a busy lady."

"But she said—"

"I know what she said. But I have big plans for us today." Ethan didn't, but he wanted to avoid the subject of Mariah and her games. He'd rather not think about her at all. Not about her shapely legs or her jet-black hair that draped over her shoulders like a waterfall.

Stop it, he told himself. "I thought we'd explore our new city today." Ethan usually took Mondays off, mostly to decompress from Sunday, but as a day to spend time with Jayden by himself. Back in Seattle, Jayden was in daycare Tuesday through Friday. Here in Main, one of the church ladies offered to watch him. Sarah was a Godsend, watching Jayden for a fraction of the cost of daycare.

"Come on, J-man. Let's get dressed and find a place to get a man's breakfast."

Jayden pumped one fist. "Yeah!"

Thirty minutes later, they sauntered into Cookie's Café, a hole in the wall on Main Street.

"Seat yourself," called out a waitress from across the room.

Ethan and Jayden sat in a corner booth as the waitress approached with a steaming pot of coffee. Her hair was a shade of purple not found in nature and she wore enough metal in her ears to attract radio signals.

"Coffee?"

Ethan nodded. Jayden looked up at the woman, his

eyes wide. "We want a man's breakfast," Jayden piped up.

The waitress' name tag read Wren. "Well, little man, we've got what you want. I'll bring menus over in a mo'."

"Daddy, what's a mo?"

Ethan smiled at his boy. "It means a moment."

"Oh. Okay."

Ethan ordered their food and turned his attention to the other patrons, scattered around the dining room. Most of the men were older and wore working men's clothing. Jeans, flannel shirts, work boots or cowboy boots. The women were a mixed bag of retirees and young moms, trying to keep their toddlers busy while catching up with a friend. Ethan remembered those days. Distracting Jayden with soda crackers so he and Angela could have lunch or dinner away from the house. Trying to get him to color on the back of the paper placemat.

Wren brought Jayden's milk and refilled Ethan's coffee.

"You new in town or passing through?"

"I'm the new pastor of Main Community Church," Ethan replied.

"I heard something about Pastor Roy's sister-in-law. You filling in for him?"

Ethan nodded. "Yeah. Not sure how long."

Wren smiled. "Welcome to Main. I've lived here my whole life. Don't want to go anywhere else."

Ethan had no wish to make small talk with her, but Wren seemed in no hurry to get back to waitressing.

"Where you from?" she asked.

"Seattle." Maybe his short answers would get his message across.

"Seattle, huh? Now there's a place I don't want to visit. Too big. Too many people." Wren shuddered.

Ethan didn't respond.

"You'll like it here. Everyone is friendly and we all chip in when somebody needs help. Ask anyone. They'll tell you."

Right now, Ethan wanted to ask her to leave.

"Order up," came the call from the cook.

"Oops, that's my cue," Wren said with a grin. "I'll be right back with your breakfast."

"Our man breakfast," Jayden piped up.

They dug into their food. Ethan reached over to help Jayden cut his pancakes into small pieces. When he looked up, he saw the woman who he tried to forget meeting walking by his table. Mariah.

"Look, Daddy, there's Miss Mariah," Jayden said in his outside voice.

She stopped and turned toward their table.

"Hi, Miss Mariah! We're having a man's breakfast." Jayden waved his pancake-filled fork.

Mariah smiled. "I see that."

"Are you having a girl's breakfast? Want to sit with us?" Jayden radiated excitement. Ethan wanted to crawl under the table.

"Oh, I don't think so," Mariah said. "I don't want to interrupt your time with your dad."

"Are you going to sit by yourself?" Jayden persisted.

"That's enough, Jayden. Miss Mariah is probably meeting some friends."

"Are you?" Jayden asked.

Ethan wanted to muzzle his son.

"No, I'm not." Mariah half turned to follow Wren, who watched them with an enigmatic grin.

"You can sit with us," Jayden said.

Ethan watched Mariah chew on her bottom lip. "Well, okay."

Mariah slid into the booth across from them. She set her expensive-looking bag on the seat next to her. Ethan spied the Band-Aid she still wore on the broken fingernail.

Wren poured Mariah a cup of coffee and sauntered toward the kitchen.

Mariah sent Ethan an apologetic look. "Sorry. I hope I'm not intruding."

"It's fine," Ethan said, his lips stiff.

"Go ahead and finish your breakfast." Mariah took a sip of her coffee. "Until my kitchen is finished, I eat a lot of my meals out."

"Must get expensive," Ethan commented.

Mariah shrugged. "I guess. But what can I do? My contractor said he'd be finished by the end of the week, but you know how that goes."

Ethan didn't. He'd always lived in a parsonage provided by the church. Angie had done her best to make it their own, but there was only so much the church would allow them to do. Pastor Roy's home was much nicer than his current efficiency apartment in Seattle.

Wren placed a plate of scrambled eggs and sourdough toast in front of Mariah. "Your usual," she said.

"Thanks, Wren." Mariah bowed her head and Ethan assumed she was saying grace. When she looked up to find Ethan staring, her face suffused with color.

Ethan cleared his throat and turned his attention to Jayden. "You almost done, J-man?"

"Almost, Daddy. Is that a girl's breakfast?" Jayden asked, leaning toward Mariah.

"I guess it is," Mariah responded with a smile in Jayden's direction. "We girls have to watch our weight."

No wonder she was thin. She had the build of a runner. Angie was on the shorter side and tended toward plumpness. Not that Ethan minded. Angie was all curves while Mariah was angles. Why was he comparing the two? Ethan mentally slapped himself.

Wren appeared and dropped the check on the table. "Can I get you two anything else?"

"Nope, that's it," Ethan said. "Thanks."

With one last glance between him and Mariah, Wren strode to the next booth. Ethan heard her taking their order and filling their coffee mugs.

Mariah took delicate bites of her eggs and toast without smudging her lipstick. How did women do that? Angie never wore makeup and was content to *shlep* around in jeans and a tee shirt when she wasn't at the church or leading a Bible study. By contrast, the woman across from him wore stylish workout wear and pricey athletic shoes.

Jayden took a last noisy gulp of his milk and wiped his mouth with the back of one hand. He let out a gusty burp.

"Jayden!" Ethan said.

Jayden grinned. "Sorry, Daddy." He looked anything but sorry.

Mariah smiled. "Did you know in some foreign countries, you are expected to belch after a good meal? It's considered rude if you don't."

"Cool," Jayden said. He belched again.

"We are not in one of those foreign countries, Jayden." Ethan sent Mariah a hard look. Her face turned red.

"Sorry."

~

Mariah poked at her scrambled eggs and set her fork down. There she went again. Saying the first thing that came into her brain without thinking it through. Pastor Ethan must think she was an idiot, trying to get his son to burp.

She'd stopped when Jayden's voice called her

name. Seeing Pastor Ethan sitting in the corner booth had brought a rush of adrenaline.

Breathe. *God has not given me the spirit of fear.*

Mariah sent up a prayer of thanks for Pastor Roy. He'd shown her what a man of God was supposed to be like. Not like the youth pastor when she was twelve. But what kind of man was Pastor Ethan? He seemed like a devoted father, so there was that.

She took a sip of her now lukewarm coffee. "What do you two men have planned for today?" Mariah directed her question to Jayden, who beamed.

"Me and Dad are gonna do some stuff." Jayden looked to his father. "What *are* we gonna do, Dad?"

Ethan rubbed a hand across his face. He hadn't shaved and the dark stubble gave him a different look than when he was in the pulpit. An image of Scott filled her mind, of his dashing good looks that always turned women's heads. Mariah shoved the memory away. Scott was yesterday's news.

Ethan twirled his coffee mug in a circle. "I'm not sure, buddy. What's there to do in this little town?" He glanced at Mariah, then down to his mug.

Mariah sat back against the hard wooden booth. "It's a short drive to the coast. You could go to the aquarium. If it doesn't rain later, you can go to the beach." Mariah ran through several possibilities for amusing a five-year-old.

"There's bowling. The bowling alley also has an arcade. Do you have bikes? There's a pretty bike trail that wanders along the creek."

Jayden clapped his hands. "Let's do everything, Daddy."

Mariah laughed. "You won't have time to do it all today."

Jayden's face fell. "What can we do?"

Ethan grabbed a napkin and wiped syrup off his son's face. "We'll go home and figure it out."

Jayden stood on the booth seat and leaned toward his dad. "Can we ask Miss Mariah to come with us? Maybe she'll let me play Spiderman at her house."

Ethan sent Mariah an apologetic look.

Mariah saved him from answering. "Oh, that's sweet, Jayden. But I can't. I have some work stuff to take care of."

"What do you do for work?" Ethan asked.

Mariah felt her face grow warm. How to explain that she didn't have an actual job. Dad's generous allowance took care of that. "I, uh—"

She was saved from having to answer by Wren stopping at their table with a steaming coffee pot.

"Come back anytime," Wren said to Ethan with an appraising smile.

Mariah grabbed her check and slid out of the booth. "Thanks for the company. I'll see you Sunday." She couldn't escape fast enough. The subject of her allowance was the cause of a lot of criticism from her former friends. Jealousy and envy never took a vacation.

Time to figure out who else to ask for a personal reference before heading to Mom and Dad's to talk about the fund-raiser.

Staring at the Notes app on her phone, Mariah willed a name to appear. Nothing. Still blank and somewhat accusing. Of course no one would be a reference. Mean girls didn't change their reputations overnight.

Mariah climbed into her car and turned the vehicle toward home. She passed the high school, stopping at the sign. With a flash of inspiration, Mariah pulled into the school's parking lot.

She climbed out of her sedan and draped the strap of her Michael Kors handbag over one shoulder. In one hand, she carried the reference request.

"May I help you?" asked the young receptionist at the front desk.

"Is Mrs. Mickelson still teaching here?"

The young woman nodded. "Yes. Can I tell her you want to see her?"

"Can't I go down to her classroom?"

The receptionist looked Mariah up and down and must have decided she posed no threat. Handing Mariah a yellow visitors tag, she pointed down the main hall.

"Her classroom is the last one on the left."

"I remember."

Mrs. Mickelson must be ancient by now. She'd been old when Mariah took English from her ten years ago. Or was her perception the assumption of teenagers that everyone over thirty was practically in their graves.

Mariah paused outside the classroom door. Of all her teachers, Mrs. Mickelson had been the most encouraging. Mariah remembered how she'd urged everyone to read A Tale of Two Cities, even though most of the students complained about how difficult it was to understand.

Mariah sucked in a breath and pulled open the door. She found her former teacher sitting at her desk, head down, scribbling notes on hand-written assignments.

Mrs. Mickelson's head jerked up and her hand flew to her chest when Mariah approached. "Oh, you startled me."

"Hi, Mrs. M. I don't know if you remember me—"

She pushed her chair back and rose to her feet. "Mariah Martin, of course I remember you. The prettiest girl in Main High School."

Mariah found herself wrapped in a hug. Mrs. Mickelson smelled of lavender.

Mrs. Mickelson pulled back to gaze up at Mariah. "To what do I owe this unexpected pleasure?"

Never one to beat around the bush with small talk, Mariah got right to the point. "I need a favor."

Mrs. Mickelson returned to her chair behind the desk and pointed to a student desk nearby. "Have a seat, my dear, and tell me what you need."

Mariah set the reference sheet on the corner of the teacher's desk before squeezing into one of the student desks.

"I've applied to a program called Safe Families for Children. It provides temporary respite care to parents who need a place for their kids. Sometimes they're living in their car and have to go to work. Other times the mom or dad might have to go to rehab, and they don't want to put their kids into the system for only a few weeks." Mariah's speech sped up.

"I saw it on a YouTube video by Katie Couric. She's a huge backer of this program. I told myself, and God, that if I won the house lottery, I'd use it as a place to take in these kids. Doing foster care is not an option. As a single woman without a job, it's practically impossible to be approved."

Mariah took a breath. "But I need three references."

Mrs. Mickelson held her gaze without blinking. "Why me? Surely you have plenty of friends you could ask. Or your father's business associates?"

Mariah's shoulders sagged. Everyone knew her as the selfish, self-centered, sharp-tongued vixen. Time to give up the dream of being a caregiver. She'd never live down her reputation.

Mariah set her mouth in a straight line. She got up from the desk and reached for the reference sheet. "Thanks, anyway."

Mrs. Michelson was quick. She slapped her hand onto the paper. "Not so fast, young lady. The Mariah I remember from high school wouldn't give up that easily."

The older woman picked up the sheet, pushed her glasses up her nose, and perused the document. When she finished reading, she set it down and folded both hands on the desk.

"Mariah, when you were in school, you were a good student. A bit lazy, but overall, your grades were decent."

"How do you remember that?"

Mrs. Mickelson smiled. "I always remember the good ones. You had a gift for creating stories. I think that's why you won the essay contest for the house lottery."

A smile worked its way up from Mariah's belly. "Thank you."

"Now, young lady, let me work on filling out this form. Come back tomorrow, and I'll have it ready."

"Again, thank you, Mrs. M."

The teacher smiled. "Don't underestimate yourself, Mariah. You have more friends than you think."

With a nod, Mariah stepped out of the classroom with a lighter step than when she entered. Her cell pinged with a text.

Brittany: Coffee?

Brittany and she had been friends since sixth grade when they both had a crush on the same boy. When he chose another girl to be his girlfriend, Brittany and Mariah bonded over their mutual dislike for the boy and disdain for the girl.

Mariah hesitated before responding. Brittany was not a part of Mariah's new but tiny circle of Christian friends. Lizzy and Simone, who'd been best friends since forever, had let her into their circle. Brittany didn't understand Mariah's new faith.

Mariah: Sure. Human Bean. Fifteen minutes.

This was followed by a thumbs-up emoji from Brittany.

Fifteen minutes later, Brittany breezed into the coffee house on a cloud of expensive perfume. Tere de Hermes. Yummy. Brittany could afford it. Her husband was a major construction material supplier in Portland.

"Hey, girlfriend. Where have you been hiding?" Brittany leaned in for a quick hug before turning to place an order for a skinny mocha.

Mariah waited until Brittany sat before answering. "Oh, you know, remodeling the house, preparing for the Safe Families program, stuff like that."

Brittany wrinkled her nose. "I still don't understand why you would want to take in some snotty-nosed kids?"

Mariah grimaced. "I told you. I need something to feel like I'm useful."

"Useful is overrated. Look at me." Brittany spread her arms out wide. "I take care of my house. Take care of my husband." She waggled her eyebrows at this.

Mariah blushed.

Brittany continued, "I might even be convinced to pop out a kid or two."

Mariah's core filled with envy. She'd wanted to have a baby with Scott. He didn't. Since committing her life to Christ, Mariah vowed to stay single until she found the kind of love Pastor Roy had told her about. Love that was unconditional. Love that didn't rely on finding sexual compatibility before marriage. Love that lasts.

Until then, helping kids would be second-best.

"Safe Families is a great program."

"Ugh. Sounds like a lot of work." Brittany stood to retrieve her coffee order from the counter. Returning to the table, she set her cup down and leaned forward. "Did you hear what happened to Carly? She got pulled over on the way home from Salem."

Mariah's stomach sank. Brittany's nickname of Gossip Queen was well-earned. Mariah and she used to love to meet for coffee and dish on their friends. Now the thought of enjoying other's misfortunes had zero appeal.

She didn't respond, but it didn't stop Brittany from continuing.

"She tried to convince the trooper not to give her a sobriety test. She ended up with a DUI. Her boyfriend threatened to make her move out if she didn't stop drinking." Brittany smirked, then took a sip of her beverage.

"That's too bad. I'll pray for her."

Brittany's well-sculptured eyebrows rose to her hairline. "Pray for her?"

Mariah grew hot. "Well, yes. Sounds like her life is messed up. I'll pray she starts to make some better choices."

Brittany barked out a laugh. "She needs an intervention, not prayers."

Mariah steered the conversation away from gossiping about their friend. "Do you remember Mrs. Mickelson, our high school English teacher? She agreed to write a reference for me for the Safe Families program."

Brittany regarded her with a straight face. "You're not going to let it go, are you?" She sighed. "Look, I know you had some sort of religious experience, but that doesn't mean you have to change your life." Brittan leaned forward and whispered, "Does this have anything to do with what happened, you know, back in middle school?"

Brittany was the only one who knew the details of 'the incident.'

Mariah took a sip of her latte and nodded. "It changed my life, Brit." She tapped her finger against the lid. "And my life changed again when I started meeting with Pastor Roy after Scott dumped me."

Brittany leaned back and rested one arm on the back of the chair next to her. "That religion stuff was fine when we were kids, Mariah. We're adults now."

Mariah searched her brain for any verses she could use to show how they needed God even more now as adults but came up empty. She hadn't been a follower for long enough to know much of anything.

"Speaking of religious stuff, did you know Pastor Roy is on a leave of absence?"

Brittany's face lit up. "Yes, I heard that. Have you met the new pastor? He's hot."

Speaking of hot, Mariah felt a flush work its way up her chest to her cheeks. Count on the Gossip Queen to know everything that happened in their small town.

"I've met him. He's nice. He has a little boy."

Brittany leaned forward again. "Married? Divorced?"

"Widowed."

Brittany's face took on a calculating look. "Husband material?"

Mariah laughed out loud. "Uh, no, Brit. I could never be a pastor's wife. I have too much baggage. Besides, I don't play the piano." Old stereotypes die hard. Mariah pictured a pastor's wife as almost saint-like. Long, demure dresses, sensible shoes, musically inclined, and perpetually pregnant. Like Roy's wife Susan, minus the pregnant part.

Brittany popped the lid off her drink and drained the last of her mocha. "Oh, well. I want everyone to be happy like me and Link."

Mariah had wanted that too. With Scott. She sent her friend a rueful smile. "I'm happy for you, Brit. Maybe someday I'll find what you have. Until then, Safe Families is my goal in life." She pushed back her chair and stood. Gripping the back of the chair with white knuckles, she asked, "Oh, by the way, would you be willing to give me a personal reference? I need three and I only have two so far."

"Of course I would."

Mariah exhaled with relief. "Great. I'll email you the form when I get home. Thanks."

They hugged goodbye and headed to their separate cars. Mariah chewed her bottom lip and watched her friend drive away. How did she and Link stay happily married without God?

With a shrug, she climbed into her car and drove back to the little house she now called home.

Chapter 5

Ethan tucked an exhausted Jayden into bed. They'd spent a busy day at the coast, building sandcastles and chasing the waves of the Pacific Ocean. For the millionth time, Ethan asked himself if he was doing enough to give his son a stable upbringing.

If only Angela was here. She'd been the one to take Jayden to the park, on play dates, and to the library story time. Was he doing enough?

Angie would have hated today. She would have complained about sand in her shoes or in her hair. Ethan felt a pang of guilt at his criticism of his dead wife. His thoughts turned to the woman at breakfast. Mariah. Would she complain about sand blowing in her perfectly straight hair? Or on her expensive looking running shoes?

Ethan shook his head. Why was he comparing the two women? Angie had been the perfect pastor's wife. She created a meal schedule for church members recuperating from surgery. She faithfully led a weekly Bible study for young married women. A random memory hit Ethan.

They'd argued about Angie's desire to complete her degree in Social Justice.

"You have tons of opportunities to do social justice stuff right here in Seattle," Ethan told her.

"But I want that degree, that piece of paper to show I finished. Why can't you understand that?"

Ethan remembered how he'd practically bullied Angie into complying with his point of view. It created a small fissure in their marriage. Angie's bitterness over the situation showed up in tiny ways. Her lips narrowed as she grudgingly agreed to yet another task he gave her. When he insisted that Saturday was a 'workday,' she'd narrowed her eyes and brought guilt on him for neglecting quality time with Jayden. Then she started talking about overseas missions.

Ethan sighed. Other than that, Angie had been the example of what a pastor's wife should be. He'd never find another one like her.

Why were thoughts of Mariah invading his brain like an earworm? He wasn't here in Main, Oregon, to find a wife. Pastor Roy had asked him to fill in for three months. Thank goodness he hadn't completely burned the bridge to his former church.

"Why am I here, Lord?" Ethan said aloud. Roy's living room didn't respond.

Ethan readied himself for bed, but sleep wouldn't come. He felt like Jacob, wrestling with God. In the Old Testament story of Jacob, he wrestled with an angel all night until the angel finally dislocated Jacob's hip. Ethan rubbed his own hip.

Hope it doesn't come to that.

The next morning, Miss Sarah knocked on his door at exactly nine o'clock.

"Good morning, Pastor. I brought you some fresh baked blueberry muffins. I picked the blueberries last summer from the bushes behind my house." She handed Ethan a plate of fragrant muffins. "I thought since I was bringing the muffins here, I'd pick up Jayden, so you don't have to bring him.

"Come on in," Ethan said. "He's brushing his teeth." Ethan indicated the plate. "Thanks for these. They smell great."

Sarah blushed. "It's the least I could do. Now, let me get that beautiful boy out of your hair so you can get some work done."

Jayden ran from the bathroom, straight toward his babysitter. "Miss Sarah, what are we going to do today?"

Ethan watched his son with a smile. Jayden didn't know a stranger. Ethan wished he had the same enthusiasm for life as his son. That had died with Angie. Or had it died before then? Ethan shook off the thought.

"Here's Jayden's backpack. You two have a great day."

"Bye, Daddy. See ya later."

When they were gone, Ethan couldn't escape the empty house fast enough. Perhaps the church would offer respite from the crushing loneliness.

Ethan walked briskly the two blocks from Pastor Roy's house to the church. He unlocked the door and turned off the alarm. Sitting at the secretary's desk, he punched in the voicemail code.

"You have five new messages," intoned the robot-like voice.

Ethan sighed and pulled a pad of paper toward him. Roy's wife Susan had been the church secretary. Their absence created a canyon-sized void.

Two voicemails were hang-ups. Ethan sighed with relief. Then the next three.

"This is Samantha Burton. Harvey tripped over a paint bucket and landed on his shoulder. I'm taking him to Urgent Care. Please let the prayer chain know. Thanks."

"Hey, Pastor Ethan. We met Sunday. My name is Noah and I'm the youth leader. Today I tested positive for Covid. I can't lead the youth group Wednesday night. Can you fill in for me?" Ethan winced when Noah coughed into the phone. Noah left his phone number and disconnected.

A shiver of excitement worked its way up from Ethan's core. Youth work was his first love. His first assignment after Bible college was as the youth pastor for a small church outside of Seattle. Angie hated it. She'd regularly complained about his irregular hours, kids coming and going from their small apartment, and the meager pay. Ethan tried to explain that the ministry experience would prepare them for the future. The only upside was the annual week-long mission trip to Mexico. Angie lived for those trips. If she hadn't gotten pregnant with Jayden, Angie might have persuaded him to apply for a full-time mission assignment. Her dream, not his.

Ethan made a note to talk to Miss Sarah about Samantha Burton and what Pastor Roy usually did about the prayer chain. He headed down the hall to Roy's office to plan for Wednesday night youth group.

He opened his laptop and opened it to a blank Word document. As he typed out some notes, his subconscious noted the constant ringing of the phone at the front desk.

~

Mariah wandered through her living room to peek into the kitchen. "How's it going, Grady?"

Grady straightened from where he bent over, examining the cabinets that had been delivered that morning. He pulled the ball cap from his head and scratched his balding scalp. "Well, ma'am, I'm about finished inspecting them cabinets. My sons will be here in a bit to start installing them."

Mariah grinned. One step closer to having a sleek new kitchen. "Great news, Grady. I'm heading out to do some errands."

Grady tucked the cap back on his head with a nod. "Gotcha."

Mariah headed back to the bedroom to retrieve her purse. As she pulled the strap over one shoulder, she stopped in the doorway to the second bedroom. A multi-colored quilt lay on the twin bed. She'd set a few stuffed animals against the pillow. The crib was on the wall closer to the door. Since there was no way of knowing if she'd host a boy or a girl, or even both, Mariah had gone with soft pastels of blue, pink, green, and yellow. How long after sending in her references would it take before she could be a respite for needy families?

With a shrug, she pulled out her car keys. First stop, the high school and Mrs. Michelson. Mariah slowed as she neared the school. School was still in session – how could she have forgotten that? She made a U-turn in the school parking lot. Now what?

Down the street, the church spire pointed toward the gathering clouds. It seemed to pull her into its orbit. Without stopping to second-guess herself, Mariah turned into the parking lot. She sat for a moment. What was she doing here? Almost against her will, she hopped out of the BMW, hit the remote door lock, and strode through the side door leading into the church office.

The ringing of the phone jarred the silence. No one sat at the secretary's desk. The phone stopped ringing, then started again a few seconds later. Mariah skirted around the counter and grabbed the phone.

"Main Community Church."

"Oh, my goodness. I'm glad you answered. This is Samantha Burton. Who's this?"

"Mariah Martin."

Mariah heard a gasp. "Mean girl Mariah?"

Mariah gritted her teeth and blew out a breath through her nose.

Samantha Burton continued. "I'm sorry, dear. You caught me off guard is all." She paused to take a breath. "I left a message earlier about my Henry. Did you get my message?" Without waiting for Mariah to answer, she continued, "I took him to Urgent Care, and they are taking him by ambulance to Salem. To the hospital. His blood pressure went sky-high and they're afraid he'll stroke out."

Mariah opened desk drawers searching for a notepad as Samantha Burton continued. While the older woman went on, Mariah jotted down the pertinent information.

Henry Burton, hospital, Salem, blood pressure.

When Samantha stopped to take a breath, Mariah said, "I think I've got everything, Mrs. Burton. I'll let Pastor Ethan know."

"Thank you, dear. And please ask Sarah to activate the prayer chain. Oh, and I am in charge of the flowers for the altar on Sunday. I don't think I can take that on this week. No telling how long Henry will be out of commission. Did I mention he tripped over a paint can and fell on his shoulder? I had to drive him to Urgent Care—"

"Yes, Ma'am, I got all that. Let me let you go so you can take care of Henry." Mariah breathed a sigh of relief when Samantha Burton disconnected. She set the phone down and tapped the receiver with the tip of one fingernail. Now what?

She jumped when a male voice spoke.

"What are you doing here?"

Mariah whirled around to see Ethan standing in the entrance to the hall, hands on hips.

She fanned herself with one hand.

"You scared me." In more ways than one. Her heart kicked up a notch. She was alone with a clergyman, in a church building, far away from anyone else. Pastor Roy's voice echoed in her head. "You don't have to be afraid, Mariah."

Was it fear or Ethan's rugged handsomeness that increased her pulse? He wore faded Levi's and a long-sleeved checked cotton shirt with the sleeves rolled up on lean forearms. She recognized his slip-on shoes as a brand known as Hey Dudes. Not cheap, but not super expensive. His casual attire was polar opposite of her former boyfriend's. Scott tended toward name brand clothes and pricey Italian loafers. Without socks. A glance down confirmed Ethan's sock choice. Good. Guys without socks were a turnoff.

Ethan frowned. "Again, what are you doing here?"

She had no idea. Mariah flipped her hair back with a shake of her head. "I heard the phone ringing." She held out the pad of paper where she'd written Samantha Burton's information.

Ethan took it without speaking. "She left a message this morning." He tapped the pad on his open palm. "Do you have Sarah's phone number?"

"No. But I can find it for you."

Ethan shook his head. "I have her number. She babysits Jayden. Can you call her about the prayer chain?"

"Sure, I guess." Mariah wrinkled her nose. If he had Sarah's number, why not call her himself?

Ethan pulled his cell from the back pocket of his jeans and tapped the screen. Setting the pad on the desk, he wrote Sarah's phone number.

The phone rang again. Mariah sent Ethan a questioning look. At his nod, she answered. "Main Community Church." Pause. "Yes, he's here. Yes, he knows about Henry." Pause. "Yes, please. Thank you." Mariah hung up the phone and turned back to face Ethan.

"That was Sarah. Someone already alerted her about Mr. Burton." Mariah shrugged in a 'what are you gonna do' expression. "Small towns."

A smile broke out on Ethan's face. Mariah's breath caught. If he was handsome with frown on his face, smiling, he was devastating. Not that she was interested in a pastor. Not with her history. Ethan took a step toward her. Maiah pushed the chair back, leaving a six-foot gap between them.

"You're hired," Ethan said.

"Excuse me?"

"You're hired," Ethan repeated.

Mariah shook her head. "No. I can't be your secretary."

"Oh, right. My bad. Administrative assistant."

Mariah shot to her feet. The rolling chair rolled back and struck the wall. "I don't need a job." Nope, no way. She had too many things going on. The kitchen remodel, Safe Families, and helping her parents with their fundraiser. Besides—

Ethan's voice broke into her tumbled thoughts. "You think being an admin is beneath you?"

"It's not that." Sweat tickled her underarms.

"What is it then? I need help here." He swung his arms around to indicate the church foyer. "Pastor Roy's wife, Susan, used to help him."

"I can't."

Ethan placed both hands on his hips. "Why not?"

"B-because. You scare me." There. She'd said it.

Ethan's shot up. "What are you talking about?"

Mariah's face grew hot as she remembered the shame of what happened at that youth retreat. How she'd been flattered by the attention from the older boy. She'd flaunted his attention to the other, less attractive and developed girls. How she let him touch her beneath their zipped together sleeping bags. She hadn't stopped him when he wanted more.

Ethan reached out a hand. His face was all sympathy. "Help me understand, Mariah."

It was his use of her name that undid her. Tears formed in the corners of her eyes and spilled down her cheeks. "I-I'm sorry." She pushed past him and dashed out the door to the sanctity of her car.

Chapter 6

Ethan stared at Mariah's retreating back. What just happened? Why would Mariah say that he scared her? From his observation, she was a woman who wasn't easily frightened.

Ethan sank onto the rolling desk chair Mariah had abandoned and rubbed a hand across his face. He examined his behavior, searching for something-anything-he'd done to cause Mariah to be afraid.

Nothing came to mind.

The door burst open. Ethan looked up, hoping for Mariah's return.

"Daddy!" Jayden ran to him and jumped on his lap.

"Oof. You're almost getting too big for my lap, J-man."

A moment later, Sarah shuffled through the door. "Good afternoon, Pastor." She heaved a canvas bag onto the counter across from him. "Here's Jayden's library books. We had a lovely time at story hour, didn't we, Jayden?"

"Daddy, can you come with us next time? Story hour was super cool." Jayden jumped down and reached for the bag.

While he rummaged through the stack of books, Ethan stood and walked around the counter. "Thanks very much for watching him for me Miss Sarah."

"Did you get a lot done this morning?"

Had he gotten anything done? His sermon notes lay on Roy's desk, mostly blank. But he'd made good progress on what he would say to the youth group. "I think so."

Sarah smiled up at him. "I got the prayer chain going for Henry Burton. I called one of the elders, you met Mark, right?" At Ethan's nod, Sarah continued. "Mark and his wife, Cindy, are going to the hospital in Salem to be with Samantha while they figure out what's going on with Henry."

Sarah turned to leave, then whirled back. "Oh, I almost forgot. Samantha Burton was in charge of the altar flowers Sunday. I made a couple of calls and got someone else to handle it."

Ethan grabbed Sarah in a hug before she could leave. "What would I do without you?"

Sarah gave him a quick squeeze before pulling back. "I must run now. I have errands to do. I'll see you tomorrow, Jayden." With a wave and a whiff of gardenia, Sarah disappeared out the front door.

"Well, J-man? What do you say we head home and figure out what to have for supper?"

Jayden already had his nose buried in one of the library books. Ethan let him be while he went back to Roy's office to gather his notes. His thoughts returned to Mariah. How had he struck fear into the woman? He hadn't seen that coming. Direct, yes. Scared, no. He'd have to figure that out somehow. And how to convince her to spend a couple of hours every day with administrative tasks. For a small community church, the phone sure rang a lot.

Main, Oregon, had a population of about eleven thousand. Polar opposite of his church on the outskirts of Seattle, population approximately one hundred fifty thousand. Impossible to know your neighbors. Here in Main, Ethan constantly ran into people from the church. They seemed unaffected by his inability to remember their names. Instead, the men pumped his hand, and the women either greeted him with a smile or a quick hug. Ethan's heart warmed at their relentless friendliness.

Everyone doted on Jayden. So far, though, the single women hadn't begun circling him like hungry piranhas. He'd become adept at avoiding their schemes at his home church. His 'grieving widower' persona kept them at bay.

After two years, his grief over Angie was a dull ache rather than a sharp stab. Ethan struggled to remember the good times rather than her discontent. To the congregation, she'd been the perfect pastor's wife. Behind closed doors, she'd vented her frustration over being what she called 'stuck' in their growing congregation.

"You knew when we got married, I wanted to pastor a church," he'd said during one of their arguments.

"But you promised we'd go on missions trips," Angie replied.

"That was before Jayden. Would you leave him for six weeks or more?" Angie had shaken her head. Ethan could see the sorrow on her face. Angie was a good mom, but he wondered if she sometimes regretted Jayden's birth. During one of their quarrels, she'd threatened to go overseas and leave Jayden with him. After her death, Ethan had found a partially filled out mission application on her computer. A representative and his wife from SIM, formerly Sudan Interior Missions had spoken at their church. Ethan and Angie had hosted a dinner for the couple and invited a close group of people to join them. Ethan remembered how Angie's face glowed while listening to their stories of helping villagers learn agriculture in the remote province of Maradi, Niger. She'd never had that look while Ethan pastored their church.

Jayden's appearance in the doorway interrupted Ethan's mental wanderings.

"Ready to go, son?"

"Sure, Daddy. I'm so hungry." He rubbed his stomach and faked passing out.

Ethan gathered his iPad and notebook in one hand and grabbed Jayden's hand with the other. "Didn't Miss Sarah feed you?" Ethan knew she had.

"Uh huh. But that was a long, long time ago."

Ethan smiled down at his growing boy. Soon he'd have to take Jayden shopping for school clothes. So far, Ethan liked living in this small town. But he needed a secretary. Scratch that. He needed an administrative assistant. Who else could handle the phone calls and other tasks, since the lovely Mariah seemed to hate even the air he breathed.

~

Mariah pulled up in front of her house and stopped the car with a jerk. Deep, calming breaths. Inhale, exhale, repeat.

Grady's truck was gone. Good. One less person she had to pretend to be normal in front of. Her stomach sank when she spied Lizzy, sitting on the porch.

Mariah picked her way up the walkway, careful to avoid the cracks that threatened to cause a rolled ankle.

She stopped at the bottom step of the porch. "What are you doing here?"

Lizzy pulled herself out of the blue Adirondack chair. "I think this is where you're supposed to say, 'Hello, friend, nice to see you.'"

Mariah frowned. "It's been a long day."

Lizzy pulled her lips to one side. "This is where I say, 'Tell me all about it.'"

Mariah shook her head. "Fine. Come inside."

As usual, Grady had left the front door unlocked. Not that it made a difference. This area of Main was far enough from downtown so as to not get much through traffic.

Mariah closed the door behind her friend and dropped her purse on the sofa. "I'll be right back." She strode across the living room to the door leading to the kitchen.

The new cabinets gleamed in the afternoon sunlight.

Lizzy's voice sounded behind her. "Wow."

Mariah smiled for the first time that day. The white farmhouse cabinets contrasted with the nautical blue walls. Brushed silver knobs matched the faucet fixtures.

"I can't believe it's finally finished," Lizzy said, running a hand over the concrete counter. "It isn't what I pictured, but I love it."

Mariah hugged herself with excitement. "I love it, too." She pulled open a drawer, then gently shoved it closed. "Soft-closing drawers. Cool."

"I'm jealous," Lizzy said. She motioned toward the empty space between the wall and the cabinets. "When do you get your fridge?"

"Any day. I have to call and let them know I'm ready."

"Bet you'll be glad to get rid of the ice chest."

"You know it. Speaking of, want a water?"

At Lizzy's nod, Mariah returned to the living room and grabbed two bottles of water. She wiped the moisture off and handed one to her friend.

"Tell me what you're doing here." Mariah said.

Lizzy plopped down on the sofa and took a long drink from her water. "I had to get out of the house. Roman is driving me crazy."

Mariah snorted. "What now?"

Lizzy rolled the bottle between her hands. "You know he's a little OCD, right? He follows me around and cleans up after me." She leaned forward, getting into her story. "I left my coffee cup in the living room while I went to the bathroom. When I came back, he'd already washed it. I wasn't even done."

Mariah could believe it. Roman was a bit of a clean freak.

"He won't let me touch his high-end coffee machine."

"The Breville? I can understand that. Do you know how much those machines cost?"

Lizzy shook her head. "I'm tempted to buy a single-serving Keurig, so I don't have to ask him every time I want a cup of coffee."

"Sounds like a first-world problem."

"Thanks for the sympathy."

"Any time." Mariah took a sip of her water and set the bottle on the floor.

Lizzy's face filled with concern. "Enough about me and my first world problem. Tell me. Why was your day hard?"

Mariah crossed one leg over the other. She and Lizzy had been friends for less than a year. Before she'd won this house in the city's house lottery, Mariah had taken every opportunity to belittle her. Since middle school, Lizzy had been an easy target. Her Goodwill clothes stood in stark contrast with Mariah and her friends' designer jeans. When Lizzy got pregnant at sixteen, it gave Mariah more fodder. She carried her meanness into adulthood, reminding Lizzy she was a loser. No one knew Mariah was secretly jealous of the other woman. Lizzy had what Mariah wanted – a child of her own. Friends who loved her for herself and not what she could give them.

Mariah took a deep breath. "Pastor Ethan offered me a job."

Lizzy's face formed a puzzled frown. "And that's a bad thing because … "

No one except Brittany knew about 'the incident.' How could she explain to her new friend why it would be impossible to work closely with someone in the ministry?

"I'm too busy," Mariah said in a rush.

Lizzy's gaze narrowed. "Busy with what?" She motioned with her arm around the room. "You've almost finished with the remodel here. You don't have any kids to take care of yet. What is keeping you so busy that you can't work at the church? I'm assuming it isn't full-time."

Mariah had rushed out of the church so fast she hadn't gotten any details. She shrugged. "I have no idea."

Lizzy turned to face Mariah square-on. "Let me get this straight. You've had a bad day because Pastor Ethan, who is super cute by the way, offered you a job in the church. Am I getting this right?"

Mariah shot to her feet. "You don't understand." She paced across the living room and back. "My brother demanded I help with some event my parents have planned."

"And? I still don't see why you don't have time to help out. Want me to give you a list of what I'm doing?"

"No."

Lizzy drained her water. "Enlighten me, then."

Mariah wrung her hands together as she paced. "There was this time. No, wait, let me back up. Do you remember when he had that youth retreat in Lincoln City?"

"No. Remember, I didn't start going to church until, you know," Lizzy made a gesture over her growing baby bump.

Mariah clamped her lips together. This was going to be harder than she thought. "When we were in middle school, I went to this youth retreat in Lincoln

City. The youth leader was probably nineteen or twenty." Mariah paused, remembering.

A knock sounded on the front door, saving her from saying more.

Mariah strode to the door and pulled it open. "Simone, hi." Mariah grabbed Simone's arm and dragged her across the threshold. "Come in."

Lizzy narrowed her eyes. "I didn't get that kind of greeting."

Simone looked from Mariah to Lizzy. "You two having a fight?"

Mariah's laugh sounded forced, even to her own ears. "Of course not. Lizzy stopped by to complain about Roman."

Lizzy screwed the lid back on her water bottle. "Good thing we're friends now or I'd take offense at that comment."

Mariah gently pushed Simone toward the sofa. "Have a seat and I'll get you a bottle of water." She moved to the ice chest and pulled out a frosty bottle. "Let me wipe it off and then you can tell Lizzy and me what's going on in your life."

Out of the corner of her eye, Mariah saw Lizzy raise both shoulders in a shrug. She wiped the bottle with a towel, hoping Lizzy wouldn't insist she continue with her story.

"Here you go, Simone. Lizzy, do you want something else to drink?" Lizzy shook her head. Mariah seated herself on the ice chest and clasped her hands around her bent knees.

"What's up, Simone?"

Simone glanced at Lizzy. "I wanted to invite you both to a dinner at my gym. We're raising money for the youth wrestling team at the high school."

"Another fund-raiser, huh?" Mariah asked.

"Is that a problem?" Simone said.

Mariah shook her head. "Not really, I guess. My parents are hosting a fund-raiser at their ranch. I don't have all the details, but my brother said something about the Chamber of Commerce. He's roping me into helping."

Simone nodded. "Totally different crowd. We'll be using the big workout room. It's kind of laid-back. Can I count on you guys to be there?" She looked from Mariah to Lizzy. "With a plus one, of course."

Lizzy chuckled. "At the moment, I think I'll leave Roman at home. He's already gotten on my last nerve."

"Your choice," Simone said with a smile. "Bring his checkbook."

Lizzy's face took on a sly look. "Mariah, why don't you ask Pastor Ethan to be your plus one?"

Mariah felt her face grow hot. Then cold. Darn that Lizzy. If they were still back in high school, Mariah would already be plotting her revenge. But that was then, and this was now. She took a deep breath. "I don't think so."

"Why not? He might welcome the opportunity to get to know more people in Main."

Mariah bit her lip to keep from lashing out at Lizzy.

"That's a great idea," Simone added. "He'd probably enjoy it." She hid a pretend cough behind her hand and said, "And he's hot."

Mariah sprang to her feet. "What is wrong with both of you? I am not, repeat, am not looking for a man." *So there.*

"Good grief, Mariah. Get over yourself." Lizzy stood. "It's a night out at a fund-raiser, not an engagement dinner." Lizzy handed the empty water bottle to Mariah. "I gotta go. Abby will be home from school soon." She leaned down for an awkward hug from Simone before turning toward the front door. "You might have a good time," Lizzy said as she stepped outside.

When she was gone, Mariah glanced over at Simone. Lizzy and Simone had been like conjoined twins since the day Simone had first stepped on the middle school campus. Like Lizzy, Simone had despised Mariah and her friends. It was only with Lizzy's urging that Simone finally warmed up to Mariah in the past year. She wondered if Simone was as jealous of her as she was of Simone. Lizzy was the glue that held the threesome together.

"You could have used the phone, you know," Mariah said. "To tell me about the dinner thing."

"I see you're as blunt as ever," Simone said.

Mariah squeezed her lips together. Some rough edges refused to be softened, even with God's help. "Sorry."

Simon got to her feet with a sigh. "I'm sorry, too. Look, let's try harder to be friends. I know you've changed and all, and Lizzy likes you, so I guess we're stuck with each other."

Mariah almost laughed. Simone thought *she* was blunt. "Sure."

Simone embraced her with a stiff hug. "Please come to the dinner. I'll text you the details. And feel free to bring a date."

"Sure. Okay. Thanks." Anyone but Pastor Ethan.

~

Ethan gripped his cell phone with white knuckles. Miss Sarah's conversation, punctuated with a barking cough, sent frustration coursing through his veins.

"Yes, I understand. Please take care of yourself." Ethan disconnected and tossed the phone onto the sofa. He was supposed to lead the youth group that evening and his go-to sitter, Miss Sarah, sounded like she was dying. Now what? He hadn't yet met a lot of people in Main, especially someone he'd trust to watch Jayden for a couple of hours.

Ethan remembered the lunch he'd shared with Roman and Lizzy. One of them might be able to help. They had a daughter, Abigail, if he remembered correctly. He quickly punched in Roman's number.

"Roman, this is Ethan. I have a huge favor to ask."

"Pastor Ethan? Sure, what's up?" Roman sounded cautious, suspicious even. Ethan chalked it up to the guy's geekiness.

"Miss Sarah is down with a cold, and I need someone to watch Jayden for a couple of hours. I'm leading the youth group tonight. Noah is sick and asked me to fill in."

There was a pause for several seconds before Roman responded. "Uh, yeah, no. Abigail is home with pink eyes and Lizzy isn't feeling well. Sorry."

Good grief, was everyone in this town sick? "Sure, no problem I understand."

The disconnected. Ethan pulled his upper lip under his teeth and chewed. There must be a solution. A moment later a text arrived.

This is Lizzy. Ask Mariah. She has that whole video game set-up, and she loves kids. Here's her contact info.

This was followed by a text containing Mariah's phone and address.

Ethan was tempted to hurl the phone across the room. The one person who couldn't stand to be in the same room with him might be the only one who could watch his son. He lifted his gaze heavenward. "What are you doing to me, Lord?"

With a sigh, Ethan composed a text, backspaced, and started over.

This is Ethan. I need to ask a favor. Can you please call me?

That was better than trying to explain the whole situation in a text. He waited five minutes, but no answer came.

"Well, Jayden, looks like you are going to work with me today."

~

Mariah's phone rang at eight thirty in the morning. The caller ID showed Main High School.

"Good morning, Mariah, this is Margaret Mickelson. I hope this isn't too early to call."

Mariah stopped in the process of putting shelf paper down in her new cupboards. "Not at all."

"I have that reference form for you. We have a short day today. Do you want to come by around ten and pick it up?"

Excitement bubbled up from her stomach. She was one step closer to providing a safe place for kids. "I'll be there." She disconnected and did a fist pump in the air.

She pulled into the high school parking lot at nine fifty-five. At ten on the dot, she strode down the hall to Mrs. Michelson's room.

"Mariah, good to see you again. Come on in." Mrs. Mickelson pulled off her glasses and set them on a messy pile of papers on the desk.

Mariah approached her former teacher with a smile. "I can't thank you enough for doing this for me."

Mrs. Mickelson chuckled. "Maybe you better read what I wrote before you thank me."

Mariah's smile faded.

"I'm teasing," Mrs. Mickelson said. She held out the paper toward Mariah. "I always thought you had more going for you than you gave yourself credit for."

Mariah frowned. "I'm not sure what you mean."

Mrs. Mickelson toyed with her glasses, turning them over and back. "You and your friends had the reputation of being mean girls. It seemed that you embraced the image instead of trying to overcome it. You're bright, Mariah. Don't let anyone diminish your worth with an old label."

Mariah pondered the words. "Okay."

"I mean it. This Safe Family thing is a step in the right direction. You've been given a lot, Mariah. The Bible says, 'To whom much is given, much is required.' Mediate on that."

Mariah squeezed her lips together and nodded. "Thank you, Mrs. Mickelson."

Her former teacher smiled. "Please, call me Margaret."

Mariah smiled. "Thank you, Margaret."

Mariah strode from the classroom and to her car. She'd ignored the buzzing of her cell indicating an incoming text. Now she pulled out the phone and glanced at the screen, then blanched. Pastor Ethan wanted her to call him. She checked the time. He'd texted over twenty minutes ago.

She sucked in a breath, held it, and dialed his number.

"What do you want?" Mariah asked when Pastor Ethan answered.

He didn't answer for several seconds. When he did, his voice sounded weary. "I need a favor. I'm supposed to lead the youth group tonight and my babysitter is sick."

Mariah considered this for a moment. "Why don't you take Jayden with you?"

"Too much of a distraction."

"There's no one else?" Not that she wouldn't mind watching the pastor's adorable little boy. But still.

Mariah heard his sigh through the phone. "No, there's no one else. Sorry I bothered you."

"Wait." Mariah's grip tightened. "I can do it. I'll come get him." She held her breath waiting for Ethan to answer.

"That would be great. Youth group starts at seven."

"I'll be there at six forty-five." Mariah disconnected with mixed emotions. On one hand, watching Jayden would give her experience in watching a five-year-old. Which would come in handy if an older kid was assigned to her. On the other hand, it brought her into closer contact with Pastor Ethan. Which was cringe-worthy in itself. She'd practically broken the speed of light dashing from the church after telling him she was scared of him.

The pastor probably thought she was a nut case. *Well, aren't you?*

Mariah nodded. Yeah, she was definitely in need of someone to talk her off her self-made ledge. Too bad she had to see her parents today. Mom wasn't the 'talk off the ledge' kind of woman.

Chapter 7

Mariah made the last turn in the drive to her parent's home and took a moment to admire the one-hundred eighty-degree view. Everyone thought they were crazy when Greg and Christy bought the hilltop house. They'd remodeled, added on a bedroom and casita, and expanded the vineyard. On sunny days like today, Mariah could see the Pacific Ocean in the distance, glistening with diamond-like peaks.

She put her luxury sedan in park and stepped out onto the stamped concrete driveway.

"Anyone home?" she called as she pushed open the carved oak front door.

Her mother swept into the entry on a cloud of Chanel No. 5.

"Mariah, honey. Good to see you." Mom pulled her into a hug and kissed her cheek.

"Hi, Mom. Daniel said you needed my help with some fund-raiser thing." Mariah tossed her purse onto the sofa and sank onto the soft leather.

"Let me get us something to drink. Is Pelligrino all right?"

"Sure, Mom." Mariah glanced around the room, noticing the thin layer of dust on the glass-topped coffee table and on the etagere in the corner. She stood and wandered into the kitchen to watch her mom fill crystal glasses with ice from the subzero refrigerator and twist open two bottles of San Pellegrino.

"How's Beatrice?" Mariah asked, referencing her parents' housekeeper.

Her mom paused in her pour. "Such a sad thing. She's been sick for over a week." Mom resumed pouring the sparkling water. "I think she might be pregnant."

Mariah fought down a stab of jealousy. Beatrice and her husband had been wanting a baby for a long time. Now she knew two people who were getting what she wanted. First Lizzy and now Beatrice.

Since meeting with Pastor Roy, Mariah had come to realize that God had ordained things in a certain order. Courtship, marriage, then children. Mariah had tried to do things in her own timing, and life had turned her upside down.

Mom handed her a frosty glass of fizzy water. "Have you heard anything from Scott lately?"

Speaking of, Mariah thought. "Actually, no. Since he's moved to Portland, we haven't even texted."

Mom moved toward the living room. Mariah followed.

"That's too bad. I always thought you two made a stunning couple." Mom sat on a recliner and crossed her legs. Mariah recognized Mom's slacks as Ann Taylor. The white silk tee screamed expensive, along with the gold chain locket around her neck. Mariah tucked her jean-clad legs under her, hoping Mom wouldn't notice the egg yolk she'd spilled on her thigh that morning.

"Yes, well, stunning couple or not, Scott and I wanted different things."

Mom made an exasperated sound. "I don't know why you're fixated on this childcare thing. Main has many other worthwhile causes to get involved with. Things that don't involve poopy diapers and snotty noses."

Mariah laughed. "You act like Daniel and I were born completely potty-trained and germ free."

Mom chuckled. "You're right. But we're through all that now, thank goodness." Mom took a sip of her water. "Let's talk about this fundraiser. Your father offered to host the Chamber of Commerce annual dinner here on the property. I need your help. I started a list."

I'll bet you did. Her mother pulled a purple-colored portfolio off the end table and flipped it open.

"I thought we should rent one of those big tents. That way, if it rains, we'll have some cover. We'll need a band, of course, and someone to cater the food." Mom wrinkled her nose. "Not anyone local. I'm thinking a restaurant in Portland."

Mariah knew better than to argue with her mother about using a local restaurant. Main had plenty of choices because of its proximity to the coast. But once Mom's mind was made up, she was a force of nature.

Mom tapped a pen on the list. "Do you think your little friend Elizabeth would help with decorating?"

"Lizzy? Sure. I can ask."

"Do that." Mom went on to read through her exhaustive list of things to do and to arrange before the big event.

When she ran out of steam, Mariah asked, "What do you want me to do?"

Her mother exhaled with a loud sigh. "Haven't you been listening at all?"

"Yes."

Mother threw a hand up. "I need help with all of it."

Mariah gulped. "Oh, well, um."

Mother handed Mariah a copy of her list. "See how much you can get done and let me know by next week."

Mariah nodded. She finished her water while Mother went on to talk about the coming grape harvest. Mariah listened with half an ear. With the other half, she thought about what she still had left to do on her house remodel, the references she still needed to scan and upload to Safe Families, and her upcoming babysitting assignment for Pastor Ethan's son.

By the time she climbed into her car to head home, Mariah's head pounded with a fierce headache.

Chapter 8

At six o'clock, Ethan sent a text to Mariah. **Still okay to watch Jayden tonight?**

Instead of an answer, Mariah sent a thumbs up emoji. Good enough.

Ethan double-checked his iPad to be sure the battery was sufficiently charged for his sermon to the youth group that night. One of the older boys offered to help organize some games. Noah had sent him information on who was bringing snacks, who would play the guitar for some worship time, and how long to speak.

Excitement bubbled up from Ethan's stomach. He hadn't spoken to youth in several years, and he was surprised at how much he was looking forward to it. He was hit with a sudden wave of grief for Angie. She'd been the one to plan healthy but fun snacks. She scoured the internet for games that involved even the most introverted kids.

Ethan rubbed the spot on his chest over his heart. Grief didn't ambush him as much as it used to and for that he was grateful.

His phone rang with his brother's distinctive tone – Circles by Post Malone.

"What's up, bro?" Ethan asked.

"I called to see how things are going with you in Mayberry."

Ethan grinned. "Aw, c'mon. Main isn't that small. We do have more than one stoplight."

"Starbucks?"

"Yup."

"Walmart?"

"Uh, no. But we have a brand-new Taco Bell."

Robert's laugh boomed through the phone. "That's great. Bet they're already lining up in the drive-through."

Ethan smiled. "Of course. What do you want, anyway?"

"Why can't I check up on my little brother?"

"You can. Don't make a habit of it."

"Seriously, bro. I have a couple of days off at the end of the month. I thought I'd take a road trip and come see my favorite brother."

"I'm your only brother."

"Exactly. What do you think? Can you and J-man put up with me for a couple of days?"

"Of course. Send me the dates and I'll make sure to clean the bathroom."

Robert laughed again. "Sounds good. Peace out."

Ethan disconnected with a smile. Robert was coming for a visit. One more thing to look forward to. He called for Jayden, and they set out for the church.

"Let's walk," Ethan said, slinging Jayden's backpack over one shoulder. "It's a beautiful evening."

With Jayden holding one hand and his iPad clutched in the other, Ethan felt a contentment he hadn't felt for a long, long time.

~

Mariah pulled into the church parking lot and turned off the ignition. She sat for a moment with her hands on the steering wheel. What was it about Pastor Ethan that made her nerves skitter? She'd chalked it up to the traumatic experience she'd had at the youth retreat. That one time had been a watershed moment in her formative years. She'd gone from trying to be popular by being nice, to climbing over everyone else to get to the top of the social ladder. She'd hurt more people since then and had made more enemies than the current president of the United States.

Pastor Roy told her to concentrate on making changes. "Forgetting that which is behind," he'd quoted from Philippians 3:13.

Mariah's phone pinged with an incoming text from Brittany.

Scanned your reference form. You go, girl! You got this!!!

Mariah smiled. All right, now she had the three she needed. Tomorrow she'd scan them to Safe Families and wait for her first assignment.

The sun had sunk below the horizon while she'd sat in the car. A salty breeze carried over the tops of the buildings and dropped tiny bits of moisture onto Mariah's uplifted face. Not even facing Pastor Ethan could dampen her enthusiasm for spending an evening with Jayden.

Mariah stepped through the open front door of the church, passed through the narthex, and stopped inside the sanctuary. Pastor Ethan stood at the front of the church, in deep conversation with some of the youth group girls. Mariah recognized them as younger sisters of some of her friends.

Mariah flashed back to her days in youth group, always clustered around their good-looking youth pastor. Before 'the incident' that is. After that, she'd stopped going to church and mocked the girls who continued to attend. Until Scott thought it would be good for his business to attend church.

One of the girls laid her hand on Pastor Ethan's arm, almost possessively. Mariah frowned, recognizing the gesture. Should she warn the pastor to be careful?

Before she could decide, Jayden spotted her and sprinted down the center aisle. When he reached her, he grabbed Mariah's legs in a hug.

"Can we play the Spiderman video game at your house again?"

Mariah smiled down at him. "Of course. Anything you want."

Jayden pumped a fist. "Yay!"

Pastor Ethan untangled himself from the girls and made his way toward her. He stopped a good distance away. "Thank you for doing this."

"You're welcome. We're going to have a good time, aren't we, Jayden?"

Jayden barely acknowledged his dad's existence. "Let's go," he said, pulling on Mariah's hand.

She shot Ethan an apologetic look. "Guess we better go."

"Have fun, J-Man," Ethan called after them. "I should be done by nine."

Mariah strapped Jayden into the back seat and turned the car toward her house. Jayden chattered the entire way. Mariah learned all about his and his dad's eating habits, their favorite television shows, what Jayden did at Miss Sarah's, and how excited he was to start school in the fall.

Not once did he mention his mom.

Mariah's answered the door to Ethan's knock at nine-oh-five. Jayden had crashed on the sofa after two hours of serious gaming.

She opened the door and put a finger to her lips. "Shh. He's asleep."

Mariah's breath caught when Ethan smiled down at his sleeping son. He was too handsome for his own good. Those hazel eyes held softness for his child and also contained wells of sorrow.

Instead of picking up his son, Ethan perched on the ice chest across from the sofa. He crossed one leg over the other. Mariah watched it bounce up and down.

"How did it go tonight?" Mariah asked, resuming her seat on a chair nearby.

Ethan beamed. "Great. Really great."

Mariah felt the energy radiating from him. The fear she'd felt in his presence began to melt away.

"Good." Mariah bit her bottom lip. What a lame response. She took in his appearance. Ripped jeans and a sweatshirt with the logo from *The Chosen* series. She frowned.

"What?" Ethan asked.

"You're trying too hard."

"What do you mean?"

Mariah pointed toward his clothing. "What you're wearing. You're trying too hard to fit in. Ripped jeans are yesterday. Same with the sweatshirt."

Ethan stared down at his clothes, then back at her. "What do you suggest, oh wardrobe maven?"

~

Ethan's voice was harsher than he planned. But seriously, could this woman be any more blunt? What was wrong with what he was wearing? Sheesh.

He watched as color diffused Mariah's cheeks.

"You're right," she said. "Sorry."

Jayden stirred and stretched out an arm. The sight of his hand dangling over the edge of the sofa filled him with tenderness. Ethan peered at the woman sitting across from him. How could this brittle woman be so good with kids? She was a study in contrast. Blunt to the point of rudeness, yet she had an easy way with Jayden.

Ethan raised one shoulder and pulled his sweatshirt down. "No one commented on my outfit tonight."

Mariah hid a smile behind her hand. "Not to your face. They're probably giggling about it now."

Ethan pressed his lips together and grunted. "Perhaps you should pick out my outfit for next time."

"Will there be a next time?"

Ethan didn't know. If Noah, the youth leader was still sick the following week, Ethan would gladly step in. Tonight had been a lot of fun. He'd forgotten how much he enjoyed working with teens. Their boundless energy and enthusiasm filled him with hope. He could almost forget the disappointment of Angie's refusal to continue working with their youth group. She'd pushed him into the senior pastor position when it had been offered by the church plant in Seattle.

Until her enthusiasm for being a pastor's wife had waned and she hinted at missionary work.

Mariah's voice interrupted his musings. "Where'd you go?"

Ethan drew himself to his feet. "Sorry. I got lost for a moment. Let me get Jayden."

Mariah stood and moved away from the sofa when Ethan leaned down to pick up his sleeping son. What was with the fear factor she exhibited? With a shake of his head, Ethan put his attention to lifting Jayden onto his shoulder.

"Oof. Why is it a sleeping kid feels like a bag of concrete?"

"Let me get the door." Mariah moved to the front door and swung it open. "Let me know if you need me to watch him again tomorrow. If Miss Sarah is still sick, that is."

Ethan paused and glanced over at her. Mariah had pulled her hair into a low ponytail. Some hairs had escaped the elastic band and fell across her cheek. If his hands hadn't been full of sleeping child, he would have been tempted to brush them back.

Whoa. Where did that come from? Sure, she was an attractive woman. But his heart still belonged to Angie.

Didn't it?

~

Mariah watched Ethan making his way to his car. She wrapped her arms around her middle as cool, damp air seeped in through her open front door. A light rain began to fall, filling the air with the moist smells of spring. Wet dirt, damp grass, and the hope of new growth.

She stood in the door until Ethan loaded Jayden into the car and drove off with a wave. Closing the door, she leaned against it for a moment, filled with the realization she hadn't felt fearful in Ethan's presence. Maybe she really was getting better. At least with regard to being fearful of men in the ministry.

But would she ever shed her mean girl reputation? At least Ethan hadn't gotten wind of who she really was. Once he did, he'd never let her near Jayden.

Mariah continued to berate herself over her criticism of Ethan's wardrobe choice. What business was it of hers what he wore? None. At least he hadn't brought up the subject of her working at the church. That would be a disaster.

A text from Ethan arrived at eight the next morning.

Sorry to impose. Can you watch Jayden again today?

Mariah bit her bottom lip as she considered her answer. Of course she'd love the opportunity to watch Jayden. But that would mean spending more time in Pastor Ethan's presence. He disturbed her in a way she hadn't been disturbed before. Now that she was over her fear – she hoped – she experienced an attraction to him as a man.

She didn't need a man in her life. That ship had sailed when Scott packed his bags and moved out of their duplex.

With a sigh, she typed out a one-word response.
Sure.

Little bubbles appeared as Ethan typed his response.

Awesome! Thanks. I'll drop him off in an hour.

That hour gave Mariah time to go for a run, return home to shower, and have a bite to eat. Ethan knocked on her door at precisely nine o'clock.

Mariah swung the door open. "Good morning."

Jayden dashed into the house without a backward glance at his dad.

"Hey, dude, come back here and give me a hug," Ethan said, crouching down.

Jayden gave his dad a perfunctory hug before shrugging out of his jacket. "Can we play Spiderman now?"

Mariah crouched down to his level. "I have some work I have to do this morning."

Jayden's face fell.

Mariah laid a hand on the child's shoulder. "I need a man's help, though. Think you can help me with some heavy lifting?"

Jayden nodded.

"Good. Let's see your muscles."

Jayden made a fist and held up his arm, flexing his bicep.

Mariah gently squeezed his arm. "Oooh, nice guns there, Jayden. I think you're up to the task."

She straightened and addressed Ethan. "I haven't finished unpacking my kitchen stuff since the cabinets were delivered. I'll have Jayden help me. When we're done, I need to go to the grocery store and fill up my new fridge. Do you have a problem if Jayden goes with me?"

Mariah watched Ethan's face as he considered her request.

"Do you have any moving violations?" he asked.

Mariah pinched her lips together to keep from smiling. Was Pastor Ethan a cop in another life? She shook her head.

"Okay. I guess that's fine."

Jayden grabbed Mariah's hand as she straightened up. "When can we play Spiderman?"

"I tell you what. Let's work on the kitchen for a bit. Then we'll take a video break, then we'll go to the store. What kind of snacks do you like?"

As Jayden rattled off his favorite junk food choices, Ethan turned to go. "I guess you have everything under control here. Thanks again for doing this. Sarah said she hoped to be better by the weekend."

Mariah leaned against the open front door. "Not a problem. I'm happy to help."

She closed the door behind Ethan and led Jayden into the kitchen. "All right, young man. Time to get to work."

~

Ethan berated himself all the way to his car and on the short drive back to the church. *Do you have any moving violations?* What a lame question. What was he – a closet highway patrolman? Sheesh.

At least Jayden seemed happy to spend the day with the lovely Mariah. Now, if he could get some work done on Sunday's sermon. Ethan remembered a song from an old Keith Green album. Something like 'my eyes are dry and my prayers are cold.' That pretty much summed up his spiritual temperature.

Ethan pulled into the church parking lot and turned off the ignition. Maybe he could use some of what he'd prepared for the youth group for Sunday. With a renewed sense of purpose, Ethan dashed through the rain and unlocked the side door to the church.

Ignoring the blinking light on the ancient answering machine, he headed into Pastor Roy's office to begin the day's work.

Two hours later, he leaned back in the squeaky desk chair and stretched his arms over his head. His stomach growled, reminding him he'd skipped breakfast in his haste to get Jayden out the door.

Cookie's Café seemed to be the local hangout. Every booth and table were filled. The place smelled of grilled onions and freshly brewed coffee.

"Good morning," said the young man behind the counter. He made a show of looking at his watch. "I guess it's still morning. Anyway, it'll be a few minutes, and I'll get ya seated. Can I get ya a cup of coffee while ya wait?"

"Sure." Soon, Ethan had a steaming mug of hot brew to warm his hands. He glanced around and recognized some of the folks from last Sunday's service. A few made eye contact and smiled or nodded in his direction.

The overly friendly waitress, Wren, wandered over and stood in front of him. "All alone today? Where's your wingman?"

"Babysitter." Ethan hoped to avoid a lengthy conversation.

"Order up!" called the cook.

"I'll have the turkey club," Ethan said. He sent up a quick prayer of thanks when Wren whirled to grab the plates from the cook.

Ethan spied Lizzy and Roman, huddled in what seemed to be deep conversation. Lizzy raised her head, made eye contact with Ethan, and waved him over.

"Come sit with us," she said, sliding out of the booth. "You can help us settle this argument." Lizzy sat next to her husband and bumped him with her hip to scoot him over.

Roman frowned. "It isn't an argument."

Lizzy laughed. "Not yet it isn't. Perhaps Pastor Ethan can give us his insight."

Ethan sat. "It's just Ethan."

Lizzy spread her hands on the table. "My daughter, Abigail, wants to spend a month this summer with her dad. I don't want her to go, but Roman thinks it will be good for her."

Wren approached the booth with a full carafe of coffee. Ethan nodded and pushed his cup toward the edge of the table for a top off.

"Don't most divorced couples share custody?" Ethan asked.

Lizzy sent Roman a side-eyed glance. "Abigail's father and I never married."

Ethan took a sip of his steaming brew. "Oh."

"It's kind of a long story," Lizzy continued. "Until a year ago, Abby didn't even know her father. Until he abducted her from school one day."

"He didn't technically abduct her," Roman said.

Lizzy sighed. "Call it what you will. He took her without my permission and caused a lot of worry."

Wren arrived to top off their coffee, giving Ethan a moment to gather his thoughts. When she'd gone, he said, "What kind of man is he, this long-lost father?"

Lizzy sat back in the booth. "He's okay, I guess. He says he's quote-unquote turned his life around."

"Christian?"

"No."

"Does he treat your daughter well?"

Lizzy nodded. "Abby's spent time with Dylan and his new wife, Taffy. She seems to adore Abby."

"Any hints of abuse or sketchy behavior?" Ethan asked.

Lizzy bit her bottom lip. "No."

"Then why the hesitation?" he asked.

Roman spread out his hands. "See? That's my question."

Lizzy gave an exasperated sigh. "You two men are ganging up on me." She rubbed a hand across her face. "For ten years, it was always Abby and me. Until Roman came into our lives. I'm super protective of her."

"That's for sure, Lizzy," Roman added.

Lizzy sent him a glare. "Okay, fine. I'll let her go. But if anything happens, it's on you."

Ethan's gaze was drawn to Lizzy's wedding ring. "That's a beautiful ring. Unusual."

Lizzy raised her hand to admire her ring. "Roman picked it out himself."

Roman grasped her hand with a smile. "Nothing is too good for my girl."

Roman closed his eyes and cocked his head, as if hearing an invisible voice. After a curt nod, he added, "Not my girl. My wife."

Lizzy's eyes were filled with adoration as they gazed into each other's eyes. Had he and Angie ever been that in synch? Ethan tried to remember their early years, before the fabric of their marriage began to shred and tear.

His thoughts were interrupted by Wren. "Here's your turkey club. Can I get you anything else?"

"No, thank you."

Wren hovered for a moment, looking from Ethan to Lizzy to Roman. She turned on her heel and strode to the kitchen.

Ethan blew out a breath. He'd have to find another place to eat in this little town. That server was plain weird.

"We'll let you eat your lunch in peace," Lizzy said, pulling her purse onto her lap. "Who's watching your son, since Sarah is sick? Were you able to get hold of Mariah?"

Another downside of living in a small town. Everyone knew your business.

Ethan spoke around the bite of sandwich. "Yes. He's at her house, probably OD-ing on video games."

Lizzy laughed. "She's good with kids. Which is unusual, given her history."

"What do you mean?"

"We've only been friends for a short time."

"But you both grew up here?" Ethan pressed.

Lizzy threw Roman a glance that he couldn't decipher. "Yes. We went to school together. But we ran in different circles."

Lizzy looked like she wanted to say more, but Roman laid a hand on her arm with a shake of his head.

Lizzy slid out of the booth. "Well, anyway, it was nice to chat with you. You'll have to come over for dinner again soon."

Roman leaned across the table to shake Ethan's hand. "See you soon."

Ethan finished his sandwich and the best potato salad he'd ever eaten. He'd have to rethink his plan to find another place to eat.

Chapter 9

As much as Mariah enjoyed having Pastor Ethan's son help her in the kitchen, they hadn't accomplished very much unpacking. Most of her time had been spent keeping Jayden from fumbling her expensive dishes and glassware. At least their field trip to the grocery store had been fruitful.

Mariah pulled open her new sub-zero refrigerator and gazed with satisfaction at all the food waiting to be cooked and eaten. She'd had enough frozen dinners and precooked meals to last the rest of her life.

"Back to eating healthy," she said aloud.

Her cell phone sat propped against a crystal vase, pumping out the latest in Christian pop. The music was momentarily interrupted by an incoming text.

Ethan: Miss Sarah still sick. Can you watch J again tomorrow?

Sheesh, did the man never take a day off? She tapped out a quick 'okay' and pulled the fixings for a huge salad from the refrigerator, along with a package of precooked chicken tenders. Until her pots and pans were unpacked, some packaged food would be unavoidable.

Her cell phone pinged again. Mariah huffed in frustration. But this time the text was from Simone.

Fundraiser at the gym in 3 weeks. Details to follow

Shoot. Mariah had forgotten all about it. In her previous life, she would have blown off the dinner, claiming it was beneath her. She and Brittany would have sneered about the pathetic attempt to pull off a fund-raising dinner in an athletic club.

But that was then and this was now. Mariah sent a thumbs up emoji back to Simone, making a mental reminder to ask her dad to provide a check as well. Dad was all about supporting the community. Hence, the Chamber of Commerce event at their place.

With a sigh, Mariah realized her plans for the following day would have to be postponed if she would be babysitting Jayden. She'd hoped to make a dent in her mom's list, but that wasn't going to happen.

While she prepared the chicken salad, Mariah thought about how difficult it must be for Pastor Ethan to be thrust in a new town without the support system he previously had. Pastor Roy had been at the church for over ten years and was loved by the community. Pastor Ethan had big shoes to fill.

A knock on the front door pulled her out of her musings.

"Oh, I was thinking about you," Mariah said when she pulled open the door to find Pastor Ethan and Jayden standing on the porch.

She felt her face grow hot. "I mean, I was thinking about…" Her voice trailed off.

Ethan grinned. "Sorry to bother you. But Jayden thinks he left his backpack here." He leaned forward and whispered, "It has his blankie in it."

A smile worked its way up to her mouth. Not many five-year-old boys would admit to still sleeping with a 'blankie.'

"Jayden, why don't you run upstairs and see if you left it there," Mariah said.

When Jayden dashed across the living room, Ethan called out, "No video games!"

"Come on in," Mariah said, closing the door behind him.

"Am I interrupting anything?" Ethan asked.

"I was fixing some dinner. Nothing that can't wait." She crossed her arms over her stomach. They stared at each other without speaking. She was growing a little uncomfortable that she was no longer uncomfortable around him.

Mariah surprised herself by saying, "I have plenty, if you want to stay. It's plain old chicken salad." She held her breath, wondering what had possessed her to invite him for dinner.

"Are you sure it isn't an inconvenience?"

"Not at all." Mariah whirled around and headed into the kitchen. "Let me get a couple more plates."

In the kitchen, Mariah fanned her face with one hand. What was she thinking? Her stomach fluttered with nerves. But at least it wasn't the terror she'd experienced before when in the same room with a clergyman.

Jayden's feet pounded on the stairs as he returned to the living room. "Are we gonna leave now, Dad?"

Mariah heard Ethan's deep voice as he answered his son. "Not yet, J-man. Miss Mariah has invited us to stay for dinner."

"Awesome!"

Mariah didn't think Jayden would think chicken salad would be awesome. She turned when Ethan sauntered into the kitchen, followed by his shadow, Jayden.

"I'm having a salad with chicken on it. Want me to warm the chicken up for Jayden?"

Ethan glanced down at his son and nodded. "You wouldn't happen to have catsup, would you? It's kind of a staple at our house."

Mariah sent him a closed-mouth smile and retrieved a small bottle of the red stuff from the fridge. "Go ahead and sit at the table. I'll be finished in a sec." She busied herself setting napkins and silverware out for the two guys.

While the chicken warmed in the microwave, she cut veggies and tomatoes for Ethan's salad. "Will Jayden eat some sliced carrots and cucumber?"

Ethan grinned. "Under protest. But, yes."

Jayden made a face. "Yuck."

Ethan ruffled his son's hair. "None of that. We're guests here."

When Ethan's salad was assembled and Jayden's chicken slightly warmed, Mariah sat and folded her hands in her lap. "Would you say grace?"

Ethan offered a heartfelt thanks for the home-cooked meal. While they ate, Ethan talked about the difference between living in Seattle and the small town of Main.

"I grew up here," Mariah said. "I've travelled a lot with my parents, but I can't think of anywhere else I'd rather live."

"What about the nosiness of everyone?" Ethan asked. He speared a piece of chicken, inspected it, then shoved it in his mouth.

Mariah snorted. "There is that."

"Your friend, Lizzy, said you two went to school together. But you didn't hang out? Seems like in a town as small as Main, you'd be forced together."

Mariah's face grew hot. What had Lizzy told him? It seemed like her reputation would follow her for the rest of her life.

"We, uh, didn't exactly, uh, like each other in school."

Mariah kept her eyes focused on her salad, but she could feel Ethan's eyes boring into the side of her head. When he didn't say anything for several beats, she dared a glance in his direction.

Ethan was watching her with a thoughtful look.

"What?" Mariah demanded.

Ethan shrugged. "Nothing." He continued eating. Focusing his attention on Jayden, he said, "Eat a few pieces of cuke, J-man. Miss Mariah peeled them the way you like them."

"Can I dip them in catsup?"

Mariah and Ethan both made a gagging sound, then laughed.

"Whatever floats your boat," Ethan said.

When they'd finished, Mariah stood to clear the table.

"Need any help?" Ethan asked.

"No, I've got this." The sooner Mariah could whisk him out the door, the better. She was becoming too attracted to this ministry man. She was charmed by his attention to his son and the easy way he made conversation while they ate. Getting involved with a man, especially one in the ministry, was not on her agenda.

"Before I go, could I talk to you about something?" Ethan asked, pausing in the doorway between the kitchen and the living room.

A spurt of adrenaline shot through her, leaving Mariah breathless. "Sure. Let me throw these dishes in the dishwasher."

What could Pastor Ethan possibly want to talk to her about? Mariah took her time rinsing the dishes and silverware, even though her new dishwasher did most of the work. Wishing for a mirror in the kitchen, she smoothed down her hair and used her cell phone to check her teeth for any green stuff that might have decided to take up residence there.

Satisfied that she was unencumbered by errant lettuce, she strolled into the living room. Ethan sat on the couch scrolling through his cell phone.

"Where's Jayden?" Mariah asked.

"I sent him upstairs. I wanted to show you something in private."

Mariah smoothed her lips together. This was getting weird.

Ethan patted the sofa next to him. "Sit."

Ethan's thigh was warm against hers. He didn't seem to notice. "Check this out." He pointed to a text from a number she didn't recognize.

Your teaching last night was amazing.

Mariah frowned. "Who's it from?"

Ethan used his forefinger to swipe down. "That's the first text. Look at this."

A series of emoji-filled texts seemed to go on and on. Each one built on the last.

I feel much closer to God when you teach. (halo-covered smiley)

I could listen to you forever. This was followed by several heart emojis.

I feel like I've finally met my soulmate.

Mariah gasped. "Who is this?"

Ethan shrugged. "My question is, how did this person, and I'm assuming it's a girl in the youth group, get my phone number?"

Mariah blew out a breath. "Wow. This is weird. Like stalking-weird." She sat back against the cushions.

Ethan motioned to his phone. "Do you want to read the rest?"

"I don't think so." Mariah's stomach churned. One of the girls was crushing on Pastor Ethan. This was not healthy. She was reminded of her crush on their youth leader and how badly that had ruined her life.

She hazarded a glance at Ethan. "Are you flattered?"

"No! No way. This is creepy."

Mariah sagged with relief. There wouldn't be a replay of what her youth leader had done to her. Ethan was a family man, not a nineteen-year-old cradle-robber-slash rapist.

Ethan's grimace said it all. "I'm not really sure what to do. I was hoping you'd have some insight. You know, being a girl and all." His face suffused with color. "I mean, woman. Female. Whatever."

Mariah inhaled and blew out the breath through pursed lips. "Send me the phone number and I'll call it tomorrow."

"You'd do that?"

"Sure. I'll find out who it is and see if I can help." Mariah had no idea what she would do to help, but it would be better if the call came from a woman rather than him.

Ethan sagged against the back cushion. "Thanks. You have no idea how relieved I am."

When his shoulder touched hers, Mariah jumped to her feet. "I'm going to check on Jayden."

Later, after Ethan had gathered up his son and the missing backpack, Mariah returned to the kitchen to wipe down the table and the counters. Anything to keep her hands and mind busy. Sleep would be impossible with the confusion rattling her brain.

Pastor Ethan had gone from being someone she was scared of to someone she enjoyed spending time with. This was not good. She had a mission in life to care for kids whose parents needed a little help. That mission didn't include being attracted to a man.

Chapter 10

Ethan tucked a very sleepy Jayden into bed after reading 'one more book.' Ethan wondered for the millionth time if he was overcompensating for Jayden not having a mother. Ethan missed the partnership of having someone to share parenting duties with. Every decision these days was made after asking himself how it would affect his son.

Returning to the living room, Ethan sank onto Pastor Roy's comfortable recliner and studied the texts he'd gotten from one of the teenage girls in the youth group. Which one of the ten or so could it be? At least he had Mariah to hopefully solve the mystery.

Speaking of Mariah, it was time to back away from that dichotomy. Was that even the right word to describe her? Ethan opened the dictionary app on his phone.

Dichotomy: a division or contrast between two things that are or are represented as being opposed or entirely different.

Yup, that was Mariah. Brittle yet vulnerable. Blunt and tender.

Time to stop thinking about her. His focus was on making the most of this temporary ministry opportunity and getting his spiritual mojo back. Not on getting involved with a woman.

Once Miss Sarah was well, Jayden would go back to her house, and he would have no reason to engage with Mariah. With that in mind, he sent her a text.

Thanks again for dinner and for helping with the text mystery. I'm taking tomorrow off to spend with Jayden.

There. That should do it. He and Jayden would go somewhere, the two of them. Ethan watched his phone for a response. Nothing. Disappointment overshadowed his relief.

Friday dawned bright and sunny. Ethan checked the weather app on his phone to be sure there was no rain in the forecast.

"J-man, we're heading to the coast."

Jayden looked up from his bowl of cold cereal. "I thought I was going to Miss Mariah's house again today."

Ethan wished Jayden didn't look disappointed. "I know, but I thought it would be fun to explore the beach. Maybe we can find some more sand dollars to add to our collection." He was trying too hard to convince himself and Jayden. Mariah had said he was trying too hard to look cool for the youth.

Stop thinking about her.

"It'll be fun. We'll get some ice cream on the way back."

Jayden stared down into the now-empty bowl. "I guess."

"Go brush your teeth and get dressed. We'll leave when you're ready."

Ethan packed the truck with a blanket, sand toys, and snacks while Jayden dawdled over his morning routine. When he'd finally loaded his reluctant son into the pickup, Ethan heaved a sigh of relief and pointed the vehicle in the direction of the Pacific Ocean.

Main was only a short thirty-minute drive from the coast. Ethan found the entrance to a state park and pulled into an empty parking spot. The wind off the water brought a briny smell through the air.

"Let's go, Jayden. You can carry the bucket and shovel, okay?"

Like any other kid, Jayden had forgotten his previous disappointment. "Hurry up, Dad," he said, grabbing the bucket and dashing toward the path to the beach.

Ethan and Jayden set about creating an elaborate sandcastle, complete with turrets and a moat. Their beach kit included plastic army men Ethan had picked up at a thrift store years ago. They stood the men along the walls of the castle, then proceeded to hurl tiny shells at them to knock them down.

Jayden loved this part of the game. "I nailed him!" he'd shout each time one of the men went down.

Ethan hoped he wasn't teaching his son to be violent. Another self-doubt to add to the hundreds already on the list.

After a couple of hours, Ethan was ready to call it a day. "You ready to go home, J-man?"

"I'm cold." Jayden brushed wet sand off his jeans. "But I still want ice cream."

"So noted. Let's get into the car and turn on the heater."

They began the opposite process of loading up pails and shovels, shaking off the sand and loading everything into back of Ethan's truck. Once they were buckled in, Ethan searched for an ice cream shop on the way home while the car heated up.

"Found it," he said, turning in his seat to face his son.

"I want a double scoop this time. I'm not a baby anymore."

Ethan raised his eyebrows. "We'll see."

He turned on the radio to one of the kids' stations on his satellite radio and wondered what Mariah was up to. Then he chastised himself for wondering.

While Jayden dug through his cup of cookie dough ice cream – two scoops – Ethan checked his phone for the tenth time. Still nothing from Mariah indicating she'd called the mystery texter. Which of the ten-plus young girls could it have been?

Frustration mounted as he swiped down through the series of texts yet again. When he could stand it no longer, he typed out a text:

Who is this?

A moment later, dots appeared to indicate someone was typing out a response.

Guess

Ethan wasn't going to play that game. Too dangerous. **How did you get my number?**

The response came in the form of a smiley face.

Ethan grunted. This little game needed to stop. Now.

I'm blocking this number.

~

Mariah sat at her kitchen table and sighed at the sight of the empty boxes stacked haphazardly around the room. She'd break them down and take them to the recycling center later. After she'd made a dent in her mom's task list.

No sooner had she poured her second cup of coffee when the front door opened and a familiar voice called out, "Anybody home?"

Mariah frowned. Lizzy's annoying habit of popping in at random times during the day got on her last nerve.

"I'm in the kitchen," Mariah called out.

Lizzy strode into the room and dropped into a chair across the table. "I need your help," Lizzy said without preamble.

"You and everybody else," Mariah muttered. She'd been procrastinating calling the girl who was crushing on Ethan. *Pastor* Ethan, she corrected herself. It was obvious he wanted to distance himself from her after their closeness on the sofa last night.

Lizzy heaved a sigh. "Roman won't let me do anything around the house. He's insisting that because I'm pregnant, I should sit with my feet propped up for the next eight months or so. I know about not touching Millie's litter box. There's some sort of infection pregnant women can get from cat poop. I don't remember what it is, but Roman did this whole Google search on it. Now he won't let me near the litter box or Millie. Then there's Abby."

When Lizzy paused for a breath, Mariah interjected. She held up a hand. "Stop. Every time you come over here, you complain about Roman. Why did you marry him if you were going to nitpick everything he does? You knew what he was like before you married him."

To Mariah's dismay, Lizzy's eyes filled with tears. "You're right. I'm the worst person ever." She began to cry in earnest.

Mariah sighed. "Not the *worst* person. But close to it."

That brought a ghost of a smile to Lizzy's face. "It's the pregnancy hormones. They're making me crazy."

"Seeing you makes me wonder why I ever wanted to get pregnant," Mariah said, handing Lizzy a tissue.

Lizzy sniffled. "I can always count on you to tell it like it is."

Mariah watched her friend for a moment. "You know what you need?"

"A swift kick in the pants?"

"No. You need a spa day. Your hair needs to be cut and your nails are a mess. Bet your toes need some love too." Mariah stood and marched into the living room. "Let's go. I'm taking you to my favorite spa in Salem."

"But I haven't shaved my legs," Lizzy wailed.

"You won't be the first person to show up with hairy legs." Mariah retrieved her purse from the bedroom and returned to the living room. Lizzy hadn't budged from her seat.

"What are you waiting for? Text that rotten husband of yours and tell him we're going out. He can meet Abby after school, can't he?"

Lizzy gulped and nodded. "I guess."

Mariah pointed to Lizzy's phone. "Do it."

Ten minutes later they were in Mariah's comfy sedan, cruising down the highway toward the big city of Salem.

Mariah watched the estheticians go to work on Lizzy. Handing her credit card to the receptionist, she said, "Give her the works. Highlights, cut, mani, pedi, and a facial. I'm going to do some shopping."

Lizzy looked up in alarm when Mariah approached the pedicure chair where Lizzy sat with her feet immersed in warm water.

"Where are you going?"

"Out. I'll be back in a couple of hours. Stay here and enjoy."

Lizzy squeezed her lips together.

Mariah draped the strap of her Prada bag over one shoulder. "It's all paid for so don't worry about that. Bye." She waggled her fingers toward her friend and strode from the salon.

~

Mariah strolled through the maternity department at one of the major department stores in Salem. Settling on a couple of cute tops and a darling pair of maternity jeans, she carried the loot to the cashier.

"Can you hold these for a moment? I want to look at the dresses."

The cashier looked Mariah up and down and nodded.

Thirty minutes later, she added two loose sun dresses to the pile. They'd be perfect for the summer when Lizzy began to show in earnest.

"Is that all, miss?" the cashier asked.

Mariah handed the girl her credit card. "I think so."

"When are you due?" she asked as she rang up Mariah's purchases.

Mariah grimaced. "They're not for me." In the not-too-distant past, she and Scott could have been expecting a baby. But that had blown up in her face. Good thing, too. God had protected her from making a huge mistake. She would have been tied forever to Scott, who didn't want kids at all. What kind of life would that have been? A single mom, raising a child whose father hated her.

The cashier continued to chatter, pulling Mariah out of her musings. "You've made some good choices."

"I hope she likes them. What's your return policy?"

When Mariah was finally able to break away from the store, she lugged the bulging sack to her car and threw it in the trunk. It was time for a little refreshment in the form of an iced latte.

The drive-through at Bentley's Coffee was mercifully short. Mariah ordered her latte and added a decaf for Lizzy. Mariah remembered reading up on all things pregnancy related.

Pregnant women should not consume more than 200 milligrams of caffeine daily.

When she returned to the spa, she found Lizzy dozing in the waiting area.

"Wake up, sleepy head."

Lizzy stirred and opened her eyes. "I must have fallen asleep. I'm super relaxed."

She took the cup Mariah handed her with a smile. "Thanks for this."

"It's decaf."

Lizzy made a face. "Ugh. But thank you anyway."

"Let's get you home, so you can take a proper nap."

Mariah inspected Lizzy's hair and nails. "Nice cut. I always wished I had naturally curly hair."

Lizzy laughed. "That's funny. I always wished I had your perfectly straight hair."

Mariah linked her arm with Lizzy's. "The grass is always greener, right?"

Lizzy raised her cup in a mock salute. "Amen."

On the ride back to Main, Mariah had to stop Lizzy from continuing to thank her.

"What's the use of having money if you can't spend it?" Mariah said.

"Okay, I'm done thanking you. Let's talk about Pastor Ethan."

Mariah rolled her eyes. "Let's not." She'd rather not be reminded of how right it felt having her thigh pressed up against his on the sofa the night before.

Lizzy laughed. "Are you still babysitting Jayden?"

Mariah raised one shoulder. "Sort of. I watched him yesterday. I was supposed to again today, but Ethan said he was taking a day off."

Lizzy swiveled her head toward Mariah. "It's Ethan now? Not *Pastor* Ethan."

Mariah huffed. "Stop. I'm merely offering him a helping hand. Isn't that what Christians are supposed to do?"

Lizzy scrunched down in her seat. "If you say so."

Mariah's grip on the steering wheel tightened. "Just because you and Roman have discovered life-long happiness doesn't mean you have to find someone for me."

Lizzy's eyes drifted closed. "Whatever."

Mariah shook her head. There was no way she'd get involved with a pastor. Not with her past. She almost laughed out loud at the thought of herself as a pastor's wife. Pastor Roy's wife, Susan looked the part. Over fifty, slightly plump, sensible shoes. Susan had probably never heard of Jimmy Choo.

This line of thought was pointless. Ethan – *Pastor Eathan* – was probably still grieving his wife. With a start, Mariah realized she'd never called that person on the sending end of the texts. As soon as she dropped Lizzy off, that would be the first thing she'd do.

Except it wasn't. After checking her email for a response from Safe Families and finding none, Mariah went back to work in the newly remodeled kitchen. Lizzy sent a couple of texts thanking her again for what she called a 'reset.' And more profuse thanks for the maternity clothes.

Saturday dawned cold and rainy. Mariah pulled back the draperies in the living room and opted to go to the gym rather than her usual run.

Simone greeted her as Mariah dropped her towel over the treadmill handlebars.

"You haven't forgotten about the fund-raiser, have you?"

"Not at all," Mariah responded, ramping the treadmill up to an easy beginning pace. "As a matter of fact, my dad said he'd send over a check."

Simone looked surprised. "Your dad? He's never set foot in here."

Mariah's smile was wry. "Yeah, but he believes in supporting the community. Speaking of which, why don't you plan to come to the Chamber of Commerce fundraiser next month? Maybe your boss would consider buying a table?"

The corners of Simone's mouth turned up. "Good thought. I'll ask. Thanks." She raised a hand in a quick wave as she wandered over to help an elderly woman with a weight machine.

Mariah smiled with satisfaction. Only a year ago she and Simone had been sworn enemies since middle school. She'd always thought of Simone as a goody two shoes, always going to church and spouting the Bible. Once Mariah had dropped out of the church youth group, every girl and boy in church had become fair game for her taunting.

Shame settled on her shoulders until she remembered Pastor Roy's words.

"There is therefore now no condemnation to those who are in Christ Jesus."

Mariah ramped up the treadmill and began to run.

By the time she returned home to shower, endorphins had kicked in and Mariah no longer felt the weight of her past. She sat down and pulled her iPad out and tapped on the Bible app. The verse of the day was Romans 8:1. She smiled as she read the words again, "There is no condemnation to those who are in Christ Jesus."

Her past was past. Period.

Her phone pinged with an incoming text.

Pastor Ethan: Did you find out who sent those texts?

Oops. It had totally slipped her mind.

I'll do it now.

Mariah tapped in the number Pastor Ethan had given her with the tip of one finger. The phone rang twice, then a girl answered.

"Yeah."

Mariah swallowed. "Who am I speaking with?"

"Tamara. Who's this?"

"Hi, Tamara. This is Mariah Martin from the church. We're reaching out to all the youth to check in to see how you're doing and if you need prayer for anything." The lies slipped easily out of her mouth. Mariah felt a stab of guilt. *Guess the past doesn't always stay in the past.*

There was silence for a couple of beats. "Uh, no, I'm good. But thanks."

"All right. Thank you. If you think of anything, you have my number."

She disconnected and sat with the phone in one sweaty hand. Tamara's parents were Craig and Debbie. Craig's firm was one of the contractors Mariah's dad recommended for her house remodel. They seemed like the perfect Christian family. Why would their daughter send awkward texts to Ethan?

Mariah jumped when her phone rang. Her brother's face filled the screen.

"Hey, sis. Wanna take a road trip with me?"

"Where are we going?"

"I have to head to the coast to pick up some stuff for Dad."

Mariah took only a moment to decide. "Sounds good. Give me a few minutes to grab my raincoat."

Daniel laughed. "I'm outside."

"You knew I'd say yes," Mariah said with a grin.

"Of course. You love the coast."

"As long as you buy me a nice seafood dinner."

"Don't I always?"

On the quick drive to the coast, Mariah let the worries about Tamara's texts blow away like the wind blowing the rain off the Pacific Ocean. The windshield wipers on Daniel's Land Rover cut through the watery deluge offering only a moment respite between the swipes.

"What are you thinking about?" Daniel asked.

Mariah leaned her head back. "Oh, I don't know. Life I guess."

Daniel sent a quick glance sideways. "You're different these days."

Mariah struggled to come up with a response. She *was* different. Most of the time.

"How are you doing since that loser fiancé of yours took off."

Mariah snorted. "Fine. Better than fine. I finally figured out we wanted different things out of life. Besides, I think he enjoyed our lifestyle more than he enjoyed me."

"I never did see what you saw in him. You know Dad didn't like him."

The corners of Mariah's mouth turned down. "I know." She should have listened to her parents. What would they think of Pastor Ethan?

Mariah allowed that thought only a nanosecond of space in her brain. She was not – repeat- not going to get involved with a man.

"Anyone new on the horizon?"

Daniel's question brought a vision of Pastor Ethan. *Darn you*, she said to herself. "No."

Daniel laughed. "The pool of available men is pretty small in Main. Not even a pool. More like a plastic bucket." He leaned back and rested his left arm on the windowsill. "That's why I cast my net farther afield."

Mariah pursed her lips. "Are you dating someone again?"

"Of course."

"You're like a serial dater. Who is it this time?"

"I met her up at Mom and Dad's vineyard. She came up with her best friend and the friend's mom to check out the place for a wedding."

"I can picture you now." Her brother's charm with the opposite sex was legendary. "When are you going to settle down?"

"Why would I want to do that?"

"You're thirty years old, Dan. Don't you want to find someone to spend the rest of your life with?"

Daniel looked offended. "No."

Mariah fiddled with the ring she wore on her right hand. "Tell me about this new girlfriend. Are you sleeping with her?" She held her breath waiting for his response.

Daniel turned and waggled his eyebrows in Mariah's direction. "Not that it's any of your business. But, no, not yet."

Mariah considered her words and spoke slowly. "It isn't healthy for you to keep having casual sex, Daniel."

Her brother snorted. "Why not? It's consensual."

Mariah chewed her lip as she thought about her response. "What I've learned is that sex outside of marriage is wrong. You're not showing respect for those women you sleep with and then dump." She shrugged. This was not going the way she'd hoped.

Daniel reached over and touched Mariah's clenched fists. "Look, sis, I'm glad you had a religious experience and all. But let me do life my own way. Okay?"

Mariah swallowed her disappointment. "Okay."

Daniel pulled his Land Rover to a stop in front of a commercial building. "Wait here and I'll go in and get the stuff Dad ordered. I shouldn't be more than twenty minutes."

"No problem. I'll work on some tasks for Mom while I wait."

Mariah watched her brother as he climbed out of the vehicle and strode into the building. What could she have said differently to convince Daniel that what he was doing wasn't right? For the hundredth time she wished Pastor Roy was here so she could ask him and Susan what to say to her family.

With a sigh, Mariah pulled out the file folder containing her mother's notes from her bag. Balancing it on her lap, she began making calls for the big Chamber of Commerce fundraiser.

Before she knew it, thirty minutes had passed, and Daniel still hadn't returned to the car. Looking over her notes, Mariah punched the quick dial favorites button to call her mom.

"Mariah, I was thinking about you. How's the planning going on your end?"

"That's why I'm calling. Here's what I have so far. The appetizers will be provided by Simply Elegant catering. I thought since we want to support local, they'd be the logical choice. But I don't trust them to do the full dinner. I contracted with Howe It's Done in Salem. You should be getting the contracts via email later today or tomorrow. Sign them and send them back, along with a deposit. The band is a three-piece string group, also local. Oh, and the caterers will need a head count by Wednesday before the event. I'm assuming the Chamber will be able to provide that."

"My, my. You've certainly made some progress, Mariah. You're so good at this. Why don't you start an event planning business? You're a natural."

Mariah was filled with warmth from her mother's praise. "Thanks, Mom. But you know I have other plans."

"Speaking of which, how's that foster thing coming along."

"It's Safe Families, and it's going slow. I'm waiting for a response from the references I had to send in."

Her mother's sigh sounded loud in Mariah's ear. "I wish you'd forget about this, honey. I don't want to see you get hurt."

Mariah spied her brother exiting the building where they'd parked. "Gotta go, Mom."

She disconnected and shoved the folder back into her oversized bag. Daniel opened the car door and Mariah stepped out onto the sidewalk.

"Sorry about that," Daniel said. "It took longer than I expected."

"Please tell me you didn't get distracted by a woman."

Daniel raised both hands in surrender. "Guilty as charged. What could I do? She was desperate to give me her phone number." He grinned.

Mariah shoved him away. "You are such a player. I'm starved, so you better take me someplace good."

"It's such a nice day now that the rain has stopped. Let's walk." Daniel glanced down at Mariah's boots. "You okay to walk in those?"

Mariah nodded and they set off down the sidewalk and onto the busy main street of Newport.

By the time Mariah arrived home from the coast, the fried calamari she'd eaten was waging war in her stomach with the Crab Louie salad.

Mariah downed a couple of antacids and crawled into bed.

Chapter 11

Sunday morning came way too quickly for Ethan. His sermon lacked depth. Self-doubt and condemnation made his palms sweat as the worship leader signaled the end of their set. Between the weird texts from one of the teen girls in the congregation to the expectant looks on the faces of the elders, Ethan wondered how he would deliver a message of hope and encouragement.

He wiped his hands down his khaki slacks and stood. Setting his iPad on the lectern, he took a deep breath and began to speak.

"Our passage today is from the book of Acts. Let's stand together as I read from Acts 4 and verses eight through twelve."

As Ethan spoke, he was filled with the familiar sense of the Holy Spirit's presence. Words flowed from him without effort. This was what he loved. This is what he lived for. The privilege of saying what God wanted him to say.

When he was finished, there was a hush over the congregation until the worship leader took the stage and began the closing song.

Ethan returned to his place on the front row and sent up a silent prayer of thanks. During the final chorus of the song, he walked down the center aisle to the church door to shake hands with the congregation as they exited. His church in Seattle didn't expect him to greet every person, but here in Main, Pastor Roy had let him know the people loved it.

The compliments came rapid fire as people filed out of the church.

"Great sermon, Pastor."

"Really inspiring today."

"I'll never think of that passage the same way after today."

"We're glad you're with us."

A group of teens clustered by the side door leading into the office. Ethan spied a few of the girls sending him sidelong glances, then leaning in to whisper to each other. He shrugged it off. Hopefully the blocking of the number would discourage any further communication.

Ethan made a mental note to text the youth leader, Noah, to see how he was feeling. He wasn't in church today. If he was still sick, there was the chance Ethan could fill in again on Wednesday night. Not that he wished Noah ill. But he'd gotten a lot of satisfaction from spending time with the energetic youth of Main Community Church.

"Good sermon, Pastor."

Ethan pulled his glance away from the youth to find Mariah standing in front of him with her hand out to shake his. He thrust out his hand and took hers. He noticed how easily her long fingers slid into his grasp. Ethan stared into her blue eyes and noticed again how pretty she was.

Mariah wore a pair of black slacks that hugged her lean legs. A bright red top peeked out from a black and white checkered blazer that rested below her waist. Ethan's mouth went dry as he noticed her lipstick matched her blouse.

"Thank you," Ethan said, forcing his gaze from her lips to her eyes.

Mariah pulled her hand from his. They stared at each other until someone jostled Mariah, and she moved to the side.

One of the church elders grabbed Ethan's hand and pumped it vigorously. "Great sermon, Pastor. I knew we hadn't made a mistake when we went with Pastor Roy's recommendation to have you fill in. Let me and the wife take you to lunch."

Ethan nodded as he watched Mariah make her way out the door. He turned his attention back to the man standing in front of him.

"That sounds great, Mr. Stanley."

"Call me Mark, son." Mark shot a glance toward Mariah's retreating back. "Nice enough girl. But I'd steer clear if I were you. She's bad news."

"How so?"

Before Mark could answer, a woman approached. "Let's get going, Mark. If we hurry, we can beat the lunch rush at the Mexican restaurant."

Mark chuckled and took his wife's hand. "Sure thing, honey. Pastor, we'll save you a seat."

Ethan pulled Jayden from a game of tag with some other little boys and strapped him into his booster seat.

"Why can't I stay and play with my friends?" Jayden demanded.

"Because we're invited to lunch."

Jayden seemed to consider this. "Where?"

"Los Olivos Mexican Restaurant."

From the rearview mirror, Ethan could see Jayden's frown. "I don't like Mexican."

"Sure you do. I'll order you a quesadilla."

That seemed to satisfy his son. On the short drive to the restaurant, Ethan pondered Mark Stanley's words about Mariah. He'd have to figure out a way to bring the subject into their conversation over lunch. What could he have meant that Mariah was 'bad news?'

When he arrived at Los Olivos, he found Mark and his wife seated with another couple from the church and their two teenagers. Mark did the introductions.

"I think you've met everyone, Pastor. Craig and Debbie are the parents of these two fine young people. You probably met them at youth group Wednesday night."

Ethan acknowledged the two kids, Jesse and Tamara with a smile. "Great to see you again."

Jesse reached across the table to shake Ethan's hand while Tamara stared down at her phone.

"Put the phone away, Tam," Craig said. Tamara blushed and leaned forward to shove her phone in the back pocket of her jeans.

"I'm hungry," Jayden announced.

Ethan pulled a basket of tortilla chips toward him. "Eat a few of these. But not too many."

Debbie smiled. "I remember those days. They're gone too fast. Now we have teenagers." She leaned toward Tamara and bumped her shoulder.

Tamara frowned. "Mom, stop."

While Jesse engaged Jayden with comparisons of their favorite video games, Ethan was free to talk with the adults. Out of the corner of his eye, he saw Tamara pull her phone from her pocket and begin to thumb-type on the screen.

"How have you found Main thus far?" Mark's wife, Cindy, asked. "It must be a big adjustment after Seattle."

Ethan considered his words before answering. "It's true Main doesn't have all the assets that Seattle has. But I'm adjusting to life in a small town."

Mark leaned forward. "Wait until summer. You can hardly stir the tourists with a stick."

Craig laughed. "That's for sure. But it's good for business."

"What do you do for work?" Ethan asked.

"I'm a contractor," Craig answered.

Mark reached around his wife to slap Craig on the shoulder. "Don't let his modesty fool you. Craig is the owner of the biggest construction firm in the area. He's also the biggest contributor to the church." This statement was followed with a wink.

Ethan cringed inwardly. He made it a point to stay oblivious to the amount that people tithed. He didn't want to fall into the trap of preferring one over another because they gave more.

Cindy touched her husband's arm and sent him a look.

Mark raised his hands in surrender. "Sorry."

In Ethan's opinion, he didn't look sorry.

Ethan was grateful when Cindy changed the subject. "We wanted to take you and your son out last week on your first Sunday here. But everyone's been getting that awful bug that's been going around."

Debbie nodded. "This is the first day all of us have been well."

Ethan turned his attention to Debbie and noticed Tamara holding her phone in front of her face. Debbie ignored her daughter's blatant disobedience. He was tempted to say something to the girl but held his tongue. Not his battle.

The food arrived, and Ethan turned to Jayden. "Be careful, J-man. That quesadilla looks hot."

"Blow on it, Dad."

Ethan fixed a stern gaze on his son. "Are you forgetting something?"

"Please."

Tamara reached across the table and latched on to Jayden's plate. "I'll do it."

"Thanks. I appreciate that." Ethan gingerly touched the edge of his own plate, turning it so the beans and rice were at the top and his enchilada at the bottom.

Mark took a bite of his tamale and waved his fork in Ethan's direction. His mouth was full as he spoke. "I saw you talking to Mariah after church. I'd be careful with that one."

Ethan kept silent and hoped Mark would elaborate.

"She's been coming to the church for a while, now. Used to come with that boyfriend of hers. Big-city type guy, if you know what I mean."

Ethan didn't, but he nodded.

"They were living together." Mark shoved another bite into his mouth.

Cindy laid a hand on her husband's arm. "She met with Pastor Roy after they broke up."

"Well, yeah, that's true. I guess she had a true come-to-Jesus moment with the pastor. Time will tell if it took."

Ethan set his fork down. "I'm not sure what you mean."

Mark opened his mouth to elaborate but Cindy stopped him. "Mariah's mother and I used to be friends. Greg and Christy spoiled that girl and her brother something awful. Mariah has always had a mean streak."

Ethan's appetite slipped away as the gossip intensified. Part of him wanted to make it stop and the other part wanted to know more. More about the pretty young woman who was comfortable around Jayden still a bit brittle around him.

Debbie looked from Cindy to Mark and back. "We've only lived here for a few years. But I have heard stories." Debbie shrugged. "She seems nice enough."

Mark spoke around the food in his mouth. "Don't let her fool you. She bullied our daughter when they were in high school. Aimee has since moved to Eugene, but she was traumatized by that young woman."

"Bullied is such a harsh word," Cindy said.

"It's the truth," Mark exclaimed. Ethan cringed as a bit of rice flew from Mark's mouth onto the table.

Craig had been quiet until then. When he spoke, it was with a quiet authority. "Let's let the Lord deal with Ms. Martin."

"I agree," Debbie said.

Ethan breathed a sigh of relief and turned his attention to Jayden. He'd eaten almost all his quesadilla. All except for some crusty browned edges.

"Want some of my enchilada?" Ethan asked.

"Sure!"

Ethan cut his half-eaten enchilada in half again and scraped it onto Jayden's plate. Looked like his son was in another growth spurt.

Cindy took a sip of her iced tea and set the glass down. "Did anyone invite you to lunch last week?"

Ethan nodded. "Yes, Roman and Lizzy had me over." He didn't mention that Mariah had been invited too.

"That's sweet of them. Lizzy has been part of Main since she was a little thing. It's too bad she got pregnant in high school and had to drop out."

Could these people be any more gossipy?

"Good thing that no-good Dylan James skipped town after he'd done the deed. Good riddance, I say." Mark thumped his soda glass on the table for emphasis.

Cindy nodded. "She got saved during that time. Her best friend Simone kept inviting her to church, and she finally came."

"I don't know how Lizzy and Mariah became friends," Mark added. "Especially since Mariah won that house right from under Lizzy's nose."

Ethan frowned. "House?"

Cindy leaned forward and rested her elbows on the table. Her face was full of animation as she spoke. "Last year the City of Main decided to have a lottery for that house where Mariah lives. It had been vacant for a long time, and frankly, kind of run down. The City Council thought it would be good for the community to have an essay contest. The top five winners would all be put into a lottery and the winner drawn by chance."

Mark interrupted. "The winner had to pay all the back property taxes and agree to live in the house for at least a year."

Cindy's eyes glowed. "It was very exciting. Lizzy, Simone, and Mariah all were semi-finalists. At that time, only Lizzy and Simone were friends."

When Cindy paused to take a breath, Ethan said, "Mariah won the house?"

Cindy and Mark nodded in unison. "That's right," Cindy said. "Mean girl Mariah won the lottery."

"She has good taste," Craig interjected.

When all the heads turned toward him, he grinned. "My subcontractor, Grady, has been doing the work. I've seen the stuff she's ordered." He shrugged. "It's top quality."

"Figures," grumbled Mark. "With her parents' money, she could probably buy us all a new house. I always wonder if she got to the judges somehow. Seems unfair that Miss Money should win the house over folks who could really use it."

Debbie spoke for the first time in several minutes. "I heard she's looking to take in foster kids."

Mark snorted. "That'll be the day."

Ethan inhaled and blew out the breath. He was more than done with this conversation. He'd have to check his calendar to see if it was 'gossip about church members' day. What would they say behind *his* back?

"I better get this guy home," Ethan said, resting a hand on Jayden's shoulder.

"Don't worry about paying, Pastor," Mark said. "Craig'll take care of the check." Mark guffawed while Craig shifted in his seat, clearly uncomfortable.

"Thanks for having me," Ethan said.

Jesse leaned across the table and spoke to Jayden. "Nice talking with ya, little man." He held out his fist to bump Jayden's.

Tamara watched Ethan with hooded eyes, still holding her phone up like she was going to take a picture.

Ethan raised one hand in a brief wave. He couldn't get Jayden out of the restaurant fast enough.

~

Monday dawned with a hint of sun. Ethan rolled over in bed and asked himself what he was doing, trying to pastor a congregation that was two-thirds people over sixty years of age. Why had he agreed so quickly to Pastor Roy's request?

Because you didn't have a job.

Right. His church offered him an unpaid 'leave of absence.' Which pretty much meant he was fired. Ethan couldn't blame them. He'd been phoning it in for months. Being a single dad was the hardest job in the world. Finding out that Angie had gone behind his back to apply for a missions position had knocked the little bit of wind he had right out of him.

Why hadn't their ministry been enough for her? Why hadn't *he* been enough? What about Jayden? Ethan would never know the answers. Some days he felt like he'd gone through Elizabeth Kubler Ross's five stages of grief, ending in acceptance. Other days, like today, Ethan had a burning anger for his dead wife.

Why, Angie? Why didn't you talk about it with me? We could have worked something out.

Her betrayal tasted like ashes in his mouth. Ethan rolled out of bed to start another day where he would try to be a good dad and an okay pastor.

Jayden munched on his cereal while Ethan sucked down two cups of coffee.

"What are we going to do today, Dad?" Jayden looked up from his now-empty bowl.

"I'm going to do some work at the church." Roy had left him a list of handyman projects that he never got around to doing. With Ethan's background in basic carpentry, Roy tasked him with a few things he thought would keep Ethan busy.

"I don't want to go to the church with you," Jayden whined.

"I know, buddy, but Miss Sarah wasn't in church yesterday, so she's probably still sick."

"Why can't I go to Miss Mariah's again?"

Sometimes his son's whining got on Ethan's last nerve. "Because." Ethan struggled to come up with a reason that would satisfy his son. Because he didn't want to contact Mariah. Because he was irritated that she hadn't responded to his request to find out who sent the texts. Because she annoyed him and attracted him, and that fact annoyed him even more.

Chapter 12

After experiencing slight queasiness on Sunday, by Monday Mariah was ready to don her running tights and hit the pavement. She checked her email again for a response from Safe Families and headed out her front door.

She stretched for a few minutes on the front porch and set out on an easy jog through the quiet morning streets. This was her favorite time of day. Light had begun to break over the rolling hills surrounding Main. Lingering fog clung to the tops of the Douglas Fir trees. Her ponytail swished to the rhythm of her Asics hitting the sidewalk.

Today she'd chosen not to listen to music. This run would be her prayer time. Yesterday when she'd shaken Pastor Ethan's hand at the church, she'd felt something like a connection. Almost like a physical shock from static electricity. Maybe today God would show her what that was all about.

Several things rolled through her mind. How to talk to her family and her bestie, Brittany, about what God was doing in her life. How to remain patient for His timing about taking in kids for Safe Families. What to do about this growing attraction for the interim pastor and his adorable little boy. Especially in light of her decision to give up dating for the foreseeable future.

Ugh. Why couldn't life be more predictable? If she were to allow herself a brief – very brief – situation with Ethan, he'd leave like Scott did. Ethan would go back to Washington State, and she'd be here in Main, nursing another wound to her heart.

Sorry, Lord, it's a hard no.

With that resolved, Mariah sped up her pace. Her smart watch showed she was on target for an easy ten miles in an hour. Jogging in place at a stoplight, Mariah glanced down the street and noticed the lights on in the church building. With a start, she remembered she'd never told Ethan about the mysterious texts.

With a sudden change of direction, Mariah headed down the street toward the church. She found the side door open.

"Hello? Anyone here?"

A child's exuberant whoop sounded somewhere down the hall. "Miss Mariah!"

A moment later, Jayden came barreling toward her and threw his arms around her.

"Can I come to your house today? Please?" Jayden looked up expectantly.

Mariah squatted down and placed her hands on Jayden's shoulders. "Let's see what your dad says."

Ethan appeared in the hall carrying a door. Mariah took a moment to admire the muscles showing below his ridiculous tee shirt. It was the same one he'd worn the first day she'd seen him in the sanctuary. Like Swiss cheese.

Ethan frowned. "What are you doing here?"

Mariah almost laughed. He sounded exactly like her. "I was out running and saw the light on. I remembered I hadn't told you about my phone call to the text sender."

Ethan shrugged. "Yeah. So what?"

Mariah clenched her teeth. What was with the hostility? She was here to do him a favor,and he was acting all stupid.

She tried to keep her sarcasm to a minimum. "I thought you might like to know who sent the texts."

Ethan propped the door against the wall and shrugged. "It doesn't matter. I blocked the number."

Mariah mimicked his shrug. "Fine. I guess I'll be on my way."

Jayden swung his gaze between his dad and Mariah. "Dad, can I go to Miss Mariah's house?"

Mariah and Ethan spoke at the same time.

"I don't think—"

"It's okay with—"

Mariah rested a hand on Jayden's shoulder. "I am happy to have you come over, Jayden. If it's okay with your dad. I need to go home, shower, and change first. Okay?" Mariah slid her gaze to Ethan.

Ethan's exhale sounded loud in the silence. "Fine."

Mariah smiled down at the boy. "Great. Give me a half hour or so, and I'll come get you."

"I can bring him over," Ethan said.

Now her sarcasm came out in full force. "I wouldn't dream of keeping you from … whatever it is you're doing." Mariah motioned toward the door.

Ethan ran a hand down the door. "Pastor Roy said the door sticks at the bottom. I'm going to use a plane to shave off a bit at the bottom. A plane is a tool that—"

Mariah made a pfft sound. "You don't have to mansplain to me. I know what a plane is."

Mariah turned to leave. Her sneakered foot caught on the edge of the rug, and she tripped. Ethan grabbed her arm to keep her from falling. Her forward momentum had them both crashing against the wall. Mariah found herself in Ethan's strong arms as he attempted to steady them.

Mariah looked up and found her face inches from Ethan's. He smelled of pine and sage and a bit of sawdust. She closed her eyes and inhaled.

Ethan's breath was warm on her cheek as he spoke. "I'm sorry to be such a jerk. I guess I woke up on the wrong side of the bed."

Mariah lifted the corner of her mouth. "That sounds like something my grandma would say."

Ethan's face broke into a grin. "Your grandma sounds like mine."

As he inched closer, Mariah's heart raced with the anticipation of a kiss. She couldn't deny her attraction to him. What would it be like to have his lips on hers? The thought both thrilled and terrified her. She struggled to push away the conflicting emotions and focus on the present moment.

"Dad!" Jayden's voice broke the spell. "Miss Mariah has to go home."

Ethan's arms dropped to his sides. Mariah scooted away, smoothing the loose strands of her ponytail back into control. If only it were that easy to control her racing heart.

She turned her attention to Jayden. Anything to avoid looking at Ethan. "Right you are, Jayden. I'll run home and get changed."

Jayden giggled. "Run home. You are literally going to run."

Ethan turned a proud look on his son. "Where did you learn such a big word?"

"From you, Dad."

"You are one smart cookie," Mariah said.

"Not literally a cookie," Jayden added.

Mariah turned and headed for the door. "I'll be back in a bit," she said over her shoulder.

Once she hit the street, Mariah began a slow jog back toward her house. At least now she had an excuse for the runaway pounding of her pulse. What in the world was that, back in the church office? She'd actually wanted Ethan to kiss her. *Literally*.

Mariah laughed out loud.

~

Ethan chastised himself with every swipe of the plane, relishing the feel of the blade slicing the rough wood at the bottom of the door. If only he could easily slice away the conflicting emotions that bubbled up every time Mariah was within a six-foot distance. Although he no longer felt guilty for looking at other women after Angie's death, there was something about Mariah that both attracted and repelled him. She was beautiful, and she seemed to love Jayden. Those two things landed firmly in the 'plus' column.

But, and there was always a 'but' when Ethan had been attracted to a woman in the past two years. Prior to Mariah, the 'buts' had been superficial. Their skirts were too short, or they showed too much upper body skin for his liking. She wasn't athletic. She didn't bond with Jayden.

Mariah checked all those boxes in a positive way. Her clothing showed flawless style and taste. She loved running. Jayden begged to spend time with her. But the church elders held a different view of Miss Mariah. Her past screamed 'worldly' and 'ungodly.' Ethan couldn't afford to be in a relationship with a woman who didn't hold the same set of values that he did.

Yet his heart continued to betray him.

Ethan dropped the plane on the floor and bent to grab the door. He wrestled it back onto the hinges of Pastor Roy's office and swung it back and forth. Satisfied he'd shaved off enough of the sagging wood, he pounded in the hinge pins.

Next on the list was replacing the wax ring on the commode in the women's rest room. Ugh. That could wait.

Jayden's voice snapped Ethan out of his mental meanderings. "Dad, do you think Miss Mariah will be here soon?"

Ethan pulled out his cell phone to check the time. "I think so, buddy." As he held the phone, a text appeared from the very woman he'd been thinking about.

Mariah: Leaving my house now. Be there in 10.

"It says here she's on her way. Let's grab your backpack and wait for her outside."

Jayden ran to get this bag, and they, headed outside. Ethan sank onto a low brick border holding at bay the flowers blooming in the weak sunshine. Jayden sat beside him, watching each vehicle as it cruised by at the posted twenty-five mile an hour speed limit. Some drivers sent him a cheery wave and a smile as they passed.

"What do you think of our new town, J-man?"

"It's awesome, Dad. Can we stay here? Me and my friends will all be in the same kindergarten class next year."

"That all depends on when Pastor Roy comes back. He originally said three months, which would mean we'd move back to Seattle right before school starts in the fall."

Jayden turned his head to gaze at Ethan expectantly. "But could we stay here too?"

"Don't you want to go back to your friends in Seattle?" What would he be going back to, anyway? If his church wanted him to come back, Ethan would have to step up his game. The elders wanted crisp sermons with engaging content. *Relevant*, they'd called it. Ethan wasn't sure what that meant anymore. The elders seemed to think that 'relevant' meant bigger crowds and more money in the offering.

A couple of the men – and women – pressured him to get married again. They felt his singleness was a distraction to the unmarried females in the congregation.

"I like it here better." Jayden jumped off the retaining wall and landed on the grass with a thump.

"Yeah, buddy, I like it here better too."

Mariah's BMW pulled up to the curb as a text appeared from Noah.

Sorry, man. Still sick. Can u cover again Wednesday?

Ethan's pulse jumped.

Yes, of course.

He had the perfect message for the youth that week. It was one he'd been working out in his mind since the previous Wednesday. As soon as Jayden left with Mariah, he'd head to Roy's office and work on the Scriptures and some content.

Working with teenagers gave Ethan's ego a boost he didn't get from preaching to adults. When they gathered around him after last Wednesday's service, he felt fulfilled. Their enthusiasm sparked Ethan's own desire to dig deeper into God's word.

Mariah stepped out of her vehicle wearing skinny jeans and a loose knit sweater that ended at her waist. Instead of showing a strip of skin, it appeared she wore a cami underneath. Angie would have done the same. She always complained that the current style of women's tops were several inches too short.

Ethan put thoughts of Angie aside as Mariah strode toward them.

"Ready to go have some fun, Jayden?" Mariah asked.

Jaden grinned. "Yeah!" He grabbed his backpack and said, "Bye, Dad."

"Wait a minute, buddy. I need a hug goodbye."

Jayden dutifully returned to Ethan and gave him a quick squeeze.

"I love, you buddy," Ethan said. Soon his little man would head off to school and the messy kisses and good-bye hugs would be over. Ethan had a vision of his boy slowly morphing into an adolescent, to a teenager, to a young man. He wished Angie could be there to see their son grow.

But Angie was gone. And Ethan didn't know if their marriage would have survived had she lived. Angie was already planning to leave him for the mission field. Her short-term plan could have grown into a long-term commitment, leaving him and Jayden on their own.

Ethan thought he'd chosen well when he asked Angela to marry him. She'd embodied what his mentors had said was the 'perfect pastor's wife.' A true Proverbs 31 woman.

Too many times in the past few years Ethan regretted the pressure he'd put on Angela to marry him. He'd dangled the carrot of 'missions someday' until she took the bait. They both watched as their college friends got engaged and married. It felt like the logical thing for them as well. Ethan wanted the stability of marriage and a family because of the upheaval of his own childhood, shuffled from Mom to Dad and back. Angie wanted a partner to escape from her own family drama. She pictured a life far away from her fractured family.

Ethan sucked in a ragged breath.

Maybe he should choose someone not perfect the next time around. Someone like –

Before Ethan could complete the thought, Mariah's voice interrupted.

"Earth to Ethan."

"Huh?" Ethan rubbed his eyes with the heels of his hands. *Focus, Ethan. Focus.*

"I'll bring him back in, what, maybe three hours? Will that give you enough time to get Pastor Roy's stuff done?"

"Uh, yeah. Roy's list. Thanks." Mariah must think he was an idiot. "Actually, I'm going to work on another lesson for the youth group. Noah's still sick."

Mariah's face clouded over. "I'm sorry to hear that. Not that you're going to lead it again." She shook her head and her jet-black hair whipped around her face. She pulled it back with one hand. "That Noah is sick. There's a nasty bug going around." She let her hair fall again. "Be careful, okay? Those high school girls can sometimes let a crush go too far."

Ethan watched as a slow flush worked its way up from Mariah's neck to her forehead. There was a story there. He was sure of it.

"Are you talking about those texts?" Ethan had forgotten about them until that moment.

Mariah nodded and then shook her head. "It's probably nothing to worry about. Forget I said anything. You said you blocked the number. That should send the proper message."

Ethan almost laughed. 'Proper message' indeed.

Mariah clasped Jayden's hand in hers and walked him to her waiting car.

"Since it's such a nice day, I thought we'd go to the park first. Then we can go back to the house."

"And play video games?"

"Maybe. But I have something else planned that might take up all our time."

Ethan couldn't hear the rest of their conversation as Mariah strapped Ethan into the back seat. He had half a mind to invite himself along. Spending some quality time with Jayden in the park sounded awesome. And spending time with Mariah wouldn't be that bad, either. He could find out what Mark was talking about when he said Mariah had a bad reputation. It'd be nice to get to the bottom of that bit of gossip.

But the youth group message pulled him back inside the church.

~

Mariah started her car but took a moment to admire Ethan's retreating back as he strolled into the church. The fear she'd experienced when she'd first walked into the church sanctuary and saw him there was gone. In its place was a growing admiration for the single father who adored his little boy.

So far, Pastor Ethan's sermons had been right on. The Scriptures he'd used spoke to Mariah's heart. She'd overheard some snippets of conversation that Ethan had a back story with his church in Seattle. She chalked it up to idle gossip – something she was very familiar with. Between her and Brittany, they could gossip the socks off anyone. But that was BC.

Mariah jerked to a stop at the curb facing the park. Drops of water from the recent rain glistened on the play equipment like tiny diamonds.

"Glad I brought a towel." Mariah spoke over her shoulder to Jayden, who was already working with the seatbelt.

"Got it," he announced, grabbing for the door handle.

Mariah slid from her car and rounded the front to the passenger side. The minute the door was open, Jayden was off like a guided missile. Mariah followed on his heels, clutching a towel.

"Let me get the slide dried off before you go down."

Once she was satisfied Jayden wouldn't get soaked, Mariah sat on a bench and watched the boy play. Soon another kid joined him, and then another.

A young mom sank onto the bench next to Mariah. "Whew. Thanks for drying off the equipment." She turned toward Mariah. "I'm assuming you're the one who did that, right?"

Mariah nodded.

"I'm Yasmin. Those two holy terrors are my twins, Clayton and Zoe."

"Wow, twins. How hard is that?" Mariah sent Yasmin a sympathetic smile. "I'm Mariah."

The two women shook hands.

"It was super hard the first couple of years," Yasmin admitted. "But now they're best friends. Most of the time." She laughed and raised one shoulder. "It changes from day to day."

They watched the kids engage in a game of who could climb up the slide the fastest.

"How old is your boy?" Yasmin asked.

"Jayden is five. But he isn't mine. I'm babysitting him for a couple of hours, so his dad can get some work done."

"His dad?"

"Pastor Ethan is the interim pastor at Main Community Church."

Yasmin nodded. "Ah. We don't go to church. We've only lived here a couple of months. Moved here from Eugene for my husband's job. He's a welder."

A quick stab of jealousy struck Mariah's heart. Husband, kids – Yasmin had what Mariah desperately wanted.

Yasmin's voice cut into Mariah's downward spiral. "Are you and Jayden's dad dating?"

Mariah exploded in a laugh. "Hardly. I don't think he's looking for a wife. And I'm not looking for a husband."

"That's too bad. Being married to my best friend is awesome. Clayton's dad and I planned to get married 'someday.' But when I found out I was pregnant, we speeded up the process. I have no regrets. I want everyone to be as happy as we are."

Yasmin had no idea her words were like acid on Mariah's soul. She found it hard to breathe and placed a hand on her chest.

"I'll be right back." Mariah sprang to her feet and sprinted to a drinking fountain. After inspecting it for cleanliness, she pushed the button to let the water flow for several seconds before taking a tiny sip.

A quick perusal of the play area showed Jayden playing happily with his new friends. Mariah returned to the bench.

Yasmin indicated the three kids. "Isn't it amazing how kids can make friends so quickly? I wish it were that easy for us."

Mariah murmured her agreement.

"Frankly, I've found Main a little cliquey," Yasmin continued.

"Small towns can be like that," Mariah agreed. "You should come to church sometime. It's a great place to meet people. I mean, if you're interested." Mariah held her breath.

"Hm. I might do that. At least the twins could get some spiritual stuff." She shrugged.

"Why don't you give me your number, and I can text you the address and the service times."

Yasmin smiled. "Sounds great. And maybe we can do this again. Meet for a play date for the kids the next time you're babysitting Jayden."

As soon as they exchanged texts, the children ran from the playground announcing they were starved.

"Did you bring any snacks?" demanded Jayden.

Yasmin's kids said the same thing.

Mariah stood. "Guess I'd better get home. I didn't think to bring any food."

She was surprised when Yasmin stood and grabbed her in a fierce hug. "You have no idea how much I've enjoyed chatting with you. I miss having a female friend."

Mariah couldn't help but wonder if Yasmin would still be as friendly once she learned of Mariah's reputation. "I've enjoyed it too." She waved her phone back and forth. "Let's stay in touch."

By the time Mariah parked in front of her house, Jayden's hungry whine had notched up to def-con ten.

"I'm starved. When can we eat? I want McDonald's."

Mariah resisted the urge to snap at him, remembering the techniques she'd learned from the dozens of parenting books she'd devoured.

"Let's get you unbuckled and into the house. I'll make you a peanut butter sandwich. How does that sound?"

"I don't want peanut butter. I want McDonalds!"

Jayden jumped out of the car and ran to Mariah's front door. Mariah followed him and unlocked the door. Jayden collapsed on the floor. "I want McDonalds!"

Mariah looked down at him and with a calm voice said, "That isn't an option, Jayden. Here's what I have. PB&J or frozen mac and cheese. Which one do you want?"

Jaden stilled and appeared to be thinking. "Mac and cheese, I guess."

"Great. Let's go into the kitchen. I'll cut up an apple for you while it cooks." Mariah took a deep breath, grateful to have avoided a complete meltdown.

Jayden was a good kid. Ethan seemed to be doing a good job raising him on his own. What was his wife like? Mariah pictured someone like Susan, Pastor Roy's wife. She shook her head. No, Ethan wouldn't have married someone dumpy, would he? Not that Susan was a complete disaster. She was on the matronly side, carrying several extra pounds around her waist. Susan called it her 'Grandma pooch,' always with a smile.

Mariah couldn't imagine what it would be like to be overweight. What would she do if she ever got married and got pregnant? Would she embrace her growing girth or resent the changes a baby would make in her body?

Enough of that. Jayden was making whiny noises again.

"Here you go, little man. Munch on these apple slices while I heat up your lunch."

Jayden dove into the apple like he hadn't eaten in a week. Mariah watched him with a smile while the microwave did its thing. While the mac and cheese cooked, Mariah threw together a salad and tossed some leftover chicken on it. She dabbed on some low-calorie salad dressing and set it on the table.

"Here's your lunch, Jayden. Let me blow on it before you take a bite."

With a mischievous grin, Jayden snagged a cucumber slice from Mariah's salad.

"Hey, no sharing," she admonished him with a smile.

Jayden spoke around the food in his mouth. "I love cukes. Especially with catsup."

"Next time I'll slice some up for you."

"After lunch, can we play Spiderman?"

Mariah glanced over her shoulder at the digital microwave clock. "I'm not sure. Let me text your dad and see what time he wants me to take you home."

Jayden nodded and dug into his mac and cheese.

"What did you think of Clayton and Zoe?" Mariah asked.

"They were cool." Jayden swiped his arm across his mouth, smearing cheese on his face and on his sleeve.

Mariah jumped up and pulled a paper towel off the roll. "Here, use this."

Mariah shuddered while Jayden continued to smear the gooey mess across his cheeks. Self-doubt lodged in her heart. How would she be able to take care of an infant or any child, really, when she was grossed out by one five-year-old boy eating macaroni and cheese? What would it be like to change diapers and have all that mess? Ugh. Time for some soul-searching about the Safe Families program. And time for some deep prayer.

Mariah's phone pinged with an incoming text. She pushed back from the table, stood, and retrieved it from the counter next to the sink.

"It's your dad," she said.

Jayden looked up expectantly. "When's he coming? Do we have time to play videos? Can you ask him?"

"One question at a time, little man. How about I call him?"

After Mariah dialed his number, Jayden said, "Put it on speaker."

"Please."

"Please," Jayden parroted.

Mariah sent him a wry smile while pushing the speaker button.

Ethan's voice came through the phone. "I'm leaving now to come get Jayden. Are you back from the park?"

Jayden leaned close to the phone. "No, Dad, wait. We haven't gotten to play videos yet."

Mariah scooted the phone closer to her side of the table. "We got back from the park a while ago, and we're finishing lunch."

There was a pause for several seconds. "Oh. Well, I'll grab something to eat here. Do you mind if he stays a little longer?"

Mariah glanced at the boy, who nodded vigorously.

"I don't mind. Take your time."

"Yes!" Jayden said with a fist pump in the air.

Mariah thought for a moment before answering. "Or you could come over now. I'll make some lunch for you and after you can play with Jayden." She held her breath, hoping he'd agree.

"Say yes, Dad. Say yes," Jayden pleaded.

Ethan's laugh boomed through the phone. "Okay. Sounds good."

"Is salad with chicken on it okay for you?"

"Anything I don't have to cook or make myself is okay with me."

Mariah smiled. "See you soon."

Jayden jumped from his seat and danced around the kitchen. "Yay, Dad's coming to play with me."

Mariah marveled at the ability of children to be happy about the smallest of things. But she had to admit, she was happy that she'd get to see Ethan for more than a couple of minutes.

Speaking of which, she hustled to throw together another salad. "Finish your lunch, Jayden, before your dad gets here."

Jayden returned to his chair and shoveled more pasta into his mouth. Mariah shook her head. *Kids.*

~

Ethan pulled to a stop behind Mariah's BMW and turned off the ignition. He sat for a moment, examining the nervous jitter that worked its way up from his gut. This woman was getting under his skin, but in a good way. Thoughts that he was betraying Angie were becoming a distant memory. Mariah seemed to check all the boxes, especially the one about caring for Jayden.

Still, what was behind Mark's insinuation there was more to Mariah's backstory? Ethan wracked his brain for a way to bring the subject into a normal conversation. But for now, he'd enjoy a meal he didn't have to prepare and spend some quality time with his son.

Mariah was quick to answer his knock on her front door.

"Come on in. Jayden is finishing up his lunch." Mariah opened the door wide and let Ethan pass.

"Hey, Dad," Jayden greeted him when Ethan crossed into the kitchen. He took a moment to admire the nautical blue cabinets and brushed silver handles. "Your kitchen is nice," he commented.

A blush rose to Mariah's cheeks. "Thank you. My friend Lizzy helped me design it. She's really good at interior design. As a matter of fact, she's going through design school."

Ethan didn't want to talk about Lizzy or her husband, Roman, or their daughter. He wanted to focus on the woman standing in front of him, clasping her hands together like she was nervous.

Mariah moved to the sink and wet a paper towel. "Let me help Jayden get the cheese off his face."

Jayden squirmed under her attempts to wipe off his face.

"I'm clean," he protested. "Can I go upstairs now?"

Mariah looked to Ethan to answer.

"Sure, buddy. If it's okay with Miss Mariah. I'll be up as soon as I eat my salad."

Mariah removed the plastic wrap covering his plate and pushed it across the table toward him. "It's fine. Can you remember how to turn everything on?"

"I think so," Jayden answered.

Mariah hesitated. "Let me know if you have any problems with the set-up, okay?"

"Gotcha." Jayden dashed toward the living room and Ethan heard his shoes pounding up the stairs.

Ethan smiled. "Wouldn't it be great to have that much energy?"

Mariah shook her head with a wry grin. "Oh, yeah. I'm tired already, and I didn't even play at the park."

They dug into their salads without talking for a few minutes. Mariah had already finished half of hers before Ethan had arrived. She set her fork down. "I met a young mom at the park and invited her to church."

Ethan's eyebrows rose. "You did? That's great. What's her name? I'll look for her this Sunday."

"Her name is Yasmin, but I don't know if she'll show up or not."

"Even so, it was brave of you to invite her."

Mariah seemed pleased with his compliment.

"She has twins, Clayton and Zoe. They're about Jayden's age. They had fun playing on the play structure."

Ethan nodded. "Thank you again for taking him. I got a lot done on the message for the youth group Wednesday."

"It was my pleasure. Speaking of which, you still don't want to know who sent those texts?"

Ethan shook his head. "It was probably a harmless crush. Knowing high school girls, she's probably over it by now. Besides, I don't want to have it affect how I relate to the kids. It might make it awkward."

Mariah looked like she wanted to say more, but picked up her fork and speared a piece of chicken without speaking.

"This salad is great, by the way. Thanks." Ethan felt like he was continually thanking this woman. Would he forever be in her debt? He'd need to think of something to do for her in return. The words came out of his mouth before he had a chance to think about them.

"Would you like to go to dinner with me sometime?" Ethan cleared his throat. "I mean, to thank you for Jayden, and you know, everything."

Mariah's hand holding the fork stopped halfway to her mouth.

Ethan shifted on the hard kitchen chair. "I mean, no obligation or anything. I feel like I've taken advantage of your kindness too many times. I'd like to make it up to you."

He watched as Mariah carefully laid her fork on the edge of her plate. Ethan felt his pulse speed up. Sweat broke out on his forehead. When had it gotten hot in here?

Mariah squinted at him. "Like a date?"

Ethan leaned back in his chair. "No, nothing like that. Think of it as, oh, I don't know, a thank you gift." Ethan took a sip of water to moisten his dry mouth.

"A gift?"

Smooth, dude, real smooth. Ethan focused his attention on the mixture of lettuce, tomatoes, and chopped chicken on his plate. "Look, I—"

"Yes." Mariah picked up her fork and continued eating.

"Yes? Well, okay. Um, I'll figure out a place. And a time."

Ethan exhaled slowly, wondering if he'd made a huge mistake.

~

Mariah almost laughed out loud at Ethan's discomfort. She'd been asked on dozens of dates, but never in quite this way. His excuse of it being a thank you for watching Jayden was amusing.

Date or not, it would be nice to be taken out to dinner by someone of the opposite sex. Someone who didn't expect payment of the physical kind for a nice evening out. Ethan probably wouldn't even kiss her goodnight. Since her breakup with Scott, Mariah hadn't been interested in dating. Especially since the pool of available men in Main was in short supply as she and her brother discussed.

Mariah swallowed her unease at going out with a minister by telling herself it was only dinner. A *thank you* dinner.

Ethan took the last bite of his salad and pushed back his chair. "I better go see what my son is up to. Thanks again for lunch."

"I'll be up in a few minutes. After I clean up."

Ethan paused in the doorway. "Can I help?"

Mariah shooed him with her hands. "No. I've got this."

She watched Ethan turn and stride through her living room. While she rinsed the dishes and placed them in the dishwasher, she marveled that her initial fear of Ethan was completely gone. Thank you, Pastor Roy. His and Susan's counsel had helped rid herself of a lot of the baggage she'd carried since 'the incident.'

If she could shake her reputation as Mean Girl Mariah, that would be awesome.

The evening passed quickly while Mariah alternated with Ethan in challenging Jayden's gaming skills. Who knew a five-year-old could be so proficient? When they'd finally worn out, Ethan practically had to pry his son away from the controls.

"We've been here long enough," Ethan said. Jayden protested loudly and all the way to the front door.

Mariah opened the door to let them out, letting in a blast of cold, wet air. Hugging her arms to her chest, she stepped onto the porch as Ethan zipped up his son's hoodie.

Without making eye contact, Ethan said, "When would be a good time for me to, you know, uh, say thanks. With dinner."

Mariah shrugged. "Tomorrow?"

Ethan straightened. "So soon? I mean, sure."

"I can see if Lizzy and Roman can watch Jayden. That is, unless you wanted him to come too."

Ethan shifted his weight from one leg to the other. "Uh, no."

"Okay, then. I'll text you and let you know what Lizzy says."

Ethan hunched his shoulders and pulled his sweatshirt down. "Okay."

He hustled Jayden to his car as Mariah returned to the warmth of her little house. The minute she got inside, she grabbed her phone and sent a quick text to her friend.

Can you watch Ethan's son tomorrow night around six?

She backed up the typing and inserted 'Pastor' in front of Ethan. No sense in giving Lizzy something to gossip about.

Lizzy's text came quickly. **Sure. What's up?**

Mariah tapped a fingernail on the phone. How to answer? Count on Lizzy to want all the details.

He's going out to dinner and Miss Sarah is still sick.

Mariah scrunched her face and held her breath as she waited for Lizzy's response.

I thought you were the backup these days.

Mariah ground her teeth while working on how to dance around that she was going to dinner with Ethan.

Can you do it or not?

Lizzy: Why are you asking me and not him?

Good grief. Lizzy's relentlessness was getting on Mariah's last nerve. With a groan, she typed out her response.

I told Pastor Ethan I would ask you.

Mariah held her breath, waiting for the little dots indicating Lizzy was forming a response. Nothing. Mariah blew out her breath and tossed the phone onto the sofa.

After ten minutes of obsessively checking the phone, Mariah gave up and wandered into the kitchen. Going to dinner with Ethan was probably a bad idea anyway. She had no desire to feed her growing attraction to him. Having a man in her life wasn't in her new life plan.

Before Scott, Mariah had had a series of boyfriends, none serious. She'd seen nothing wrong with becoming intimate. That's what women did. But not until after the second or third date. Mariah had standards.

It wasn't until she met Scott that she'd settled into a more permanent relationship. He understood the trauma Mariah had experienced from the youth leader. He'd been tender and patient. When he'd offered her a key to his apartment, Mariah had taken it as the first step toward marriage. Unfortunately, Scott's goals and hers didn't line up. Mariah wanted marriage and kids. Scott did not. He wanted to pursue his legal career and found the little town of Main too limiting. When Scott found one of Mariah's pregnancy tests in the trash, he'd freaked out and accused her of 'trapping' him.

Looking back, that was exactly what Mariah had been doing. It backfired big time. She'd gone to Pastor Roy, broken. He and Susan had helped put her back together and had shown her the love of God.

Mariah wouldn't make the same mistake of trusting a man, even someone like Pastor Ethan, to help her feel loved. She strode toward the sofa, intending to text Ethan and decline his invitation.

As she reached for her phone, the doorbell rang, then swung open. Lizzy stepped into the room, bringing with her the smell of rain.

"Brrr. It's freezing out there." Lizzy hugged her arms to her chest, closing the door with a shove of one foot.

"What are you doing here?" Mariah demanded.

Lizzy grinned. "I'm trying to find out why my *friend* Mariah is not being honest with me." Lizzy walked toward the kitchen, pausing in the doorway. "What do you have that's hot to drink with no caffeine?"

Mariah followed Lizzy into the kitchen and gave her a gentle shove toward the table. "Sit down and I'll make you a cup of tea. Is chamomile okay?"

Lizzy settled onto a chair. "Sure. Thanks. Then you better tell me what's going on. I'm not leaving here until you do."

Mariah filled the electric kettle with water and set it on the stand to heat. She pulled two matching mugs from the cupboard along with a box of tea.

While the water heated, Mariah considered what to tell Lizzy. Having Lizzy for a friend was a lot harder than having her as an enemy. Bullying was easy. Sharing her heart was difficult.

Mariah carried the box of teabags to the table and set it down. She removed two spoons from the drawer and carried them to the table. The water bubbled in the clear carafe indicating it was ready.

Lizzy pried open the box of tea and pulled out a bag. "Stop dawdling and pour the water, Mariah. Sheesh."

"Fine," Mariah snapped. She filled the mugs, splashing boiling water onto the counter. "Darn it!" Grabbing a paper towel, she mopped up the liquid before carrying the mugs to the table. Once they'd dunked their teabags a couple of times, Mariah inhaled and blew the breath out through pursed lips.

"Okay, here's the deal. Pastor Ethan wants to take me to dinner to say thanks for helping out with watching Jayden."

Lizzy quirked an eyebrow. "I don't recall him taking Miss Sarah to dinner for babysitting."

Mariah slapped a hand on the table. "Exactly."

"Soooo, it's like a date?" Lizzy took a sip of her tea, hiding the smile Mariah could see peeking around the edges.

"No. At least I don't think so."

Lizzy shrugged. "I fail to see the problem here, Mariah. He's single. You're single. You're going out to dinner."

Mariah chose her words carefully. "As you may not know, I don't always make the best choices in men."

Lizzy choked out a laugh. "Me neither."

"That's the truth," Mariah said.

Lizzy's mouth tilted up in a wry smile. "I can always count on you to be brutally honest."

Mariah raised both hands in surrender. "Who's the one who got pregnant in high school?"

"Okay, okay. Point taken."

Mariah dropped her hands to the table, clasping them together as if she was praying. "Anyway, I didn't have the best moral compass prior to getting saved. Since, you know, that thing in middle school—"

"Wait. What thing in middle school?"

Mariah felt her face grow hot. "Um, that was something that happened a long time ago." She jumped from her chair and strode to the pot of hot water. "More hot water?"

"No, thank you. Stop deflecting. What thing?"

Mariah set the pot back on the warmer. Might as well get it out there. Lizzy was supposed to be her friend. *Let's see how she reacts.*

She told Lizzy everything. How her life had spiraled out of control since that horrific night.

Mariah leaned back against the counter. "There was this youth retreat. The youth pastor made me do something I didn't want to do."

Lizzy's lips formed a grim line. "He forced you?"

Mariah nodded.

"Did you report him?"

Mariah shook her head. "I was ashamed. I thought it was my fault because I flirted with him. He was nineteen, and I was twelve."

Lizzy sprang from her chair and rushed to pull Mariah into a hug. "You know it wasn't your fault, right? You were only a kid!"

Mariah leaned into Lizzy. Lizzy smelled of cinnamon and nutmeg. A comforting smell of home-baked muffins.

"Pastor Roy helped me understand that. But the thing is, that one incident turned my life into a ball of barbed wire. I became this awful person, lashing out at everyone and making life miserable for anyone who I decided was better off than me." Tears burned behind Mariah's eyelids.

Lizzy pulled back and focused her gaze on Mariah. "Oh, sweetie, I'm sorry you went through that. How awful."

"It explains a lot, though, doesn't it? Like why I was so mean to you?"

The corner of Lizzy's mouth tilted up. "Yeah. It does." She released her hold on Mariah and stepped back. "But what does this have to do with Pastor Ethan? Have you told him?"

Mariah grabbed the hot water carafe and headed toward the table, refilling their mugs.

Lizzy pulled another tea bag from the box and dunked it in the hot water. Mariah did the same.

Mariah's mouth tightened. "I like him, okay? And I adore Jayden. But—and this is a big but—if he is looking for a wife, I am not it. I have way too much baggage in my past. He won't want anything to do with me when he finds out what I did. How I was before, you know, I changed my life."

Lizzy barked out a laugh. "Talk about lame, Mariah." Lizzy formed the letter L with her finger and thumb and raised it to her forehead. "It's dinner. One dinner. Sheesh, overthink much?"

Mariah chuckled. "You're right. I am overthinking it." She took a deep, cleansing breath. "Fine. One dinner for him to express his undying gratitude to me for watching his son."

Lizzy batted her eyes. "I'll go online and start looking at wedding invitations."

"Ha."

Lizzy scooted her chair back. "One more thing before I go. What's happening with the Safe Families thing?"

Mariah let out a groan. "Crickets. I sent in the references, but I haven't heard a thing. I should probably email them. Or call. Something."

"Let me know, okay?" Lizzy carried her cup to the sink. "And, yes, I will watch Jayden so you can go out to dinner." She made kissy noises, dashing out the door before Mariah could toss a wet teabag in her direction.

Chapter 13

Ethan spent a restless night flopping from one side to the other on Pastor Roy's too soft bed. He alternated between excitement over going to dinner with Mariah and terror that he had made a huge mistake by asking her out. He tried focusing on Angie's face, but the vision was fading.

They'd never discussed what they'd do if one of them died before the other. Ethan figured they'd have years before that eventuality. Unless Angie decided to leave him to go on the mission field.

Ethan punched the pillow and jammed it under his head. He'd ignored the signs of his wife's discontent, certain she'd never act on her desire to serve the Lord in a foreign land. Angela knew the Bible as well as he did. "Wives, submit to your own husbands as to the Lord." He huffed out a laugh. How easy it was for people of God to deceived themselves that what they were doing was right.

That train of thought brought him back around to the dinner with Mariah. Could it be that he'd convinced himself the dinner was merely a 'thank you' for helping watch Jayden in Miss Sarah's absence? Perhaps it was time to lay Angela to rest in his memory and move on. Jayden needed a mom, and Ethan desired a partner in ministry.

But what about Mark's hints that Mariah wasn't the person she showed to church people? It wasn't something he could bluntly ask. *Say, how about that bad reputation you have?*

Maybe she'd bring up the subject at their dinner tonight.

Ethan gave up the pretense of falling back asleep and rose to get ready to face the day. Sermon prep, preparing his message for the youth group the following evening, answering phone calls – how he wished for someone to do that administrative task. He'd broach the subject with Mariah again.

Not only would it relieve him of some of the mundane tasks required of a pastor, he'd get to see her every day.

Jayden stumbled into the kitchen as Ethan was enjoying his second cup of coffee.

"What's for breakfast, Dad?" He rubbed eyes still filled with sleep.

Ethan pulled Jayden into a hug and lifted him onto the counter. "Oof, you're getting big."

Jayden giggled. "Pretty soon I'll be as big as you."

"That's right, J-man. Keep eating like you do and you'll be even bigger."

Jayden's eyes grew round. "Think so?"

Ethan did a mental inventory of the contents of Pastor Roy's cupboards and fridge. "What do you say you get dressed and we go out to breakfast?"

Jayden leapt off the counter and landed with a thud on the wood floor. "Yes! I want a man's breakfast again."

Ethan ruffled his son's hair before Jayden took off in a run toward his bedroom. He really needed to stop eating out. But providing three meals a day for a growing five-year-old boy added more stress to his already full plate.

Which returned his thoughts to Mariah. What would it be like to have her as a partner in his ministry? She seemed organized. Clean house. Given to hospitality. Great with kids, at least what Ethan had observed with Jayden. For the first time since Angie's death, Ethan thought of another woman as more than another female in his congregation.

Still, there was a brittleness about the lovely Miss Mariah. Tonight's dinner would prove interesting.

But first, breakfast with his boy.

They arrived at the coffee shop as the morning rush wound down. Ethan was led to a booth by a young man with a man bun perched on the top of his head. Without a word, he handed Ethan two menus and walked away. Ethan glanced around the dining room and sighed with relief when the nosy waitress, Wren, was nowhere in sight.

"What do you want today, J-man?" Ethan draped his arm across his son's shoulders.

"Pancakes. Big ones."

"You've got it, buddy."

Ethan slid his coffee mug closer to the edge of the table, hoping the gesture wouldn't go unnoticed by the server. The young man seemed to be the only one working the dining room.

A few minutes later, the front door opened and Roman stepped into the diner in a blast of frigid air. Roman's gaze settled on Ethan and he strode over to their booth and slid in across from him and Jayden.

"Can I join you?" Roman asked.

"Looks like you already did."

Roman shrugged out of his jacket. He folded it and laid it on the bench beside him. "I had to get out of the house."

Roman said this as if it explained his presence at their booth.

As the silence between them lengthened, Ethan shifted on the seat.

"Dad, can I play a game on your phone?"

Ethan slid his phone from his front shirt pocket and handed it to his son.

Roman raised his coffee mug in the air and the young kid immediately brought a pot brimming with steaming coffee. Roman must have some superpower or something.

The server set the pot on the table after filling their mugs. He pulled a pencil from his apron pocket along with an order pad. "What can I get you to eat?"

"Just coffee for me," Roman said.

"I'll have the Santa Fe Scramble and this young man will have your short stack of pancakes."

Jayden pulled on Ethan's sleeve. "No, Dad, I want the big stack."

Ethan winked at the server. "Okay, J-man." The server gave him an imperceptible nod.

Ethan watched the young man's back as he returned to the kitchen and placed their order on the circular ticket rack. Roman sipped his coffee in silence.

"So, Roman, how's life?"

Roman blinked a couple of times. "I needed to get out of the house. I usually go to the Main Bean, but the line was too long. I came here instead."

Ethan was used to drawing people out. He put on his pastor's hat and mentally prepared a list of potential questions.

"Why did you need to get out of the house?"

"Lizzy needed to study."

Roman answered as if that explained everything.

"What do you do for work, Roman?" Basic question, used to get a conversation rolling.

"IT security."

Roman's Adam's apple bounced up and down as he swallowed. His hand shook when he raised the coffee mug to his lips.

"Something on your mind, Roman?" Ethan leaned forward in an active listening posture.

Roman set his mug down and gripped it with white knuckles. "Lizzy and I have been married for nine months and six days."

Ethan's brain whirled with possibilities of what this odd guy was going to say. "Yes?"

"She's going to have a baby. Our baby."

"Uh huh."

"I'm terrified I won't be able to love the baby as much as I love Abigail."

Ethan forced down a laugh. Roman wouldn't appreciate being laughed at. He placed his hands on the table, thumbs up, about six inches apart.

"This is your love for your wife and her daughter." Ethan scooted his hands apart a few more inches. "Our hearts have an amazing ability to expand for love. Think about it. I assume you love your parents, right?"

Roman nodded.

"Then you met Lizzy and Abigail, and your heart expanded to include them."

Roman's gaze was laser-like on Ethan.

"You'll be amazed at how much your heart will expand when this new baby makes an appearance."

Roman's posture relaxed. He loosened his grip on the coffee mug and began to twirl it in lazy circles. "I hope you're right."

Ethan smiled. "I'm right. You wait. The minute that baby comes into the world, it will be love at first sight."

Roman's face split into a grin. "Until I met Lizzy, I didn't believe in love at first sight. It's not logical to love someone you don't know."

"The heart is rarely logical, my friend." Ethan's thoughts turned to Mariah and his growing fondness for her. His mind said she was all wrong, but his heart insisted on its own way. What held him back was the concern she'd be like Angie – coming into a relationship with her own agenda. Tonight at dinner would be a good time to talk.

The server arrived and plopped their plates down without speaking.

"Can I get some more coffee?" Roman asked.

The server nodded and returned a moment later with a coffee pot.

"Thanks," Ethan said as his cup was refilled too.

Jayden set the phone down. "Can you cut my pancakes, Dad?"

Ethan set to work, buttering the huge cakes and pouring a small amount of syrup on top. When he'd cut enough to get Jayden started, he dug into his own breakfast.

"Are you going to order something?" Ethan asked, pointing his fork at Roman.

"I ate at home." Roman looked like he wanted to ask something. Ethan gave him time to formulate his words.

"I liked your sermon Sunday," Roman said.

Ethan spoke over a mouthful of food. "Thanks." Good thing the guy didn't know it was a rerun from a sermon he preached at his old church. Except when the Holy Spirit took over. That was amazing.

"I don't always get to be in the service," Roman continued. "I work with kindergartners."

Ethan almost choked on his scramble. This geeky guy taught five-and-six-year-olds? The hidden depths of some people never ceased to amaze him.

Ethan eyed Roman and cut his eyes to Jayden. "You didn't tell me Mr. Roman was your Children's Church teacher," Ethan said.

Jayden shrugged. "You didn't ask."

Ethan and Roman exchanged a look.

Roman reached into his pocket at pulled out two twenties, laying them on the table. "I better get home." He slid from the booth.

Ethan eyed the money. "I don't think they charge that much for coffee here."

"My treat." Roman leaned over to retrieve his jacket and slipped it on. "Thanks for listening to my drama."

Ethan stuck out a hand to stop Roman's departure. "Hold up a minute. Can I ask you a question?"

Roman sank onto the bench. "Sure."

"How well do you know Mariah?"

A red flush rose from Roman's neck to his hairline. "About as well as anyone, I guess."

Ethan drew in a breath and dove into the question that had been niggling at the edge of his brain. "What about this bad reputation?"

Roman's gaze dropped to the table before returning to focus on Ethan. "I didn't know her back in the day like Lizzy did. She used to be mean. This is all I know, that she started meeting with Pastor Roy and Susan and accepted the Lord. Total personality change, if that's even possible. I'll admit I had my doubts. But she and Lizzy used to be sworn enemies and now they're best friends." Roman raised his hands in an 'I don't know' gesture.

Ethan nodded. "Thanks, man. That helps."

Roman stood and grinned down at him. "Enjoy your date with her."

He was out the door before Ethan could respond. *It isn't a date.*

~

Mariah turned down the television news. She didn't want any details about the fierce storm that was predicted to hit their area later that week. Mariah had her own storm to contend with. Simone and Lizzy had burst through her door a few minutes earlier.

"We're here to help you decide what to wear on your date with Pastor Ethan," Lizzy declared.

Simone had rolled her eyes, but quickly changed her attitude when she eyed the open door to Mariah's walk-in closet.

Simone's mouth dropped open. "How many pairs of shoes do you have?"

Lizzy ran her hands along the lines of slacks neatly hanging on a low rod. "And pants."

Mariah felt herself grow hot. It didn't used to bother her that she'd grown up with money. Her small circle of friends were also from wealthy families. Her new friends Lizzy and Simone grew up in homes where money was tight. Mariah shoved down the shame that filled her when she remembered how she'd bullied Lizzy over her Goodwill used clothes.

"Stop drooling in my closet," Mariah snapped.

"Right," Lizzy said. "We're here on a mission. What would look best for a first date?" She pulled a sweater dress out and held it up with raised eyebrows.

"It isn't a date," Mariah said.

Lizzy burst out a laugh. "Yeah, that's what Roman and I said when we went out to dinner." She waved her wedding ring in Mariah's face. "Look what happened."

Mariah's jaw tightened. "Number one, I am not—I repeat, not—looking for a relationship. Number two, Ethan doesn't like me that way. This is a simple thank you for helping him with his son. Number three, and you two should know this better than anyone, I am not pastor wife material." She snatched the dress from Lizzy's hand and shoved the hanger back on the rod.

Lizzy and Simone exchanged a glance. Then they both laughed.

Lizzy patted Mariah on the shoulder. "You keep telling yourself that, girlfriend."

Mariah made a disgusted sound. "You're both crazy."

Thirty minutes later, they'd settled on a pair of black slacks with a patterned sweater and a pair of red Prada ankle boots. The clothes lay spread out on the bed.

Lizzy sank onto the end of the bed. "Now, what about her hair?" she asked to no one in particular. "Up or down?"

Mariah crossed her arms over her stomach, uncomfortable with the two women's perusal.

Simone walked a circle around Mariah. "You usually wear it down. Why not change it up a little? Pull it back into a low pony. Wear some sparkly earrings to catch his attention."

Mariah huffed. "I'm not interested in 'catching his attention.'" Her air quotes brought another round of laughter from her friends.

Mariah made a 'go away' motion with her hands. "You two find someone else to bother while I get dressed."

Lizzy pulled herself to her feet and grabbed Simone's arm. "Come on, let's go snoop in her kitchen while she's getting dressed."

Mariah sent them a glare that she hoped would melt their bones as she hustled them out of her bedroom.

When she finished getting changed into the outfit her friends had chosen, Mariah left her bedroom and strolled the few steps into the living room for her friends' perusal.

Lizzy struck a model pose. "You look mahvelous, dahling."

Simone giggled. "I agree. Now go fix your hair."

Lizzy grabbed Mariah in a quick hug. "I gotta run home. Your man will be dropping his son off at my house any minute."

Mariah's protest that Ethan was not 'her man' fell on deaf ears as the two women pulled open the front door. A blast of frigid air hit them.

"Yikes! What happened to our sun?" Lizzy clutched her sweater around her neck. "Simone, will you give me a ride home?"

Mariah shut the door behind them and headed into the bathroom to pull her hair back with an oversized clip. Deciding against dangly earrings, she opted for a pair of ruby studs.

A quick check of her smart watch showed ten minutes to the hour. Ten long minutes to rethink her decision to have dinner with Ethan. Ten minutes to send a text telling him she was deathly ill. Or someone in her family died. Or any excuse to avoid going out with him.

Never had she experienced this many nervous tingles while waiting on a date.

Not a date, she reminded herself. A thank you dinner. Whatever.

On one hand, Ethan was an attractive man. He seemed kind and thoughtful. He loved his son. On the other hand, he was a pastor. He preached wholesome living, something Mariah had only recently practiced. If her growing attraction for Ethan went any further, it would come to a screeching halt once he knew her back story.

With a sigh, Mariah walked to the window to gaze out at the gusts of wind whipping the branches back and forth like a madman. She'd go and enjoy a nice dinner she didn't have to cook and call it good.

Chapter 14

Jayden barely spared Ethan a backward glance as he burst through Lizzy and Roman's front door. Ethan followed, carrying Jayden's backpack.

"Here's a change of clothes, you know, in case he needs them," Ethan said to Lizzy. "And his blankie, although he will not admit to still sleeping with it." Ethan shrugged. "He still takes it everywhere."

Lizzy chuckled. "I hear ya. Abby insisted on taking her blankie everywhere until she was seven."

"Did not!" came a small voice from down the hall.

Lizzy rolled her eyes. "Whatever."

"Thanks again for watching him. I feel guilty I've left him a lot lately."

Lizzy took the backpack from Ethan. "It's tough being a single parent. I dealt with a lot of guilt and I'm sure you do too."

Ethan nodded. "It's much easier with two parents, that's for sure."

"Amen to that," Lizzy agreed. "Go, have a good time tonight. Stay as long as you want."

"Thanks."

Ethan yelled a quick goodbye to Jayden, who had disappeared down the hall. No response.

Ethan returned to his pickup, backed out of the driveway, and made the short trip around the block to Mariah's little house. He sat with the vehicle running, hands on the steering wheel.

What was he doing? Whatever he'd chosen to call it – a way to say thank you for babysitting – taking a woman out was a date. He, Ethan Walsh, was taking Mariah out on a date. The first date since Angie's death. He had to ask himself why. The answer came swiftly. Because he was attracted to her. She was one hundred percent different from Angie. His wife had a hidden agenda, while Mariah was as blunt as a ball pein hammer.

Ethan left the truck running and pushed open the car door, battling the wind buffeting him. Mariah's walkway was strewn with bits of twigs, broken off the mature trees in her yard and the adjoining ones.

Before he could raise his hand to knock, the door swung open, and Mariah stood framed in the doorway. Ethan's breath caught. Mariah had pulled her hair back, revealing high cheekbones and black eyebrows that formed slashes above her blue eyes.

"Here, take my arm," Ethan said.

Mariah pulled the door closed behind her and linked her arm in his. "Chivalrous," she commented with a small smile.

The low-heeled boots she wore brought her up to his same height. Ethan's shoulder brushed hers as he navigated the path to his vehicle. Once they were both seated with belts fastened, Mariah sent him a challenging look.

"Having second thoughts?" she asked.

"Why would you say that?"

"I saw you pull up to the house and sit in your truck for over three minutes. I don't think you were talking on the phone. My guess is you're wondering what you're doing. Am I right?"

Ethan pursed his lips. Answering her question was like walking through a minefield.

Honesty would be the best response. Mariah would expect no less. "Truthfully, this is the first time I've been out with a woman since my wife passed. I'm terrified." He sent her a rueful grin.

Mariah's laugh both soothed him and irritated him.

"This is the first time I've been out with a man since my ex dumped me," Mariah admitted. "I'm nervous, too. This whole Christian dating thing is new to me."

Ethan navigated the streets of Main like a native before turning on to the highway leading away from the coast.

"Let's clarify something," Ethan said. "This isn't a date."

"So you said."

"This is me, saying thank you."

"Sure."

"I'm serious."

"I'm sure you are."

Ethan glanced over to see Mariah's grin. It nearly did him in. He was falling, and it left him breathless.

"Where are we going, anyway?" she asked.

"I looked on Yelp for some restaurant suggestions and found one on the way to Salem. Hope you don't mind driving that far."

Mariah settled into her seat. "Not at all."

While he drove, Ethan asked about the Safe Families program.

"I'm super frustrated," Mariah said. "I sent them all the paperwork they asked for, and I've heard nothing. I sent an email earlier today but haven't gotten a response yet."

Ethan considered her words. "Remind me why you want to do that?"

Mariah turned her head to stare out the passenger window. "All I've ever wanted was to get married and have kids. Saying it out loud sounds old school, you know?" She turned to stare at his profile.

Ethan nodded. "Same here."

"When my ex and I had a difference of opinion about our future, I did some soul-searching, which brought me to Pastor Roy and Susan. After I committed my life to Christ, Pastor Roy encouraged me to find someplace to volunteer that involved kids. He suggested foster care, but it's extremely difficult for a single woman to get a foster license. I remember hearing about this program where you can help single moms, and even couples, with respite care when they need it. Safe Families lets them get back on their feet without having to put their kids into the foster system."

"Sounds very altruistic." Ethan's respect for Mariah increased several notches.

Mariah shook her head. "Not at all. Think about it," Mariah's voice increased in passion. "You're a single dad, and you lose your job, and you can't pay your rent. You suddenly find yourself on the street, living in your car. Now you don't have childcare, and you can't look for another job. What are your choices?"

"Pretty limited," Ethan agreed.

"Safe Families will take your child and place him with a loving family until you can find a job, get established, and get your son back. No government involvement. No visitation requirements, no money involved."

"Sounds like an amazing program," Ethan admitted. "How do you support yourself?"

Mariah's gaze dropped to her hands clutched on her lap. "It's embarrassing."

The woman who was outspoken now was hesitant to explain her financial situation?

"I promise not to judge."

"My parents set up a monthly allowance for my brother and me."

Ethan bit his lip to keep from laughing. That explained the designer running shoes and what he was sure was an expensive purse she'd grabbed before heading out the door.

"Ah."

"See? I knew you'd judge me."

"Not judging." Ethan smiled in her direction before turning his attention back to the road. He signaled to turn right into the parking lot of Café 22. "This place is known for its pies. Although you probably wouldn't know about that."

"Why wouldn't I?" Mariah unlatched her seatbelt.

"You look like you don't eat a lot of sweets, pies or otherwise."

Mariah swung her door open. With a backward glance, she said, "I run so I *can* eat sweets."

They were seated in a booth and handed menus by a harried waitress. "We're short-staffed tonight. I apologize in advance for slow service."

Ethan nodded. "Not a problem. Thanks."

He perused the menu and settled on the grilled Reuben. The server returned with water and took their drink orders.

Mariah pulled off her jacket and laid it on the bench beside her. Ethan drew in a breath. She was stunning.

"Tell me about your wife," Mariah said, reaching for the water glass.

"She was ..." How would he describe Angela? He'd been attracted by her boundless energy. She embraced life in a way Ethan couldn't. Angie was always ready to take on a new challenge, whether it was a deep dive into Scripture or climbing Mount Rainier.

"She was driven. Focused." It felt like betrayal to talk about Angie's flaws. Yes, she was driven, even to the point of wanting to abandon him and Jayden to conquer the mission fields of Africa. Her need to continually challenge herself became a point of contention in their 'perfect' marriage.

Mariah's next question pushed Ethan back against the booth. "Were you happy?"

Ethan rubbed his jaw with one hand. Was he happy? The first few years of their marriage, he'd been delirious with gratefulness to God for bringing Angie into his life. Looking back, he saw when things began to splinter. After Jayden's birth, Angie suffered from postpartum depression which lasted months. She seemed to come out of it when a missionary couple spoke at their church about the joys of serving the Lord on the mission field. That's when things changed.

Mariah tapped a red fingernail on the Formica table. "Earth to Ethan."

He shook his head. "Uh, sorry. Yeah, I guess I was happy."

"That wasn't very convincing."

"Let's change the subject." Ethan took a long drink from his water and wiped the condensation on his slacks.

"Do you have siblings?" Mariah asked.

Finally, a question Ethan could answer without cringing. "I have an older brother. We're sixteen months apart."

"Are you close?"

"Very. Our parents got divorced when we were ten and eleven."

"Where does he live?"

"He lives in Seattle. He's coming to visit this weekend. He wants to check out my new town." Ethan paused. "You'll like him. He's an attorney with a sense of humor."

Mariah smiled. "Sounds like an oxymoron."

"Yup," Ethan agreed.

Ethan made small talk while they waited for their food. He learned the name and age of Mariah's brother – Daniel, age thirty-two – and her parent's names and ages.

Mariah dug into her sandwich with a gusto Ethan wasn't used to. Angie had always fought gaining weight and was obsessive about counting calories. She always ordered a salad, dressing on the side, the few times they went out to eat.

"My dad does a little bit of everything," Mariah explained. "When he bought the vineyard, he was able to turn a profit in the second year. Then he went to viniculture school to learn winemaking." She inspected her sandwich before continuing. "My dad has a super high IQ. Like between 160 and 180. He's one of those people who can make money with the snap of his fingers."

"I envy him. I'm doomed to earning a small paycheck as a minister of the gospel."

"There's a lot to be said about job satisfaction," Mariah commented before taking another huge bite of her Reuben.

Ethan had to ask. "Have you ever held a job?"

Mariah set her sandwich down and wiped her hands on her napkin. Her voice carried a tone of terseness. "I have worked for my parents picking grapes and dressing the vines. I've organized many events at the vineyard and prepared food for special events. I've served the food. I've done my family's bookkeeping. I've babysat guests' kids during special events like weddings, funerals, and fund-raisers. To answer your question, yes, I've held many jobs."

Ethan felt himself flush. "Sorry. I was out of line."

Mariah sniffed, took a drink of her Diet Coke, and picked up her sandwich. "Apology accepted."

On the ride home, Ethan wanted to ask Mariah about the rumors he'd heard regarding her reputation, but after his misstep with the job question, he kept his silence. Better to not poke the bear again.

When he pulled up to Mariah's house, he put the truck in Park and turned in his seat to face her. "Thanks again for watching Jayden for me. I talked to Miss

Sarah earlier today. She's feeling much better and said she could watch him again starting Thursday. Noah asked if I'd take the youth group again tomorrow night. He still has that lung-wracking cough. Can you take care of Jayden tomorrow night?"

"Sure. I look forward to hanging out with him." Mariah laid a hand on his arm. "You've done a good job with him."

Ethan basked in her praise. "Thanks. Now stay there so I can open your door for you."

Mariah's eyebrows rose to her hairline. "Still the gentleman."

The wind had picked up while they were at dinner. It buffeted them as Ethan escorted Mariah to her door. Mariah fumbled in her purse for the keys as the wind whipped loose strands of hair around her face. Ethan resisted the urge to smooth them back. His arm still felt warm from where her hand had been. Or was it his imagination?

After she unlocked the door, Mariah grabbed him in a quick hug. "Thanks for dinner."

Before Ethan could react, she closed the door. She heard the decisive click of the lock. He stood for a moment on her porch before dodging small branches on the walkway to his car.

Once he was back home with Jayden tucked into bed, Ethan made himself a cup of decaf from Pastor Roy's Keurig and settled onto the sofa. He used the remote to turn on the gas fireplace. Staring into the flickering flames, Ethan pulled his iPad to him and opened the Bible app.

He did a word search for 'wisdom.' Ethan had a good idea of the verses that pertained to wisdom, but it helped to refresh his memory.

James 1:5 from the Message version suited his situation to a tee. "If you don't know what you're doing, pray to the Father. He loves to help."

Yup, God, that sums it up. I don't know what I'm doing.

Mariah attracted him like no woman had since Angie. To be honest, maybe even before Angie. They'd met in Bible College where a lot of the people their age were 'courting' and getting engaged. They'd seemed like the perfect couple because he and Angie were both ministry-minded. Both came from broken homes, determined to do things differently from their parents. All that had worked in their favor.

Until it didn't. A disturbing thought entered Ethan's mind. If he could do it over again, would he have made a different choice for a spouse? He shoved that thought into the dark recesses of his brain. He had Jayden. Without Angie, Jayden wouldn't be here.

But now, here in tiny Main, Oregon, Ethan was falling for a woman who was different from his wife in practically every way. He was terrified of making a mistake – one that would lead him to disappointment when she turned out to have very different ideas about the future.

Chapter 15

Mariah tossed her bag on the sofa and slipped off her jacket with a smile. She dropped onto the sofa, hugging her arms across her chest. She'd had a great time with Ethan. What a relief to go out with someone who didn't expect to be invited in for a 'nightcap.' Or expect sex as a payment for dinner. Ethan was respectful and genuine and seemed truly interested in her as a person.

Such a difference from the men she'd dated BC, before Christ. The only danger was that she was falling for him. Mariah pulled the clip from her hair and shook her head, loosening her black mane. Too bad Ethan was a pastor. He'd want a woman who was pure, not someone with a tainted past like she had.

At least she could be a blessing by watching Jayden for him. One more time, that is. Then she'd fade into the background, and Ethan could concentrate on what he did best – preaching the Word of God.

Maybe she should find a different church until Pastor Roy returned.

Mariah picked up the heavy Bible Susan had given her. She thumbed through the unfamiliar pages, not sure where to read. The Bible app on her iPad suggested a number of reading and studying plans, but there was something tactile about holding the actual book.

She laid her hand on the cover and said a quick prayer before letting the Bible fall open to the book of James chapter four. When she got to verse seventeen, Mariah gasped.

"Therefore, to him who knows to do good and does not do it. To him it is sin."

What could that mean? Was God speaking to her about a relationship with Ethan? Or was He warning her off?

Arrgghh. This Christian life was uber confusing. Mariah closed the Bible with a thump and set it on the end table. She'd ask Lizzy about it tomorrow. Maybe. Since Lizzy had met Roman, she wanted everyone to live happily ever after. But Mariah knew all too well, life wasn't a Hallmark movie and not everyone in a small town finds true love.

The next morning, Mariah received a text from Ethan. Her stomach fluttered with nerves when she opened up the text.

I'll drop Jayden off around six thirty, if that's okay with you

Disappointed that he hadn't referenced the prior evening, Mariah sent a thumbs up emoji. What did she expect? A gushy 'I adore you and can't live without you' text?

Disgusted with herself, Mariah focused on making a list of things to accomplish.

Clean house

Check in with Mom re: fundraiser

Email or call Safe Families for an update

Get snacks for Jayden's visit

But first, a nice long run. Mariah pulled up the blinds in the living room to see the mess the wind had made of the branches. Although the wind had died down, the sky was dark with ominous-looking clouds. Plan change - go to the gym and use the treadmill. Then stop at the store on the way home for the snacks Jayden liked.

The news on the car radio blasted dire predictions about the coming storm. *Stockpile water! Buy a generator! Prepare for a deep freeze!*

Mariah took the reports with a grain of salt. Main had seen its share of coastal storms blow through the area. She felt confident she could ride out whatever Mother Nature threw at them.

By the time she returned from the gym and the grocery store, the temperature dropped several degrees. Rain spattered the roof, a sound Mariah found comforting as she was tucked cozily into her little house.

Her iPad dinged with an incoming email. Hoping it was a response from Safe Families, she set her grocery bags on the counter and retrieved the device to check.

Yes! She gave a fist pump and opened the email.

"Dear Ms. Martin, Thank you for your interest in serving as a host home for Safe Families. At this time, there are no needs in your area. We will inform you when a need arises. Again. Thank you for your willingness to be a part of our organization to serve families in Oregon."

Mariah felt a shaft of disappointment. Oh well, at least she'd been approved. Perhaps it wasn't in God's timing right now. But when?

She had a sudden urge to express her disappointment with someone. The first person who came to mind was Ethan. No, not him. He was not in her league.

The verse in James that she'd read the night before popped into her mind. Could it be wrong if she gave into her desire to share the email with him?

Gritting her teeth, Mariah tapped out a text.

Heard from Safe Families. Nothing available right now.

She held her breath, waiting for the little dots to appear showing he was responding. Nothing.

"Get over yourself," Mariah said aloud. She busied herself putting away groceries and starting a load of laundry, willing herself not to obsess over checking her phone for a text.

But by the time Ethan showed up at her door with Jayden, Mariah was ready to snap.

"Didn't you get my text?" she demanded.

Ethan grimaced. "Uh, yes. Sorry. Busy day."

Mariah huffed out a breath. "Fine."

Ethan seemed in a rush to drop Jayden off and get to the church. Mariah swallowed her anger and gathered the boy into the house, closing the door against the onslaught of freezing rain.

The power flickered on and off a few times throughout the evening. Mariah's mother called while she and Jayden shared a snack.

"We lost power a few minutes ago," Mom said without preamble. "I'm calling to be sure you're okay."

Mariah glanced up at the overhead light. "I'm okay so far. What are they saying?" She put the phone on speaker to touch the weather app on her phone. "Wow, they're predicting a hard freeze tonight."

"You'll be okay, won't you?"

"Mom, I'm fine. Don't worry."

"But your power—"

"I'm on City power, not like you up there in the boonies. I'll be fine."

"Keep your phone charged, in case there's an emergency."

"I will, Mom. Stay safe." Mariah disconnected, promising to call her mom if anything changed.

Soon after, Mariah's phone rang again. Grady's name popped up on the screen. Why was her contractor calling? Mariah's hand flew to her chest.

"Grady, is everything okay?"

"Yup. I'm calling to see if you're okay. You got power?"

She let her hand fall. "I'm fine. Thank you for checking on me."

"The missus and I were worried, you being a single gal and all. The storm is gonna be a doozy."

"How sweet. Thank you. So far so good." Mariah couldn't remember the last time someone in the community had shown that much concern over her well-being.

"You call if you need anything, okay young lady?"

Mariah assured Grady she would let him know. Tears gathered in the corners of her eyes at his call.

When Ethan arrived to pick Jayden up, the temperature had dropped another few degrees and Mariah's front walk turned into a sheet of pebbled ice.

She and Jayden crouched on the sofa, watching out the front window for Ethan's headlights to appear. Ethan slid a couple of times on the ice before reaching her door.

"Brr," Ethan said, his breath forming puffs of white as he breathed.

"Want something hot to drink?" Mariah offered.

"That'd be great. Coffee if you have it." Ethan gathered Jayden into a hug.

"Let me go! Your jacket's cold, Dad," Jayden protested. Ethan shrugged out of his coat and hung it over a chair. He followed Mariah into the kitchen.

"That's some fancy coffee maker you have," Ethan commented as Mariah set the machine to warm the water.

"Thanks. It does the trick."

Ethan rubbed his hands together to warm them up. "Tonight was really good. The teens really seemed interested in hearing truth."

"You're kinda late," Jayden said, dragging his blanket into the kitchen.

"I'm sorry, buddy. Some of the girls wanted to ask questions afterward." Ethan ruffled his son's hair.

Mariah felt Ethan's excitement vibrating from him. "I'm glad. I hope some of the kids in the youth group will take to heart what you've been teaching." She thought back to the incident that changed the course of her life. If only she'd said something to someone. But shame had kept her silent, believing it had been her fault for flirting with the older guy.

She set a mug under the spout. When Ethan's cup was full, Mariah handed the cup to him. He wrapped his hands around it.

"Want to sit?" she offered.

"Sure."

They sat across from each other at the table. "I'm glad it went well. Are you disappointed that Noah is feeling better and will teach next week?"

Ethan took a sip of the steaming brew. "Umhm. Sometimes I wish I'd never left youth work. But Angie . . ." his voice trailed off.

"Your wife didn't want to work with youth?" Mariah prodded.

Ethan shook his head. "Her heart was for foreign missions." He stopped, looking like he wanted to say more.

"Yet here you are. Stateside, serving in a local church."

Ethan frowned and shrugged. "Sometimes things don't work out the way we want."

Was he talking about his ministry or his marriage?

Mariah carried her mug to the table and took a seat. "Tell me about youth group."

Ethan warmed to the topic again. "As the kids say, it was epic. Lots of good questions and discussions. A couple of the girls stayed after to ask more questions. One in particular seemed especially interested in learning more."

Alarm bells sounded in Mariah's head. "Were you alone with her?"

"Only for a bit."

Mariah shook her head. "Not good, Ethan." Mariah hesitated. She wanted to tell him about her experience but was wary of his judgement.

"It was totally innocent," Ethan protested. "We sat on the front pew, and I showed her some Bible verses to check out."

Mariah bit her lip. "Did you touch her?"

Ethan's hand shook as he slammed his mug onto the table. "Of course not!"

"Did she touch you?"

"Why are you asking me all these questions? You think I'm some kind of sicko?"

Mariah's heart raced as she fidgeted with her hands, feeling the familiar shame and fear bubble up inside her. She couldn't believe she was about to tell her secret to a man she barely knew.

She took a deep breath and blurted it out, unable to hold back any longer. "I was molested by a youth leader when I was only twelve years old." The words left a bitter taste in her mouth.

Ethan's expression turned from curiosity to shock and horror. "Oh my gosh, Mariah! Did you report it? Is that creep in jail now?"

Her grip on the table tightened as she shook her head, fighting back tears. "No, I didn't report it. I was too ashamed. I thought it was my fault because I flirted with him. I thought I deserved what he did."

Ethan's hand reached across the table and grasped hers tightly. "No, no, no," he said firmly. "It was not your fault, Mariah. You were a kid." His thumb stroked the top of her hand soothingly, sending shivers up her spine.

Tears fell freely down Mariah's cheeks as she looked into Ethan's unwavering gaze. "I know that now," she whispered hoarsely. "But that experience changed everything for me. It made me someone I never wanted to be." She dropped her eyes to the table, unable to meet Ethan's sympathetic gaze any longer. "You've probably heard the rumors," she added bitterly.

She heard Ethan grunt in response, his hand squeezing hers in understanding. Mariah couldn't help but wonder if he truly understood how much that one traumatic event had impacted her life. "You can see how I'm concerned about young women being alone with a church leader."

Ethan's grip tightened on hers. "I get it. But I can assure you she wanted some clarification on some Scripture verses."

"Was it the same one who sent you those texts?"

Ethan huffed out a laugh. "I don't know. I didn't want you to tell me, remember?"

"Oh, right."

Ethan sprang to his feet. "I better check on Jayden. He's been suspiciously quiet since we've been talking."

Mariah followed Ethan into the living room. They found Jayden fast asleep on the sofa.

"I better get the little man home. This weather is gonna get worse, according to the 'experts.'"

Mariah helped Ethan bundle a sleeping Jayden into his jacket. She wrapped him in his blanket and opened the door.

"Thanks again," Ethan said. "See you soon?"

Mariah braced herself on the doorframe. "Sure."

What that would look like was as turbulent as the sky overhead.

Chapter 16

Mariah spent the morning baking, praying all the while the power wouldn't go out in the middle of making chocolate muffins. While they cooled, she headed upstairs to straighten up. She found Jayden's backpack partially tucked under one of the beanbag chairs.

She strode to the window with the backpack dangling from one hand. The wind seemed to have died down, but the dark sky held ominous-looking clouds. Mariah debated for a few minutes about going out and decided it would be worth it to see Ethan, even if only for a brief moment while she handed off Jayden's pack.

What would be his reaction to her now, after she had revealed the truth last night. Would he refuse to meet her gaze, ashamed of what she had confessed? Or would he give her pitying glances, looking down on her with superiority. Or worst of all, would he condemn her for not fighting back against the older boy, casting her out as weak and unworthy.

When she arrived at the church, she found Ethan on his hands and knees hammering away on the baseboard in the foyer.

"What are you doing?" Mariah set Jayden's backpack on the reception counter and put her hands on her hips.

Ethan glanced up. "Pastor Roy left me a list of projects he wanted done while he was gone." He sent her a rueful grin. "Maybe I shouldn't have told him I had carpentry experience."

His smile sent quivers through her belly. No minister should be that good-looking. His wavy brown hair fell over one eyebrow. Mariah's fingers itched to brush it out of his face.

She cleared her throat. "Probably not."

Ethan set the hammer on the floor and got to his feet in one fluid move. "What brings you out on such a nasty day?" He moved to within a foot of her.

Mariah's mouth went dry. She swallowed twice. "Uh, Jayden's backpack." She made a vague motion toward the item on the counter. "He left it at my house."

Ethan chuckled. "I swear that boy would forget his feet if they weren't attached."

Mariah's lips quirked up into a smile. "You sound exactly like my dear old grandmother."

Ethan placed a warm, open palm over his heart. "What can I say? I've always been an old soul."

Mariah leaned closer to him, her breath coming in short bursts, almost as if she were running a race. The electricity between them was palpable and unfamiliar to her. She couldn't quite put her finger on it, but something special was happening.

They stared at each other for several beats. Before either of them spoke, the front door of the church burst open and two uniformed police officers strode into the foyer.

Mariah had only a moment to register their appearance. Both wore heavy jackets, making them seem huge. The men's hands rested on their weapons as if expecting to use them in the next few minutes.

The larger of the two barked, "Ethan Walsh?"

Ethan's face drained of color. "Yes?"

The second officer approached. They stood within a foot of Ethan and Mariah.

"Mr. Walsh, we'd like to take you to the station and ask you a few questions."

Ethan visibly shook. "What's this about?"

Mariah placed her hand on her chest, hoping to slow down her racing heart.

The taller of the two officers spoke. "If you'd come down to the station with us, we'll explain there."

Ethan stepped back. "I don't understand."

"We have some questions," said the older officer, glancing at his partner.

"About what?"

Mariah was frozen to the spot, mouth open. What was happening?

"Mr. Walsh, if you'd come down to the station with us, we can ask some questions and explain. Please."

The 'please' at the end seemed tacked on. Pretend politeness.

Ethan glared at the two officers. "Do I have a choice?"

Neither answered.

"Maybe you should go," Mariah said. "I can pick you up when you're done."

The older officer sent her a humorless smile. "Listen to your girlfriend, Padre."

The younger officer took Ethan's arm and pressed him toward the door.

Ethan called out over his shoulder, his voice tinged with fear, "Go to Sarah's and get Jayden. And call my brother. Unlock my cell. Six-two-five-four-nine-nine."

Mariah stood frozen in shock, her mind struggling to process what was happening. Her body moved on autopilot as she stumbled to the door, her heart racing with panic and dread.

~

Ethan sat at a metal table, facing a two-way window in a soulless room. White walls, white floor, white ceiling. The room reeked of ammonia cleaner and stale sweat. While he waited, Ethan tried and discarded a dozen reasons why he was sitting in an interrogation room at Main Police Department.

Dread lay heavy on his shoulders. His leg bounced up and down as the minutes crawled by. Without his phone or a watch, he could have been waiting an hour or ten minutes. Impossible to tell.

When the door opened, Ethan breathed a sigh of relief. Then his breath caught at the severity of the suited guy entering the room.

"Mr. Walsh, or should I say Pastor Walsh, I'm Detective McDonald." He sat in the chair across from Ethan and dropped a manila file on the table. "I suppose you're wondering why you're here."

Ethan spoke around the desert that was suddenly his tongue. "May I have some water?"

Some unspoken message must have been transmitted to the person behind the two-way window.

A few moments later, a uniformed officer brought a bottle of water into the room and set it on the table.

Ethan cracked it open and took a sip of the tepid liquid. His mind went back to Mariah, pulling a dripping water bottle from her ice chest and wiping it with a towel. He forced his concentration back to the detective.

McDonald flipped open the file and pulled a pen from the inner pocket of his dark suit jacket. "Let me get some background information from you, okay?"

Ethan nodded.

"You're the pastor of Main Community Church, right?"

"Interim pastor," Ethan said.

"How long have you been there?"

"About three weeks." Ethan remembered his brother, Robert, instructing his clients never to talk too much with the police. *Not that they're bad people, bro, but the less said the better.*

"What is your role there?"

Ethan frowned. What did this guy think a pastor did? "Well, I preach on Sunday."

The detective asked a few more questions that were ridiculous in Ethan's mind. Then he got to his main agenda. Ethan felt a shift in the air when Detective McDonald asked, "Does your role as Interim Pastor involve working with high schoolers?"

Ah, this was about those texts. The ones Ethan didn't want Mariah to talk to him about. But why would the police be involved?

Ethan opened his mouth, then closed it. How much information should he share? Did McDonald need to know that Noah, the youth leader, had been sick? Did

Ethan need to explain how he filled in for the past two weeks?

He settled for one word. "Yes."

Detective McDonald peered at him under bristling eyebrows. "Do you like working with teenage boys and girls?"

Did Ethan detect a slight emphasis on the word 'girls'?

"Yes. I enjoy teaching high schoolers how to live out Biblical principles." Take that, Detective.

Detective McDonald scratched a few notes on a paper before leaning back in his chair. "Let's talk about where you were two Wednesdays ago. March 13."

Ethan stared at McDonald as his brain clicked back to the date. "I believe I was leading the youth group that night. During the day, I was probably in Pastor Roy's office preparing a lesson."

"Pastor Roy is the real pastor of Main Community?"

Ethan felt his blood pressure rise. "Pastor Roy is the senior pastor of the church. I am the 'real' pastor in his absence." He forced his hands to stay in his lap so not to use air quotes.

"You taught the youth group. Then what?"

"I believe I went home."

"No stops? No staying after to clean up?"

Ethan squinted his eyes, trying to remember. Was that the night he picked Jayden up from Mariah's? "I might have picked my son up from the babysitter." He shrugged. "Why? What's this about?"

Detective McDonald's eyes were like twin lasers. "Pastor Walsh, did any of the girls in the church youth group stay after? Maybe to get some additional teaching or clarification? Maybe ask for counseling?"

Ethan's stomach churned. This conversation had turned a corner into a dark and dangerous place.

God, I need wisdom.

"No. Everyone left at around the same time. I closed up the church and went to pick up my son."

McDonald closed the folder and placed his hands palms-down on the table. "Pastor Walsh, one of the girls in the church youth group said you touched her inappropriately."

"What? No!"

McDonald's words continued to hammer Ethan's already aching head. "She said that after everyone left, you asked her to stay. She said at that time, you pushed her down on one of the pews and sexually assaulted her."

Ethan felt bile rise up his throat. He was going to retch. He reached for the water bottle and took a sip, hoping to settle the whirlpool that was his gut.

"That never happened," he managed to choke out.

McDonald sent him a grim smile. "And yet, here we are." He raised his hands in surrender. "I'm merely trying to get some facts before we proceed."

Proceed to what? Arrest, then being charged as a sexual predator? Going to prison for something he hadn't done? Losing his son?

Ethan choked back a sob. "The fact is, I never touched any of the girls. Except for a chaste hug."

Ethan's mind was a jumbled mess as he tried to piece together the events of the Wednesday two weeks ago. He had been excited about Tamara's possible decision to follow Christ, and now he couldn't believe that he was being accused of something terrible. He remembered hugging her goodbye, but nothing else. Had he done something wrong? This was a mistake. Ethan couldn't shake off the feeling of guilt and confusion as he struggled to make sense of the accusations against him.

Chapter 17

Mariah leaned against the church door, listening to the wind sneaking around the edges. The storm brewing outside had nothing on the tempest inside her. Why would the police want to question Ethan? They'd given no indication of what the interview was about.

Several ideas formed in her mind, but she rejected each one. Except … No, that wasn't possible. It couldn't be a rerun of what she'd endured at the hands of the youth leader years ago. Ethan wouldn't.

Tears filled Mariah's eyes and trickled down her flushed cheeks as she stumbled towards the reception counter. Her vision blurred and her steps were unsteady, but she managed to reach Ethan's phone which lay next to Jayden's backpack. These ordinary objects now seemed out of place in the aftermath of the chaotic events that had unfolded moments ago.

Jayden's smiling face stared up at her from Ethan's screensaver. Mariah punched in the code Ethan had called out to unlock his phone. What was his brother's name? Mariah searched her memory and came up blank. She typed 'brother' in the search bar and the words 'Annoying Big Brother' came up. She smiled despite the seriousness of the situation and tapped the number.

"What's up little bro?"

"Uh, this is Mariah. Ethan asked me to call you."

"Ah, the famous Mariah. Ethan has mentioned you a couple times. Wait, where's my brother? Is he okay?"

Mariah sucked in a breath. "He was taken to the police station. Just now."

"I'll be there in about an hour. I'm outside of Salem right now. What's this about?"

Mariah put a hand on her forehead. "I-I'm not sure. They said they wanted to question him."

"What about Jayden? Did he see this go down?"

"No. I'm going to pick him up now from the sitter's."

Ethan's brother's voice was all business. "Get Jayden and take him to your house. I'll make some calls. Then I'll go to the police department and find out what's happening."

"Okay." Mariah sagged with relief against the counter. Someone else would take over. "I can't remember your name."

"It's Robert. Text me your number so I can let you know what I find out."

"Okay." Mariah nodded, even though she knew Robert couldn't see her. They disconnected, and Mariah sent Robert a text with her contact information.

She scrubbed her cheeks with a tissue and squared her shoulders. Robert would take care of this.

Doubts filled her mind as Mariah returned to her car and headed toward Sarah's house. What if Ethan . . .

No. Not possible. That was the enemy whispering in her ear.

All ministers are the same. They all hide behind the Bible when in private they're evil.

That's what she believed for years. Until Pastor Roy and Susan had shown her pure love. But what if they were the only ones who were good? Maybe Ethan had a dark side that he'd hidden from everyone.

Mariah gripped the steering wheel with white knuckles, willing herself not to throw up. This couldn't be happening. Her budding attraction to the handsome and charming Pastor Ethan had instantly blown up in her face. Had she been attracted to a sexual predator?

Mariah needed someone to talk to. Not her parents. They still didn't know about the incident. Not Brittany either. Mariah didn't trust Brittany to not spread rumors all over town. Instead of turning left to head toward the mobile home park where Miss Sarah lived, Mariah turned right toward her home and around the block where Lizzy lived.

Rain pounded on the windshield and barely kept Mariah's vision clear enough to move forward. She pulled in front of Lizzy's house and braced herself to get drenched on her dash from her car to Lizzy's front door.

Lizzy's mouth was a round O when she pulled open her front door. She grabbed Mariah's arm and dragged her into the house.

"What are you doing out on such a nasty day?" Without waiting for an answer, Lizzy left Mariah standing in the entry, returning only a moment later with a warm, fluffy towel.

"I brought this from the dryer. Dry your hair and take off your coat."

Mariah did as Lizzy instructed without speaking. When she was seated in Lizzy's living room with a hot cup of coffee in her hands and a warm throw over her legs, Mariah finally let down.

Tears stung her eyes and spilled down her cheeks.

"What happened?" Lizzy demanded.

Mariah wiped her face and glanced around the room. "Where are Roman and Abigail?"

"Abby is still at school. Roman went to pick her up. They're closing early because of the storm. Now tell me what's going on."

Mariah took a ragged breath. "Two police officers came to the church. They took him to the station and said they wanted to question him."

"Pastor Ethan?" Lizzy collapsed back against the sofa. "What did they want to question him about?"

Mariah took a sip of the scalding brew, burning her lips in the process. "I have no idea."

"You don't sound sure."

Mariah chose her words carefully. "I can't help but think … but, no. It's the enemy whispering in my ear. Telling me not to trust him."

Lizzy leaned forward again. "Trust Ethan about what?"

Hot tears formed in Mariah's eyes and scalded her cheeks as they fell. "I'm confused."

Lizzy jumped up and grabbed a box of tissues, shoving a few into Mariah's lap. "Is there something you're not telling me?

Mariah closed her eyes and shook her head. Now wasn't the time to dump her past on her friend. "It was awful, Lizzy. These guys looked serious."

Lizzy murmured sympathy. "I'll bet you were scared."

"I was! They herded him out to the patrol car and everything."

"Where's Jayden?"

Mariah forced herself to stop crying. "I'm supposed to pick him up from Miss Sarah's." She made a move to stand.

Lizzy held out a hand. "Wait. Before you go, let's pray."

Lizzy led them in a prayer for peace and comfort for everyone and that the truth would come to light sooner rather than later.

Mariah pulled her jacket around her and stood. "Thanks. You're a true friend. I don't deserve you."

Lizzy's face held a wry smile. "No, you don't. But you're stuck with me anyway."

After they embraced, Lizzy said, "Call me later with any updates, okay?"

By the time Mariah picked up Jayden and arrived at her house, the storm was reaching its peak. They dashed into the house and stood on the small patch of entry tile, dripping water from their pant legs and jackets.

"Stay here and let me grab some towels," Mariah said to the shivering child. She removed her shoes and jacket and rushed to the linen closet.

Once they were dried off, Mariah directed Jayden to go to the spare bedroom and change. Thank goodness he always carried a spare set of clothes in his backpack. Ethan was a good dad.

Unless there was something he did that was very bad. Mariah shoved that thought out of her head to focus on caring for Ethan's son.

"Where's my dad?" Jayden asked when they returned to the living room.

"Your dad is—" Mariah's answer was interrupted by pounding on the door.

She rushed to open it and found a tall man resembling Ethan shivering on her porch.

"Uncle Robbie!" Jayden dashed to his uncle and wrapped his arms around the man's dripping raincoat.

"Careful, there J-man. Let me get out of this wet stuff."

Mariah closed the door behind him and helped Ethan's brother shed his coat. He slipped off his shoes and dropped a satchel on the floor.

"I'm Robert Walsh, Ethan's older brother."

Mariah took his outstretched hand and shook it. "Nice to meet you." She leaned in to whisper, "Any news on Ethan?"

Robert gave a small shake of his head toward Jayden. "Later."

Mariah nodded. "Is anybody hungry?"

"Starved," Jayden announced.

Mariah left the two men in the living room to get caught up. She quickly warmed some canned soup in the microwave and made four grilled cheese sandwiches. While they cooked, she watched the storm from the sliding glass door leading out to the back yard.

Leaves and debris were strewn on the patio. Rain had flattened the lawn and bent the bushes like they'd been run over with a tractor.

"Guess I'll be doing some yard work soon." She returned to the stove to flip the sandwiches over.

"Food's ready," she announced a few minutes later.

While they ate, Jayden kept the two adults entertained by his nonstop chatter. Mariah and Robert exchanged smiles over the child's head.

"Let me help you clean up," Robert said when they finished.

"I've got this. Why don't you and Jayden go upstairs and play videos."

Jayden whooped and grabbed his uncle by the hand. "C'mon, Uncle Robbie. I'll show you my mad skills."

Mariah cleaned up the kitchen, hoping she and Ethan's brother would have a chance to talk. Her stomach churned with what Ethan might be going through. Was he still at the police station? Had he been mistreated? The biggest question loomed like the black clouds outside.

What was the interview about?

A few minutes later, the lights flickered and went out. Mariah heard a 'Hey!' from Jayden upstairs. Momentarily disoriented, Mariah reached for the junk drawer and fumbled for the lighter she knew was in there somewhere.

The sound of feet clomping down the stairs ended at the bottom. "I'll grab some candles," Mariah said. Using the lighter as a beacon, she reached into the cabinet above the refrigerator and retrieved two tapers and a couple of tea lights.

"These should be good for now," she said, carrying them into the living room.

Jayden bounced up and down. "This is cool! How long will the power be out? Can we sleep in the living room? When will my dad be here?"

Jayden's last question brought a pall in the room that wasn't due to the furnace going off.

Mariah glanced at Robert hoping he'd have an answer.

"Your dad will be here as soon as he can, buddy."

Mariah handed the lighter to Robert. "Here, see if you can get a fire started in the fireplace. Jayden, maybe you can help?"

Distracted by the excitement of starting a fire, Jayden crouched next to his uncle in front of the fireplace. When the fire caught, Robert straightened.

"I should probably go." He moved to the window and looked out. "Uh, maybe not."

Mariah joined him. A huge limb rested on the hood of Robert's car.

Freezing rain pelted the walkway, bouncing up like a ping pong ball. Gusts of wind pushed the rain sideways.

"Let's see what the weather app says." Mariah pulled out her cell and tapped on the app. "Doesn't look good. There's an advisory saying everyone should shelter in place." She sent Robert a close-mouthed smile. "Guess you're staying here tonight."

Robert looked at Jayden and back at her with a shrug. "Guess J-man and I will bunk together. Do you have a sleeping bag?"

"Uh, no. But there's a twin bed in the spare room. I can make up a pallet on the floor for Jayden."

They settled a sleepy Jayden into bed and returned to the living room.

"I'd love to make a cup of coffee for you, but . . ." Mariah shrugged.

Her cell rang and she reached for it.

"Hi Dad. Yes, I'm fine. I have the fireplace going. It should be enough to keep warm until tomorrow."

Once her dad was satisfied she could exist without power, she disconnected. "Sorry. My parents still worry."

Robert huffed out a laugh. "My parental units couldn't care less."

"Parental units?"

Robert grimaced. "Long story. Anyway, let's sit and I'll bring you up to speed on my brother."

Robert sat facing her with his hands dangling between his knees. "Ethan is being questioned about a sexual assault on a minor girl in the church youth group."

"When was this?" Mariah demanded. "He came here right after youth group to pick up Jayden." Wouldn't she have noticed if he had done something like that a little while earlier? Or was her sixth sense dulled because of her attraction for him. How had that youth leader acted after he seduced her? Mariah tried to remember, but the details were blurry.

"I don't know when, but it must have been recently. The alleged victim claims he used his authority to convince her to have sex and that it wasn't consensual. I'm supposed to pick him up later." They both cringed as a dead branch slammed against the house. "Although I may have to wait on that."

~

Ethan hated every moment of sitting in the half-light trickling in from the generator. He'd heard of the Catholic concept of purgatory but never thought he'd arrive there. No one seemed to have any information about when he'd be released or if he'd be released. Here in the bowels of the police department, all Ethan had was meager information fed to him by the detective.

Without his phone, Ethan had no idea how much time had passed since he'd been put in this stark room. It could have been three hours or thirty. He stood and began to pace. The door remained locked from the outside. Ethan considered pounding on the door or on the two-way window and demanding to be let out.

Ethan's mind ran from prayer to worry and back to prayer. Like the wind sprints they'd had to do in football practice. Back and forth, until they collapsed, panting on the damp grass.

Where was Robert?

When would they let him go?

Lord, show me how to trust you.

What about Jayden? Did Mariah get him from Miss Sarah's?

What must she be thinking right now?

God, there must be a reason for this. Please reveal Yourself to me.

The door swung open and a uniformed officer entered the room. "There's a huge storm outside, as you probably guessed from the lack of electricity. We're letting you go, for now. Don't plan on leaving the area.

Not that you can. No one can get in or out until this storm passes. There's a citywide curfew in place. Trees are down everywhere, and ice has made the roads dangerous."

"How am I supposed to get home?" Ethan asked.

The guard shrugged. "I don't know. We're doing the best we can here. Come with me."

Ethan followed the officer to a reception area inside the front door. Visible through the glass windows, the storm unleashed its fury.

"Wait here." The officer left him, disappearing through another door.

Ethan's thoughts returned again to Mariah and what she would think when she heard why he was being questioned. After her confession about the incident with the youth leader, she'd probably assume he was guilty. End of story. Whatever their relationship might have developed into was a nonstarter.

The gray stone walls in the reception area oozed dampness. Ethan shook off a chill. It would be his luck if he caught whatever bug was going around the church. Or maybe he'd get sick and be put out of his misery by dying a slow, lingering death.

He forced himself away from that train of thought. How many times had he preached a sermon on the Apostle Paul's prison experiences? Too many to count. Paul praised God in his circumstances and one time, an earthquake caused the prison doors to miraculously open.

Ethan huffed out a humorless laugh. An earthquake in Main, Oregon? Not likely.

Ethan slumped onto a hard chair and closed his eyes. He must have dozed off because his eyes flew open when an announcement came over the loudspeaker.

"Attention all personnel. We are evacuating the building. I repeat, we are evacuating the building."

A few minutes later, two men were escorted into the reception area.

The detective who interviewed Ethan spoke. "Gentlemen, due to extenuating circumstances, we have to let you go. Please stay available for any additional questions we may have."

The detective took a moment to stare into each man's eyes. "I don't need to remind you that there is a citywide curfew due to the storm. That means, go home and stay home."

Ethan had no idea what the others were there for, nor did he care. Once he was out of there, his brother would help him figure out what the next steps were.

He shuddered, thinking of the lie that was told about him. What possessed a teenager to say something horrific and untrue?

An officer handed Ethan an envelope with his wallet, keys, and some loose change. He'd left his phone at the church so one of the other men let him use his to call Robert.

Ethan's voice shook. "Come get me at the police department. I'll explain everything once we get back to Pastor Roy's house."

While they waited for their rides, the man who lent Ethan his cell asked, "You a minister?"

Ethan paused for a few beats. This scandal would probably end his career as a pastor. Roy would send him packing and his Seattle church would bar the doors.

"Yeah," he finally said.

The guy looked to be around Ethan's age, or maybe older. It was difficult to tell from his unshaven face and stringy hair. "Could you, maybe, pray for me? I don't know if my girlfriend will let me come home. You know, after this." He made a sweeping motion with his arm.

Ethan sighed. "Sure. What's your name?"

"Patrick. My lady's name is Joanna. We got two kids, a girl and a boy."

Ethan felt a nudge from the Holy Spirit. "Give me your phone again, Patrick. I'll put my cell number in it. Call me anytime."

Patrick handed Ethan the phone. "Thanks, man. This here was a wakeup call. I gotta make some changes."

Ethan nodded. "I know what you mean." He needed to make some changes too.

Chapter 18

Robert disconnected and turned to face Mariah across the dimly lit living room. "That was Ethan. They're releasing him."

"Good."

"I can pick him up. But there's the little problem with my vehicle." He sent Mariah a wry smile.

"Take mine." Mariah strode into her bedroom and grabbed her keys from her purse. "Be careful. Not that I'm worried about my car. The roads are dangerous."

Robert gave her a mock salute. "Is it okay if I bring him here?"

"Of course. My dad is bringing a generator tomorrow."

Robert shrugged into his overcoat and headed outside. Mariah knelt on the sofa and watched him step carefully over the broken tree limbs on the walkway. He sent her a wave when he made it to her car without tripping.

Mariah paced the living room while she waited for Robert to pick up Ethan. Candlelight flickered on the walls creating a homey scene that was at odds with

Mariah's inner thoughts. On one hand, she couldn't wait to hear Ethan's side of the story. On the other hand, she was afraid of the guilt she might see in his face.

Hugging herself against the chill, Mariah wondered again about the circumstances surrounding Ethan's arrest. Too many questions fought for dominance. Who accused him? Was it true? If he was innocent, how could he prove it? What if he was guilty?

Mariah sank onto her sofa and pulled a soft throw over her legs. Her Bible sat on the end table. She opened it to the book of Psalms and began to read. Psalms 141:3 made her laugh out loud. "Set a guard, O Lord, over my mouth; Keep watch over the door of my lips." If only she'd known this verse when she was younger. She could have shed her mean girl persona a long time ago.

Hugging the Bible to her chest, Mariah prayed for Ethan and Jayden. Then she prayed for herself. That whatever came from this awful thing Ethan was accused of, the truth would prevail. And that she'd be okay with it.

Mariah wanted to believe he was innocent. From what she'd seen, he wasn't a sexual predator. He'd been nothing but respectful toward her. Unless there lurked some evil twist that made Ethan prefer teenage young women.

The thought twisted her stomach. Could she be blind to Ethan's dark side because of her growing affection for him? Look how it had turned out in her own past. She hadn't known of the youth leader's predatory actions when she'd flirted with him. She'd learned at the age of twelve that actions had consequences.

Would Ethan forever have the reputation as a rapist? Mariah shuddered. Small towns could sometimes be slow to accept newcomers. If this accusation was false, it might take him a long time to shed the cloud of suspicion. He'd probably run as fast as he could back to Seattle. Exactly like Scott, he'd get away and leave her with another broken heart.

Her phone rang and Lizzy's name filled the screen.

"How's your power situation up there?" Lizzy asked.

"Probably same as you. No power. Are you guys okay?"

Lizzy chuckled. "Roman is jonesing for some coffee, but other than that, we're making it into a camping adventure. We'll all sleep in the living room tonight in front of the fireplace."

"Thank goodness for fires."

"Any update on Ethan?"

"His brother is here, and he went to pick him up at the police station." Mariah hated having to tell her friend why Ethan was questioned. She sucked in a ragged breath. "One of the girls in the youth group accused him of . . ." Mariah couldn't bring herself to say rape. "Assault."

"Like he hit her?" Lizzy exclaimed.

"No. Sexual assault."

There was silence for several beats before Lizzy responded. "That's ridiculous."

Before Mariah could answer, she heard someone knock on the front door. Then it swung open to Robert, followed by Ethan. Mariah's heart jumped into her throat.

"I have to go. They walked through the door this minute."

"You're back," she said, disconnecting from Lizzy's call.

Robert closed the door behind them. "I hope you don't mind I brought my brother here. He'd love a shower and there's no hot water at Pastor Roy's. I remember you saying your dad might be bringing a generator."

"Not until tomorrow. But my water heater is gas. There'll be hot water."

Ethan's chin rested on his chest as he stepped into the living room.

"Are you okay?" Mariah whispered.

Ethan raised his head to make eye contact. A shake of his head was all it took to propel Mariah forward and into his arms.

~

Ethan wrapped his arms around Mariah and inhaled her minty fragrance. Almost as tall as he, she fit against him like she was made for him. Even more, she felt like home.

He heard his brother chuckle. "Get a room," Robert muttered under his breath.

Ethan broke away from Mariah and held her upper arms. "How's Jayden?"

"He's fine. Sleeping in my guest room. You and your brother will have to fight over who sleeps on the couch."

Robert dropped a bag on the sofa. "We swung by Pastor Roy's house and picked up clothes for Ethan and Jayden."

Ethan's gaze settled on Mariah's lips. He wanted to lower his head and rest his lips on hers. After his experience at the police department, her response would be the answer he needed to the question he'd asked himself a dozen times since then. Would Mariah believe he was innocent of the accusations?

Robert's voice interrupted his thoughts. "Why don't you jump in the shower and then we can talk."

Ethan reluctantly dropped his arms. "Sounds good."

Showering in flickering candlelight was a new experience. Ethan hoped the steaming spray would wash the smell of the police department off his body. Too bad it couldn't wash away the shame of the accusation.

Robert and Mariah stopped talking when he returned to the living room. Ethan looked from one to the other, trying to read their mood.

"Do you think we can talk tomorrow?" Ethan asked. "I'm beat."

Mariah frowned but kept silent.

"Sure, little brother. Let's all try to get some sleep. I'll take the couch."

Mariah moved to the linen closet and brought out a set of sheets and blankets.

"Thanks," Robert said. "I'll try to keep the fire going through the night."

Ethan watched Mariah disappear into the bathroom and close the door.

Robert quirked an eyebrow. "She's into you."

Ethan ran a hand through his still damp hair. "I don't know. This thing may turn her off completely."

Robert clapped him on the back. "Have some faith, brother."

Ethan huffed out a laugh before heading into the spare room to check on his son.

~

Early the next morning, Mariah stood in her kitchen, jittery from the lack of coffee. How was she supposed to take care of the three men under her roof with no electricity?

Her phone showed only a small amount of power, but it was enough to ping with a text from her dad. A few minutes later, the roar of his Hummer came from the front of the house.

Mariah hurried into the living room to find Jayden peering out the window, his mouth open in an O. The couch was empty and the bathroom door was closed.

"Is that your dad's car?" Jayden asked.

Mariah smiled and ruffled his hair. "That's one of my dad's vehicles."

She opened the front door to a blast of cold air. "Hey, Dad."

Her dad grabbed her in a hug. "How's my princess?"

When he released her, his eyes landed on Jayden, staring up at him with rounded eyes.

"Who's this little guy?"

"Dad, this is Jayden. He's staying here during the storm."

Her dad stuck out a hand. "Nice to meet you, Jayden."

Mariah rested her hand on Jayden's shoulder. "This little man might be able to help you hook up the generator."

Dad grinned. "I could use some help. Let's get you into a jacket."

Mariah helped Jayden bundle up.

"Can I ride in your Hummer?" Jayden asked.

"You bet! I'm going to pull it around to the side of the house to unload the generator. We'll have power to you guys in two shakes."

Dad leaned in to kiss Mariah on the cheek. "Where's his parents?" he whispered.

"I'll explain later."

With a nod, her dad and Jayden made their way to his huge Hummer. The temperature had risen, leaving the walkway and sidewalk wet but not icy. Mariah looked up to see a bit of sun peeking through the clouds. The storm seemed to have passed, leaving destruction in its wake.

The living room lights burst on, and Mariah heard the sound of the furnace kicking on. Dad must have gotten the generator hooked up and running.

A few minutes later, Dad and Jayden came through the front door.

"All done," Dad announced. "Couldn't have done it without my wingman." He ruffled Jayden's hair.

Jayden puffed up his chest. "We make a good team, Mr. Greg."

"That we do, my boy. That we do. Let me give some instructions to my daughter before I hit the road."

Mariah stood and shed the throw covering her lap. "Thanks, Dad."

"Don't overload the generator or it will shut off. Only use enough power for basic needs." He shook a finger at her. "No running the blow dryer, straightening iron, and microwave all at the same time. And don't use the toaster and microwave at the same time either."

Mariah grinned up at her dad. "No blow dryer. No toaster. Got it."

"I'm serious, young lady." Her dad grabbed her in a hug and whispered in her ear. "Tell me about Jayden."

Ethan came out of the guest room, rubbing his eyes.

"Guess I was tired-er than I thought." He took in Mariah, her dad, and Jayden.

"Greg Martin," Dad said, shaking Ethan's hand.

"Ethan Walsh."

Mariah's dad turned to Robert, who came out of the bathroom wearing a pair of Under Armor sweatpants and a University of Washington School of Law sweatshirt. "And you are?"

"Robert Walsh."

"Which one of you is my wingman's father?"

His question was answered when Jayden jumped into Ethan's arms.

There was a moment of awkward silence. Mariah clasped her hands together.

"Coffee anyone? If it won't overload the generator, that is."

There was a chorus of enthusiastic male voices. "Yes! Hot coffee."

Mariah busied herself in the kitchen, filling the Breville coffee machine with fresh water and whole beans. She could live without her blow dryer. But without coffee? Hard no.

She listened with half an ear as her dad, Robert, and Ethan discussed the storm that passed through Main. Lots of downed trees causing problems for the linemen working to restore power. Cars colliding with other vehicles on icy streets. Mariah thanked God for safety for herself and her family.

She carried two brimming cups of java into the living room and set them on the coffee table.

"You gentlemen will have to fight over these while I make two more."

Her dad quirked an eyebrow at Ethan. "Looks like you probably need this more than I do."

Ethan picked up one of the mugs with a grateful nod while Mariah returned to the kitchen.

"Can I have coffee too?" Jayden asked when Mariah returned to the living room with two more steaming mugs of coffee.

Handing one of the mugs to her dad, Mariah said, "Not yet, Jayden. Maybe in ten years or so. How about I make you some hot cocoa?"

"Sure!" Jayden replied.

Ethan touched his son's arm. "Let Miss Mariah drink her coffee first, J-man."

Jayden's shoulders slumped. "Okay."

Ethan took a long sip of his coffee and set the mug on the coffee table. He touched his chest with both hands. "I supposed you're wondering why my brother and I are staying with your daughter," he said, looking toward Mariah's father.

Greg murmured his assent.

Robert laid a hand on Ethan's arm. "As your attorney, I'd advise you not to say anything."

Ethen sent him a tortured glance. Mariah's heart went out to him. What must he be feeling?

"As my brother, you know I need to explain."

Robert raised his hands in surrender. "Whatever."

Ethan spoke to Greg but kept his eyes focused on Mariah. "Someone in the church youth group, a girl, said that I sexually assaulted her." His words sounded as if he were forcing them through a sieve.

Mariah chewed on her lip as he continued. "I didn't. I never touched any of the girls except for a hug."

"Dad, what's assaulted mean?" Jayden piped up.

Ethan dropped his gaze to his son. "It means I hurt her."

"It's wrong to hurt girls," Jayden said.

"That's right, son. It is wrong."

"Why would she say you hurt her if you didn't?"

The adults exchanged glances. "I don't know, Jayden," Ethan said with a defeated sigh.

Greg finished his coffee and got to his feet. "I better get back to the ranch and see how your mom is doing." He dropped a kiss on Mariah's head. Ethan and Robert stood and shook Greg's hand.

Greg laid his left hand over his and Ethan's clasped ones. "I'm sure it'll all get worked out."

Ethan's lips tightened. "I hope so."

Mariah showed her dad to the door. "I'll call you later," she told him. He sent her a jaunty wave and climbed into his huge SUV.

"Do you mind if I shower again? I still feel dirty." Ethan asked when she returned to the living room.

"Not at all," Mariah answered.

Robert handed Ethan a satchel. "We stopped by where Ethan's staying and picked up a few things."

"I'm bored," Jayden said, flopping back on the sofa.

"Why don't you run upstairs and get the tub of Legos," Mariah suggested.

She watched with amusement as Jayden dragged his feet to the door leading upstairs.

"Are you sure we can't play video games?" he asked.

"I don't think so, buddy. Remember what my dad said?"

Jayden gave an exaggerated sigh. "Okay."

When he was safely upstairs, Mariah turned to Robert. "What happens now?"

Robert rubbed a hand across his unshaven cheeks. "As soon as the power returns to the police department, I'll go down and talk with the detective who questioned Ethan. I'll try to see what their plan is. They can't arrest him based on an accusation. There has to be a forensic investigation of the attack. DNA, stuff like that. Unfortunately, something like this can ruin a man's reputation even if he is innocent."

"I can't believe this is happening," Mariah said. Her head pounded with every pulse. "I need more coffee."

While the coffee machine went through its process, Mariah braced her arms on the kitchen counter. Her head drooped as she considered the past twenty-four hours. A lot had changed. There'd been times when her growing attraction for Ethan had brought hope that he felt the same. Then the storm, loss of power, and this absurd accusation. It was all too much. Where was God in all this?

The coffee maker gurgled its final drops into the mug. Mariah closed her eyes and inhaled. She heard Robert step into the kitchen.

"You okay?" he asked.

Mariah reached for the mug and shook her head. Tears prickled behind her eyelids.

Robert laid a gentle hand on her shoulder. "It's going to be okay. My brother is innocent. The truth will prevail."

Mariah wanted to believe him. But she knew that sometimes people did bad things. What if Ethan didn't assault the girl, but still acted inappropriately? She'd seen him hug at least two of the high schoolers after youth group. What if there was more to the story? And those texts.

She pulled away from Robert and held her coffee mug in both hands like a shield. "I guess we'll see, won't we?"

Robert looked like he wanted to say something but held back. After a few beats, he said, "Do you mind making me another cup of coffee?"

While the coffee brewed, Robert leaned back against the counter, watching the process.

"That's quite a contraption you've got there."

"Yes, it is."

Robert blew out a breath. "Look, I know it's none of my business. But my brother really likes you. After what he's told me about you, I hope you'll believe he's innocent."

Mariah swung her head toward him. "What has he told you?" Had Ethan shared her deepest secret with his brother? She felt a flash of anger.

"He said how much he appreciates your watching Jayden. He's talked about how he's enjoyed spending time with you." Robert shrugged. "I kind of got the impression he was into you."

Mariah chewed her lip as the coffee maker finished its cycle. Robert picked up the mug. "Thanks."

She was saved from having to say anything by Ethan. He sauntered into the kitchen, pushing his damp hair back from his face.

"Thanks. I feel a lot better." His gaze swung from Mariah's mug to Robert's. "More coffee? Is that an option?"

Mariah checked the Breville for water and beans and started the process again.

They spent the rest of the day keeping Jayden occupied with board games and Legos. Mariah threw together sandwiches and soup. The generator continued to hum, creating a soothing background noise. Mariah let herself relax and enjoy hanging out with Ethan and his brother. Their easy camaraderie reminded her of her relationship with Daniel.

When it was Jayden's bedtime, Mariah offered to get him into his pajamas, which Ethan had grabbed when Robert had taken him by Pastor Roy's house.

"That would be great," Ethan said with a grateful smile. "I need to check my cell for any updates from Main PD."

His comment was like the slap of a wet towel on Mariah's mood. The reality of Ethan's situation returned to the forefront of her mind.

When she'd settled Jayden on the guest room floor, she returned to the living room to find Ethan and Robert huddled over Ethan's cell. Their heads jerked up.

"Jayden wants you to come say goodnight," Mariah said to Ethan.

Ethan went into the bedroom and came out a few minutes later. He dropped onto the sofa with a sigh.

"This stinks," he said to no one in particular.

Mariah's gaze swung from Robert to Ethan. "What's going on?"

Robert leaned back in his chair. "Ethan got a text from one of the elders, letting him know he would not be returning to Main Community Church until this ordeal is over."

Mariah blew out a breath through pursed lips.

"I need to call Pastor Roy," Ethan said, struggling to his feet.

Mariah watched him go into the kitchen. She heard his murmured conversation but couldn't make out the words.

"My brother is going to need all the support he can get until this is sorted out." Robert pinned her with his gaze.

Mariah didn't answer.

Robert leaned toward her. "My brother is innocent. What do I need to do to convince you of that?"

Mariah gathered her hair into a ponytail with one hand and let it drop. "I don't know."

In the silence that followed, Mariah could hear Ethan end his call with Pastor Roy. It sounded like he was crying. She and Robert exchanged a glance. Mariah looked away.

"I'm going upstairs," she said. She pounded up the narrow staircase to the game room she'd created on the second floor. Mariah sank onto one of the beanbag chairs, resting her chin in one hand.

She desperately wanted to believe in Ethan's innocence. But a dark whisper in her ear blew doubt into her mind.

He's exactly like that youth leader.

He's hiding his true nature.

It's only a matter of time before he hurts you.

Chapter 19

Ethan wiped tears from his eyes with a paper towel. His conversation with Pastor Roy ended with a heartfelt prayer from his friend and mentor. While Roy didn't come out and say he believed Ethan was innocent, he did say that the truth would be revealed. He quoted a Scripture verse from Ephesians. Something about everything being exposed to the light.

Ethan heaved a sigh and tossed the damp paper towel into the trash. The truth had to come out, but at what cost to his ministry? And to his relationships.

His thoughts turned to Mariah. He could no longer deny his attraction to her. He wanted to get to know her better to see if there might be something permanent there. Jayden needed a mom. And Ethan was tired of being alone. He wanted a partner. Someone who wanted the same things he did.

Was Mariah that person? This accusation would most likely kill any attraction Mariah had for him. With her history and the trauma she'd experienced at the hands of a man in ministry, Ethan wouldn't blame her if she ran for the hills.

He straightened his shoulders and headed back to the living room. Robert sat by himself swiping the screen of his phone.

Robert looked up when Ethan stepped into his line of sight. "You okay?" Robert asked.

Ethan shrugged. "As okay as I can be with a rape charge hanging over my head."

"Innocent until proven guilty," Robert said, pointing his cell in Ethan's direction.

"Not since the Me Too movement. Everyone believes the woman now." He dropped onto the sofa. "Where's Mariah?"

"Upstairs."

"She's probably trying to figure out how to get rid of us."

Robert snorted. "Not likely, little bro. I see the way she looks at you."

Ethan glanced at the door to the stairs and lowered his voice. "What are you talking about?"

Robert sent him a lopsided grin. "If I had a woman look at me like she looks at you, I'd never let her out of my sight."

Ethan shook his head. "Yeah, no. I might have had a chance two days ago. But that ship has sailed."

"Can I give you some advice?"

Ethan nodded. "You will whether I say yes or not."

"Okay then. You like her, right? And it's obvious to me she likes you. Give it some time, bro. She may be the next Mrs. Ethan Walsh."

Ethan rubbed his eyes. "If only. There's some history that negates your advice."

They fell silent as Mariah's footsteps sounded on the stairs. She reached the bottom and turned to close the door behind her.

"Who gets to sleep on the couch tonight?"

Robert stood and stretched. "I'll take the couch again."

Ethan kept his eyes pointed down as Robert headed to the bathroom. "Need some help making up the couch?" he asked.

"No, I've got it."

Ethan wanted to say 'We need to talk,' but awkwardness filled the room like a dark cloud.

"Guess I'll leave you to it then." Ethan stood. With once glance toward Mariah, he walked to the guest room where his son lay on the floor, sleeping.

"What's going to happen to you, J-man, if I get sent to prison?" Tears filled Ethan's eyes as he considered his son's future. How would Jayden ever live down the shame of having a convicted sex offender as a father?

Before collapsing on the bed, Ethan sank to his knees and began to pray.

~

Mariah pulled her wrist to her face to check the time on her smart watch. Closing her eyes, she forced her brain to stop chewing on the events of the past two days. The hum of the generator outside her bedroom window should have lulled her to sleep. Instead, it was an annoying ear worm.

At two, Mariah gave up the pretense of sleeping and swung her legs over the side of the bed. A cup of soothing chamomile tea might help her relax. Tiptoeing past the sleeping form of Robert on the couch, she padded into the kitchen. The electric tea kettle lit up when she pushed down on the button to start heating the water. It provided enough ambient light to find the box of tea bags and a clean mug.

"Hey."

Mariah whirled and almost dropped the mug at the sound of a male voice.

"You scared me!" She hugged the mug to her chest, feeling her heart pound against the cool ceramic.

"Sorry."

Mariah could barely make out Ethan's features. He sat at the kitchen table, his hands folded as if in prayer.

"I couldn't sleep," Ethan said. "Guess you can't either."

Mariah held the box of tea in his direction. "Tea?"

"Sure."

When the water was hot and poured into two mugs, Mariah sat at the table across from Ethan.

Ethan took a tentative sip of the steaming liquid. "It's my fault, you know."

Mariah's stomach flipped. Ethan was going to confess. He was the same as that youth leader years ago. She should have known her attraction to him was too good to be true.

As soon as she heard his confession, she'd toss him out of the house. "What's your fault?"

"I pushed Angela away."

"Angela? Your wife?" This wasn't what Mariah expected to hear.

Ethan slowly nodded. "She wanted to be a missionary. I didn't. She was going to leave me and Jayden and go overseas."

Mariah's head whirled. This was not the conversation she expected to have. "I-I don't understand."

Ethan took a gulp of his tea and set the mug on the table with a *thunk*. "We got married because all our friends were getting married. I thought I could placate Angela with some short-term missions trips. Everything changed when she got pregnant."

Ethan held the tea bag string and bounced it up and down in the water. "I ignored her frustration over being tied to Jayden."

Mariah felt Ethan's angst radiating off him. She understood the feeling of wanting to ignore the signs of discontent. Hadn't she done the same thing with Scott? He'd been restless, talking about moving somewhere – anywhere. Mariah thought he'd get over it once she got pregnant. That had escalated quickly into Scott breaking up with her and moving out.

"I'm sorry." Mariah felt the lameness of her comment.

Ethan continued as if she hadn't spoken. "The thing is, all I ever wanted was to get married and have a family. I tried to hold onto the shreds of that dream, even though I felt Angie slipping away. When she died, I was a little relieved." Ethan raised anguished eyes to Mariah. "Does that make me a terrible person?"

Mariah had no answer. What terrible things had she not only thought but had done in her past. Things that still came back to bite her in the backside. Shaking off a bad reputation wasn't something accomplished in a few months. Instead of replying, she laid her hand over Ethan's. "You're not a terrible person, Ethan. You're flawed like all of us."

"I didn't do it. Hurt that girl. I don't know why she's lying. I would never…" Ethan gulped, and Mariah felt his hand shake under hers.

Everything in her core wanted to believe him. Mariah silenced the whisper in her ear, that insidious voice that wanted to cast doubt. The spirit that told her she wasn't good enough to have the love of a good man like Ethan. That he was like every other man who would use her and cast her aside like yesterday's coffee grounds.

Mariah straightened and tightened her grip on Ethan's hand. "I believe you." And she did. She'd fight for the truth at whatever cost to herself. She might have the reputation of being the woman who stood with a sexual predator, but it couldn't be much worse than being Mean Girl Mariah.

Ethan's chin dropped to his chest. "Thank you," he breathed.

At that moment, the lights flickered once, twice, and came on, illuminating the room with harsh brightness. Mariah blinked, glancing toward the living room. At least she hadn't turned on any lights in the other part of the house. Robert and Jayden would be blissfully unaware of the return of power.

"I'll go out and turn off the generator," Ethan said.

When he stepped through the back door a few minutes later, Mariah had two cups of coffee ready for them. "We need a plan," she said.

"Plan?" Ethan took the mug she offered to him and returned to his seat at the table.

Mariah opened the Notes section of her iPad. "A plan. First, find out who made the accusation against you. That's something that will be up to Robert. Next, create a timeline for when this 'supposed' attack occurred."

Mariah was on a roll now. "Then we confront the girl."

Ethan held out a hand. "Wait a minute. Confront her? I'm not sure that's a good idea."

Mariah leveled her gaze at him. "How else will we get to the bottom of this?"

Ethan shrugged. "I don't know."

"Okay, then. We make sure her parents are there. Maybe a couple other witnesses."

Ethan pushed his hair back with one hand. "Why is this happening to me?"

"Stop feeling sorry for yourself. You need to fight this."

~

Ethan sent Mariah a grateful look, glad she was taking charge. His brain felt like a bowl of lukewarm oatmeal.

Her voice cut through the fog. "When did this supposedly happen?"

The interview with Detective McDonald came back with painful clarity. "Wednesday before last."

"Was that the first night you filled in for Noah?"

"Yeah. First time." Ethan leaned back in his chair and took a drink of his brew. "This coffee is amazing. What kind of machine is that?"

Mariah tapped her fingernail on the table. "Let's stay on topic. This is more important than amazing coffee."

Gulp. This woman was a force to be reckoned with. "Got it. Sorry."

"Tell me exactly what the Detective said. What he asked." Mariah bent over her iPad, waiting.

Ethan rubbed a hand over the stubble on his cheeks. "Detective McDonald asked if I liked working with youth. I said yes. Then he asked if anyone stayed after to ask questions or ask for counseling. That sort of thing. I told him, no, not that I could recall."

Mariah looked up from the device. "You have to think, Ethan. Did any of the girls stay late?"

Ethan's head pounded as he tried to remember. "I don't remember. That was two weeks ago!" He shot up from his chair and paced around the small kitchen and dining area. "This past Wednesday, Tamara stayed after. I remember that."

"Tamara, the daughter of Craig and Debbie? One of the elders?"

Ethan nodded. "She seemed interested in learning more about what it means to be a Christian. But I never touched her. I swear." As soon as the words left his mouth, Ethan realized he *had* touched her. But only a hug.

He sank down on the chair and closed his eyes. "I hugged her."

Mariah folded her hands on the table. "That isn't enough to cause Tamara to accuse you of assault. Besides, that was this past Wednesday. The police said it was two weeks ago, right?"

Ethan let out a groan. "Yeah. This is all too crazy."

"Obviously, whoever it is, she's lying."

"But why?"

Mariah rose and carried her empty cup to the sink. "I don't know. But we need your brother's help to figure this out. I'm going back to bed, and you should too. We'll need sharp brains to work on this tomorrow."

Ethan glanced at the clock on the microwave. Its green blinking light gave no indication of the time. He stood and joined Mariah at the sink.

"Thanks for this. For helping. Letting Jayden and me, and Robert, stay here."

Mariah gave him a small smile. "You're welcome."

Ethan took one of her hands. "I don't know what I'd do without you." When Mariah didn't respond, he continued. "Thank you for believing in me. I'd understand if you assumed I was guilty, what with your own history."

"To be perfectly honest, at first I assumed you were guilty."

Ethan nodded. "I understand. But now?"

Mariah's face was grim. "No way. That girl is lying. The question is, why?"

Ethan pulled Mariah close. Her blue eyes reminded him of the pool he and Robert used to swim in during warm summer days. Her breath came in small puffs as she stared up at him.

Ethan bent his head, his lips hovering over hers. "I'm going to kiss you now. Is that okay?"

Mariah's answer was barely a whisper. "Yes."

Ethan's heart raced as his lips met Mariah's. Her lips were warm under his. Ethan's heart sped up as the kiss lengthened. Mariah's response was all he needed. He cupped her face with both hands, laying gentle kisses on her cheeks and forehead before returning to her lips.

He couldn't deny the intense desire he felt for her, but at the same time, a nagging doubt crept in. Was this the right time and place for their love to bloom?

She was everything he wanted in a woman - fierce yet gentle, a perfect match for him. Together they could conquer anything, and Ethan knew with absolute certainty that God had led him to Main, Oregon, at this exact moment to meet her.

Right as he was about to pour his heart out, Mariah pulled away, reminding him of their physical boundaries.

"We should get some sleep."

Ethan couldn't help but feel disappointed, but he respected her decision. As she walked away towards the kitchen, he watched her with longing.

"Goodnight," she said before disappearing into the darkness.

Alone with his thoughts, Ethan couldn't help but wonder about God's timing.

~

Mariah slipped between the thousand thread count sheets and pulled the blankets up to her chin. Resting two fingers on her lips, she marveled at the feelings Ethan's kisses had exposed. She'd fallen hard for Pastor Ethan Walsh. His kisses were unlike any other she'd experienced. Gentle, respectful, and the fact that he'd asked permission. Oh, my. That was unexpected.

When doubts about what the future would look like threatened to overwhelm the warm feelings flooding her body, Mariah turned on her side and forced them out of her mind. As soon as this ordeal with Ethan was over, she'd have to take a long, hard look at herself and see if she could fulfil a role Pastor Ethan would need for a life partner.

The next morning, Mariah woke to the sound of moisture dripping off the trees outside her bedroom window. Squinting against the sunlight, she swung her legs over the side of the bed. It was Saturday morning, and she and Ethan had a lot to do today. First on the agenda, get dressed and make coffee. A lot of coffee.

She found Robert on the sofa with the sheets and blankets folded neatly next to him.

"Good morning. Did you sleep well?"

Robert looked up from his laptop. "Yes. Thanks. Looks like we have power again."

He stood and followed Mariah into the kitchen.

"I'll make some coffee."

Robert leaned back against the counter while Mariah filled the machine with beans and fresh water. She found his scrutiny disconcerting.

"What?" Mariah asked.

"My brother is lucky to have you."

Mariah raised her eyebrows. "I'm not sure what you mean."

Robert crossed his arms. "To have you on his side. I don't know how much he's told you about his wife."

Mariah shrugged. "A bit."

Robert chewed on his lips, seeming to consider his words. "I'm not sure Angie would have been as adamant as you about Ethan's innocence. Angie was … different."

Mariah pulled three mugs from the cupboard above the coffee machine without responding.

"She was planning to leave him and Jayden. She had this idea that her life would be better as a missionary than a pastor's wife."

"She told you this?" Mariah's mouth opened in disbelief.

Robert stared down at his feet. "Not in so many words. She wanted legal advice about a separation."

"Does Ethan know?"

Robert nodded. "He was in denial for a long time. When she died, I think he was relieved."

Mariah glanced toward the kitchen door and lowered her voice. "He shared that with me. I think he feels guilty for feeling that way."

Jaden's voice from the living room interrupted their talk.

Robert leaned closer to Mariah. "I hope you will not be like Angie."

Before she could respond, Jayden bounced into the kitchen.

"What's for breakfast?" he demanded.

Robert grabbed Jayden and tickled him. "Not so fast, little man."

Jayden dissolved into a pile of giggles. Mariah smiled at the scene.

Ethan strode into the kitchen, his hair damp from the shower. "I hope you saved me some coffee."

Mariah thrust a steaming mug into his outstretched hands. Mariah's fingers tingled when their hands briefly touched. She felt her face warm, remembering their kiss the night before. Ethan's gaze locked on her mouth as if he was remembering the same.

Robert looked from Ethan to Mariah and back again. "Come on, little man. Let's go into the living room and find something to do."

"But I'm hungry," Jayden protested.

Mariah pulled her gaze away from Ethan. "I'll make us some breakfast. Go with your uncle."

Jayden scampered into the living room, followed by Robert, who smirked at them as he backed out of the kitchen.

Mariah's heart kicked up a notch when Ethan set his mug on the counter and pulled her close.

"I can't stop thinking about last night," he whispered.

"Me neither."

"But I need some help refreshing my memory." Ethan lowered his head and placed his lips gently on hers. "Yup. That's what I remember."

Mariah leaned into Ethan, inhaling the scent of her eucalyptus body wash from his shower. This felt right. More right than any of the other men she'd been with. With a jolt, Mariah's past hit her with a dose of reality as shame and guilt filled her with remorse.

"Ethan, I—"

"Don't say anything," Ethan said, kissing the corner of her mouth.

Mariah pushed him away. "There's something you should know." She took a deep breath and braced herself for his reaction. She knew that what she was about to reveal would change how he saw her forever.

"I have to tell you something." Mariah sucked in a breath. "I'm not a virgin." She blurted the words on an exhale.

Ethan's forehead wrinkled. "I know. You were raped when you were a kid."

Mariah's gaze fell. "That's not it. I have this reputation. That I'm Mean Girl Mariah. And that I sleep around." Her stomach tightened. "It's true."

Mariah waited for Ethan to turn away in disgust. Instead, she felt his finger under her chin, lifting her gaze to his.

"That doesn't matter, Mariah. You are a new person in Christ. All that past is where it stays. In the past."

Mariah's eyes burned with tears. If only she'd met this man years ago. Before she'd lost herself in casual sex and throwaway relationships.

Ethan's thumbs were gentle as he wiped away the tears spilling from her eyes. "I love who you are now, not who you were."

Wait. Did he just use the L-word? Mariah gulped. Before she could respond, Jayden skipped into the kitchen.

"What are you guys doing? I'm starved."

Mariah pulled away from Ethan and moved to the refrigerator. She pulled out bacon, eggs, and a loaf of bread.

"I'm working on it, little man," Mariah told him.

She felt Ethan's gaze on her back as she separated the bacon slices and laid them in a frying pan.

"Dad, come play with me. Uncle Robbie is busy. Can we play video games? We have power, right? C'mon Dad, let's go." Jayden pulled on Ethan's hand.

"How long until breakfast is ready?" Ethan asked.

Mariah didn't turn from the stove. "Give me about twenty minutes."

When she was alone, Mariah let her shoulders slump.

The rumble of her dad's Hummer vibrated the front windows. Mariah turned down the burner under the bacon and went to the front door to let him in.

"Do I smell bacon?" her dad asked, sniffing the air.

"I'll throw on a few more pieces," Mariah said with a smile.

"I'm here to pick up the generator."

Jayden bounded down the stairs. "Can I ride in your Hummer again?" He ran to Greg and threw his arms around Greg's legs.

"I don't see why not. How long until breakfast?"

"You have time," Mariah answered.

Her dad leaned down to Jayden's level. "Let's go for a ride around the block. Survey the damage from the storm."

Ethan came around the corner from the stairs and stopped.

Greg straightened. "If that's okay with your dad."

Ethan smiled. "Sure."

Mariah's dad helped Jayden into his coat, and they left with Jayden dragging Greg by the hand.

Ethan sent Mariah an apologetic look. "He has this fixation on big trucks."

"My dad doesn't mind. He loves kids."

Mariah returned to the kitchen with Ethan on her heels. He leaned back against the counter, legs crossed at the ankles.

"Smells good," Ethan commented.

"Nothing like bacon in the morning." Mariah busied herself whipping eggs in a bowl and flipping the bacon.

"Robert and I are going back to Pastor Roy's house this morning. I want to make sure his power is back on and there's no damage to the house. Besides, we should get out of your hair."

Mariah smoothed a few errant hairs out of her face. As much as she'd enjoyed having the guys stay, she looked forward to having her house to herself.

"I'll have to drive you. Your brother's car has that big limb taking up residence on his hood."

Ethan smacked his forehead. "Oh, yeah. I forgot. Do you mind giving us a lift?"

"Not at all."

Mariah turned back to the stove. A moment later, she felt Ethan's hands on her shoulders. "Thanks for everything," he murmured in her ear.

Mariah's heart kicked up a notch.

"Your belief in me means a lot."

Mariah remembered his words from earlier. *I love who you are.* At that moment, Mariah realized she loved Ethan too. No other man had made her feel clean, new, and worthy of respect. She leaned back into his arms. No scandal, no teenage girl's lies, no accusation would steal the feelings Ethan had awakened in her.

~

When he'd finished eating, Ethan returned to the guest room to pack up his and Jayden's things. Robert did the same. When they were finished, Ethan and Robert lowered their voices to talk about what their plan was once they'd returned to Pastor Roy's house.

Robert glanced over his shoulder out the window at his car. "The insurance adjuster can't be here until Monday. You're stuck with me for a couple more days."

Ethan looked toward Mariah's closed bedroom door. "I'll probably have to go to the police station again on Monday. Will you go with me?"

"Of course. This whole thing is a sham."

"I'll have to get someone to watch Jayden."

Robert sent him a lop-sided grin. "I think you know who to ask."

Ethan rubbed a hand across his unshaven face. "I hope she's still speaking to me when this thing gets ugly."

"I don't think you have to worry about that, little bro."

Their conversation stopped when Mariah swung open her bedroom door. Ethan's breath caught in his throat. Even dressed in jeans and a pullover sweatshirt, the woman was gorgeous. When she smiled at him, Ethan felt his heart stop. He realized he'd do anything to make her smile like that every day.

"Are you men ready?" Mariah asked, looking from Ethan to his brother.

They rose from the sofa in unison. Jayden came out of the bedroom with his backpack slung over one shoulder. "Ready, Miss Mariah."

They loaded up Mariah's BMW and started off down her street toward the center of town. Jayden kept up a steady stream of chatter from the back seat.

"Me and Mr. Greg already saw this. There's a tree on top of that person's garage." Jayden pointed out the window, commenting on the damage the storm had brought to the stores along Main Street.

Ethan exchanged an amused glance with Mariah. "I hope everything is okay at Pastor Roy's."

"Have you spoken with him?" Mariah asked.

Ethan hoped Mariah hadn't heard him crying like a baby after his conversation with his friend and mentor.

"He and Susan are coming home today. They offered to let Jayden and me stay there until things get sorted."

Ethan hoped things would get sorted sooner rather than later. Although without a job and no way to support himself and his son, Ethan had serious doubts about his future. Even if this accusation went away, he knew how rumors spread like silent cancer cells in the Christian community. Some would believe the rumors and use them to trample his reputation in the dirt.

He breathed a prayer for God's protection over himself and Jayden, adding in a quick prayer that his friend's house hadn't sustained any damage from the freak Spring storm.

Mariah pulled to a stop on the street in front of the pastor's home.

"Looks okay from here," Robert commented.

They piled out of the car and stood in the bright sunlight.

"You don't have to stay," Ethan said.

"I don't mind. I'll help bring your stuff in." Mariah opened the trunk and they all grabbed bags, backpacks, and Robert's briefcase.

The house was cold, but at least they had electricity. Ethan cranked up the thermostat while Robert and Mariah inspected the kitchen.

When they'd made sure no pipes had broken and no tree limbs had shattered any windows, they regrouped in the living room. Jayden wandered off to play in the bedroom he'd claimed as his.

Ethan watched Mariah as she shifted her weight from one leg to the other. "I should go," she said. "You two have a lot to discuss."

Before she could get to the front door, the doorbell rang. Ethan's stomach tightened. What if it was the police again, wanting to question him?

His feet dragged as he approached the front door. Standing on Roy's porch was one of the elders he'd had lunch with – was it only last week? Craig and Debbie, along with their daughter, Tamara. The girl's face was blotchy and tear-streaked.

"May we come in?" Craig asked. Without waiting for Ethan's response, he pushed his way inside the house with his wife and daughter following.

"Please, come in," Ethan said with a hint of sarcasm.

Craig didn't wait to be invited to sit. Ethan looked at Mariah, who's face had gone hard. She looked ready to pounce. He glanced at Robert, who shrugged.

When everyone was seated, including Mariah, Craig leaned forward and rested his forearms on his thighs. "My daughter has something to say to you."

Tamara's eyes filled with tears.

Everyone jumped when Mariah said, "I knew it! You're the one who accused Ethan of assault. It was you. You sent those texts."

Ethan sucked in a breath. Tamara sent him the questionable texts? He'd totally misread the girl's earnest questions about Jesus.

Tamara began to cry in earnest. Great gasping sobs. Debbie rubbed Tamara's back and made soothing sounds.

Craig held up two hands in surrender. "Let's not get ahead of ourselves."

Robert opened his mouth to say something, but Mariah cut him off.

"By all means, let's hear what your daughter has to say." Sarcasm dripped from her voice.

Ethan's mouth went dry. He was seeing a side of Mariah he didn't know existed. He was glad she was on his side. If he was Tamara, he'd cry too.

Debbie spoke in a low voice to her daughter. "Go ahead, sweetie. You can do it."

Ethan held his breath, waiting for Tamara to spin some ridiculous story about him.

Mariah's eyes shot daggers at the girl, and Robert held his phone out to record the conversation.

When she spoke, Tamara's voice was hardly a whisper. "My friend, Kaitlin, in the youth group. She used my phone to send those texts to Pastor Ethan." Her voice faltered.

Ethan remembered Kaitlin. She was a waif of a girl, hardly five feet three and probably under a hundred pounds.

"Kaitlin sent the texts?" Mariah demanded.

Tamara cringed. "She wanted backup for her story. She's p-p-pregnant."

There was an explosion of noise from Mariah, Ethan, and Robert.

"You can't think—"

"No way—"

"Everyone calm down." That was from Robert.

Tamara took a ragged breath. "No, not you, Pastor Ethan."

Craig took his daughter's hand, which seemed to bolster her courage to continue.

"Kaitlin and her boyfriend have been hooking up for a few months. When she found out she was pregnant, she told her parents you attacked her." Tamara fixed watery eyes on Ethan. "She didn't want to tell them it was her boyfriend because she loves him."

"Oh good grief," Mariah said. She opened her mouth to say something else, but Robert silenced her with a wave of his hand.

"Let's hear the rest of it," Robert said.

Tamara's voice was hoarse with tears. "She thought if she said you did it, it would be better." Tamara started crying again. "I'm sorry. She begged me not to say anything."

Mariah sprang to her feet and stood a foot away from the girl. "You mean to tell me this Kaitlin person thought it would be better to ruin a man's reputation than admit she'd been hooking up with her boyfriend?" Mariah waved her hand in front of Tamara's face. "Hello. This is the real world. Pastor Ethan could have been arrested and his life ruined. He has a son, you know." Mariah vibrated with fury.

Ethan had to admire her ferocity. She was more beautiful to him then than ever before. That she defended him so passionately was something to behold.

"What do we do now?" Ethan asked, looking to Robert.

Robert took a deep breath and blew it out. "Let's pause for a moment. Emotions are running high right now." He sent a cautionary look toward Mariah. She pinched her lips together and returned to her seat.

Before anyone said a word, the front door opened and Pastor Roy stepped into the house, followed by his wife, Susan.

"What's going on?"

~

Mariah was never so glad to see anyone as she was at that moment. Pastor Roy would know what to do. And he'd keep her from ripping Tamara's hair out. She'd encountered other mean girls in her life, but this accusation of sexual assault topped everything.

Ethan stood and took a couple of steps toward Pastor Roy.

"I'm glad you're here."

Mariah couldn't stand to see Ethan look defeated. His face was pale and he'd seemed to have aged ten years since two days ago. Being accused of rape would do that to a person.

Ever the perfect hostess, Susan said, "I'll put on a pot of coffee."

Mariah followed Susan into the kitchen while Pastor Roy dropped their bags inside the front door.

"I'm going to check on Jayden," Mariah said. She found the child sitting in the guest room wearing headphones, watching something on Ethan's iPad. He didn't look up when she peeked into the room. Breathing a sigh of relief that he hadn't heard anything going on in the living room, she returned to the kitchen.

The coffee pot gurgled as it began to brew. Susan approached Mariah and wrapped her in a comforting hug.

"How did you get involved in all this, Mariah dear?"

Mariah leaned into Susan's plumpness. "It's a long story."

"Let's hope it has a happy ending," Susan said. "Now, help me get a tray of mugs out and some cream and sugar. It looks like we're going to be awhile."

Mariah pulled away, immediately missing Susan's embrace. "How much do you know?"

"Not a lot. Only what Roy told me. That Ethan was accused of … hurting a girl in the youth group."

Mariah almost smiled at Susan's reluctance to use the words 'assault' or 'rape.'

While she and the pastor's wife put together a tray to take into the living room, Mariah listened to the murmured voices coming from the next room. The men seemed to be discussing how the next day's service would be handled. Was tomorrow really Sunday? It seemed like ages since the previous Sabbath.

"You take the tray and I'll bring the coffee pot," Susan instructed.

Once they were in the living room and everyone who wanted coffee had helped themselves, Pastor Roy spoke.

"Before we do anything, we're going to pray." He led them in a heartfelt prayer for wisdom and guidance and that the truth would prevail.

Mariah gave a hearty 'amen' when he finished.

Robert stood and spoke. "Since my brother hasn't been formally charged, here is my advice. Mr. and Mrs. Armstrong, you need to contact the detective who questioned Ethan. His name is McDonald, correct?"

Ethan nodded.

"Tell him what you told us, that your friend, Kaitlin lied. Leave it to the police to contact Kaitlin's parents."

Ethan interrupted his brother. "But—"

Robert silenced him with his hand. "You need to take a back seat, Ethan."

Mariah's heart hurt over Ethan's pained expression.

"What if Kaitlin doesn't tell the truth to the police?"

Pastor Roy looked at Tamara's parents. "I think I can convince them that it would be best for the girl to be truthful. I'm pretty sure the charges will be dropped."

Mariah clamped her jaws together to keep from expressing her frustration.

Robert assumed his position of being in charge of the conversation. "First of all, if the girl is pregnant, there's no way my brother could be responsible. Even if an early pregnancy test can show positive after ten days, Ethan has only been here for a couple of weeks. This alleged attack would have to have been immediately after he started here at the church. According to my brother, the first time he filled in for the youth leader was over a week and a half ago. Prior to that, he only taught from the pulpit." Robert looked to Ethan for confirmation.

Mariah felt a bloom of hope for the first time since Ethan was taken by the police for questioning. She looked around the room at Pastor Roy and Susan, then at Tamara and her parents. Tamara had stopped crying, thank goodness. Mariah's anger still burned that the girl kept a secret that could have ruined everything Ethan stood for. But with her pastor back in town, he'd make everything right.

Craig and Debbie left with their daughter in tow. Once they were gone, Pastor Roy turned to the rest of them.

"I'm going to call Kaitlin's parents and set up a meeting. Hopefully later today. Ethan, you'd best stay home from church tomorrow. I'll take the pulpit."

"I agree," Robert said.

Susan stood and began to gather the now empty coffee mugs. "You two boys are welcome to stay here until this gets sorted out."

Mariah rose to help Susan clean up while the men discussed the freak storm that passed through the town.

Pastor Roy's house was one of the older ones in Main. No dishwasher meant having to wash the mugs by hand. Susan filled one side of the sink with hot soapy water.

"I'll wash so you don't have to ruin your manicure," Susan said, plunging her hands into the water.

Mariah gathered the mugs and the other assorted dishes Ethan and Jayden had left on the counter. Jayden wandered into the kitchen and wrapped his arms around Mariah's legs.

"Miss Mariah, I'm hungry."

Mariah knelt down to Jayden's level. "I'll get you something, Jayden. But first, say hello to Miss Susan. This is her house."

Susan smiled down at the boy. "Nice to meet you, Jayden." To Mariah, she said, "Looks like someone has become attached to you."

Mariah straightened. "I've been watching him while Sarah's been sick."

Susan rinsed a mug and motioned toward the refrigerator with one elbow. "See what's in the fridge to fix for this hungry guy."

Mariah examined the contents of the refrigerator, but it was practically empty. "I guess bachelors don't go grocery shopping," she commented.

"There's peanut butter in the pantry. How does that sound, Jayden?"

Jayden slumped onto one of the chairs and laid his head on the table. "Okay."

Mariah found a loaf of bread and an unopened jar of jelly in the pantry. She glanced into the living room to see the men huddled together with their heads down. It looked like they were praying. She set to work making a pile of PB&J sandwiches. Everyone was probably hungry after the emotional morning.

"Where are the plates?" she asked as Susan rinsed the last dish.

"Right above where you're standing."

While Mariah put the sandwiches on a plate, Susan retrieved an unopened bag of chips from the pantry. "They may be a bit stale, but I bet these guys will eat them anyway," she murmured.

"How is your sister?" Mariah asked.

"She's much better. Thank you for asking. Our brother and his wife offered to step in. Once she's released from the hospital, they'll take her to their house until she can return home."

"I bet you're relieved. I'm sorry you had to come home to this mess."

Mariah looked up to find Susan giving her an appraising look. "Looks like we came home to more than a mess. Is there something you want to share with me?" Susan's eyes twinkled with amusement.

Mariah felt her face grow hot. She was saved from having to answer when Pastor Roy walked into the kitchen and laid a kiss on Susan's head. "How are you ladies doing in here?"

Susan smiled up at her husband. Mariah felt a pang of jealousy. She longed for a man to look at her the way her pastor looked at Susan. Not any man, she told herself. *Ethan.*

As if she conjured him up, Ethan sauntered into the kitchen looking like a weight had been lifted.

"How's J-man?" he asked, ruffling his son's hair.

Jayden was busily cramming bites of his sandwich into a mouth smeared with jelly.

"Slow down, buddy," Ethan cautioned.

Susan poured a glass of milk and set it on the table. "Here you go, Jayden."

Robert joined them in the kitchen. They sat at the table while Susan brought plates and napkins. Once everyone had taken a sandwich and some chips, Pastor Roy blessed the food.

"I'm going to get a hotel room," Robert said. "I know you weren't expecting an extra body here."

"Nonsense," Susan said. "We'll make room. Ethan can bunk in the guest room with Jayden, and we'll set up the rollaway bed in my sewing room."

Once it was decided that Robert wasn't leaving, Mariah pushed back from the table. "I should probably go."

Ethan stood. "I'll walk you out."

~

Ethan jumped at the chance to talk to Mariah by himself. Since Tamara's revelation, he'd been hit with wave after wave of relief. He still had some things to get straightened out, but the truth would come out and he'd be exonerated.

But there was still the problem of being unemployed. With Pastor Roy back in town, there wasn't the need for him to pastor Main Community Church. And his home church in Seattle had basically said that if he returned in three months, it better be with renewed vigor. The thought exhausted him.

Mariah reached her car and turned. "What a crazy story. I feel guilty about not telling you that those texts came from Tamara." She shrugged. "I guess it doesn't matter now, since it was really Kaitlin who sent them. What a mess."

Ethan pulled Mariah close. "Hey, it's okay. I told you not to tell me. It's on me, not on you."

"Still . . ."

Ethan silenced her with a quick kiss. "I don't know what my future looks like. I'm unemployed and basically homeless. But I know that I'd like to have you in my future."

Ethan watched Mariah's eyes for the answer he hoped for. She held his gaze for what seemed like an hour. It wasn't her words that gave him her response.

She stood on tiptoe and placed her hands on either side of his face. Pulling his lips to hers, she kissed every bit of doubt from his mind.

Roy's front door burst open, and Jayden dashed toward them.

"Dad, are you kissing Miss Mariah?"

Mariah pulled away and laid her fingers on her lips.

"Yes, J-man. I was kissing Miss Mariah."

"Cool! That means you're getting married. You told me I'm not allowed to kiss a girl unless I'm going to marry her. You'll be my mom. This is so cool."

Jayden began to dance around them, singing a made-up song about getting a new mom.

Ethan cringed. "I'm sorry."

Mariah laughed. "Don't be sorry. I think being Jayden's mom would be the best thing that has ever happened to me."

Ethan sent her a wounded look. "What about me?"

"Oh, is it a package deal?" She tapped one finger on her nose. "I guess that would be okay."

Chapter 20

Dear Ms. Martin,

Due to the recent storm and widespread damage, we have had several families apply to Safe Families for help with their children and for their housing needs. Please contact our office at your earliest convenience to let us know how many children you can accommodate.

Sincerely,

R. Smith – Executive Director – Safe Families For Children – Salem Office

Mariah closed her laptop with a snap and looked out the back door of her little home. Much of the storm damage had been cleaned up and dead branches removed. The City was slowly returning to normal after the havoc wrought by what they were calling the Polar Express.

Mariah sighed with contentment. Not only was she in a relationship with a man who accepted all her faults and forgave her past, she was learning to be a mom to an active five-year-old boy. And now, her dream of making a difference in the lives of others less fortunate was finally coming to fruition.

She picked up the phone to call Safe Families, then changed her mind, punching Ethan's number instead. This was a decision they should make together. She was no longer navigating life alone.

They still had a lot of details to work out. The youth leader, Noah, decided to move to Eugene to be closer to his parents. Pastor Roy created a youth pastor position which he offered to Ethan. Ethan and Jayden found a cute house to rent around the corner from the church.

The phone rang once, and Ethan answered. "We still on for dinner tonight?"

"Of course. I have something I want to discuss with you."

"Sounds serious. I have something I want to discuss with you, too."

Mariah smiled. "That sounds even more serious."

Ethan laughed. "I'll see you later."

"I'll see you forever," Mariah replied.

THE END

Heart of a Hero

Chapter 1

With a twist of the knob, Simone cranked up the volume on the car stereo, filling the aging Honda with the energizing beats of Toby Mac's Promised Land. Even the traffic backed up on Marion Bridge heading west toward Main, Oregon, and the sun glaring through the windshield couldn't dampen her relief at leaving her parents' house.

Sunday lunches at the folk's used to be fun but lately the continual drama got on Simone's last nerve. Simone loved her family, but the safety net of her parents nearby felt more like being caught in a snare.

Her seven-year-old Honda surged forward when the traffic thinned out. Simone passed a white pickup humming along at exactly the speed limit. No one did the speed limit on this stretch of highway. She pressed harder on the accelerator. She gasped when a motorcycle darted around her, barely missing her front bumper. Sheesh. Guess sixty-five in a fifty-five-mile zone wasn't fast enough.

A two miles later, Simone caught up to the motorcycle, now stuck behind a slow-moving tractor and a UPS truck in the fast lane. The cyclist weaved from side to side, looking for an opening before pulling onto the shoulder to pass. To her horror, the bike slipped on loose gravel, hit the ditch, and flew at least twenty feet into the air. A plume of dust rose from the field where he landed.

Simone yanked the steering wheel to the right and slammed on her brakes, her car coming to rest with a shuddering stop. She jammed a finger on the emergency flashers, jumped out of the car, and sprinted to where the motorcycle lay on its side.

A man lay face down in the weeds. His helmet rolled a few feet away. Simone laid two fingers on the man's neck, searching for a pulse. Nothing. Fearful of a neck or spine injury, she waited only a moment before grabbing his arm and pulling him onto his back.

The guy's lips were blue and his face devoid of color. She started chest compressions, willing his heart to resume its job of giving life.

~

Gabriel Harrison set the cruise control of his pickup at fifty-five. He couldn't afford another speeding ticket. His insurance rates had skyrocketed since the last one, already stretching his budget.

A motorcycle buzzed past him, followed by an orange Honda. He briefly succumbed to a moment of self-pity over selling his beloved Harley. He understood why his fireman buddies called hogs 'organ donors.'

As a first responder, Gabriel had seen his share of fatal motorcycle collisions. Dying on the hard pavement was a poor substitute for feeling the wind on his face and the feeling of total freedom.

The clock on his dash showed he'd arrive at his parents' house in Main, Oregon in time for a shower before dinner. In celebration of his return, though temporary, they'd promised him a full-on roast beef dinner.

One month and he'd be back on the job in Portland. This thirty-day leave of absence to help his parents on their seed farm would give him time to train for the most grueling personal challenge ever. Since the events of September 11, thousands of firefighters around the country reenacted the stairs climbed by the first responders in the Twin Towers.

Last year, Gabe had intended to sign up, but his ex-girlfriend made plans for a romantic cruise. Now that Tiffany was no longer in the picture, there'd be no distractions to keep him from crossing this event off his bucket list.

Another five miles passed. Gabe spied the same orange Honda which whizzed past him, parked on the side of the road, emergency flashers on. He pulled to a stop a few feet behind the vehicle, stepped out of his truck and approached the car. No one sat inside.

"Help! Over here!" The female voice called from somewhere in the grassy field.

Gabe sprinted through the weeds and found a dark-skinned woman performing CPR on a thirty-something-looking man. He quickly evaluated the crumpled motorcycle, upside-down helmet, and the downed man's blue lips.

"Did you call 9-1-1?" Gabe asked.

"I left my phone in the car," the woman said.

"Here." Gabe shoved his phone at her and shouldered the woman out of the way. He pressed the man's chest, then leaned down to listen for the sound of breath.

Gabe continued chest compressions until the man took a gasping inhale as the panicked woman gave Dispatch shaky-voiced information.

The blue dissipated from the man's lips and color returned to his face. "Good job, buddy," Gabe said. He tilted the man's head back enough for him to breathe more easily.

~

Simone stayed on the phone with the operator until the sound of approaching sirens filled the air. She disconnected and leaned over to hand the phone to the stranger. He seemed to be a pro as he gently lifted each of the guy's eyelids to check his pupils. He ignored her outstretched hand.

Simone continued her observation of the pro. He rubbed his hands down each of the downed cyclist's legs before gently palpitating his abdomen. While half of her brain registered shock at the accident, the other half couldn't help notice how the guy's muscles flexed under the thin tee shirt stretched over his large frame.

His calf muscles bunched as he pushed himself to his feet. Simone took only a moment to admire his shorts-clad legs before thrusting the phone toward him again.

"Thanks," he said with a look of disdain. "How could you leave your phone behind?"

Before Simone could respond, the whine of sirens rose to a crescendo when two firetrucks and an ambulance pulled over, followed by an Oregon State Trooper.

Soon the grassy field was filled with male first responders. The handsome stranger was bombarded with a flurry of questions as they approached.

"What happened?"

"How long was he without air?"

"Any broken bones?"

"Did you see the accident?"

Simone found herself pushed out of the way of the paramedics who carried a backboard and IV supplies.

"Ma'am, you'll have to step out of the way."

"But—"

The paramedic didn't wait for her to finish.

Simone watched as the muscular stranger was congratulated by the men who now surrounded him. The conversation was garbled with traffic noises. Was he taking full credit for saving the cyclist's life?

After the downed cyclist was loaded into the ambulance, its siren wound up again and sped toward town.

Simone sucked in a breath and blew it out through pursed lips. She tried making eye contact with the presumed life-saver, but he was too busy shaking hands and grinning like an idiot.

Fine. Let him get the glory. Humility verses peppered the Bible, but Simone couldn't zero in on one.

Still fuming, Simone hurried toward town to meet with her two best friends. Wait until Lizzy and Mariah heard about the glory hog.

www.ingramcontent.com/pod-product-compliance
Lightning Source LLC
Chambersburg PA
CBHW070414310726
48977CB00003B/680